T0209340

POLYCARP

A Student of John

JOHN MENCH

WESTBOW
PRESS®
A DIVISION OF THOMAS NELSON
& ZONDERVAN

WestBow Press books may be ordered through booksellers or by contacting:

WestBow Press
A Division of Thomas Nelson & Zondervan
1663 Liberty Drive
Bloomington, IN 47403
www.westbowpress.com
1 (866) 928-1240

ISBN: 978-1-9736-4271-8 (sc)
ISBN: 978-1-9736-4272-5 (hc)
ISBN: 978-1-9736-4273-2 (e)

Library of Congress Control Number: 2018912276

Print information available on the last page.

WestBow Press rev. date: 10/22/2018

DEDICATION

Dedicated to my wife, Rose, who for thirty-four years, focused our lives around Jesus' message and to my second wife, Ann, who encouraged me for the last twenty years. Her illness provided me with the time to write and her love of life encouraged me to tell my stories. God's grace to both of you.

Acknowledgement

To my friends who after reading my book gave me critical guidance and loving care.

INTRODUCTION

The Foundation of Christianity

In an effort to stimulate your imagination, I have written a series of books concerning the formation of the Christian Church.

Our understanding of Christianity was probably formed when we attended Sunday school. Hopefully, what we learned was based on the principles of the Bible. The Bible's New Testament provides us with a disjointed series of stories about Jesus. The stories are incomplete and have caused me to be concerned about the incidents not preserved in history. Some will say they are a figment of my imagination.

After reading the books, I encourage you to form and record your imagination concerning the unrecorded events.

My books were written as fiction related to history. In my opinion, history concerning any specific topic in ancient times is fiction. The amount of written history that is accurate is pure speculation. The amount of fiction that is contained in written history is based on several items:

1. elapsed time (from event to now)
2. government influence (the winners of war write history)
3. greed (writing to make money)
4. perspective (being human)

When you read a history book, you are reading a written perspective that has been deemed acceptable by your generation and your environment. Most history books are the perspective of well-paid victors.

POLYCARP
A STUDENT OF JOHN

Polycarp's story originates in Philippi during the middle of the first century and concludes after the middle of the second century. The story involves birth, love, travel, religion, and death. Polycarp's father Augustus was killed while serving in the Roman Army. His mother, Dianna, was a strong willed woman and didn't remarry. She and her attendant, Rachael, raised Polycarp and his three sisters. Polycarp became a priest and a professor. He was a student of John's and spent time with him, in Ephesus, and later analyzed his writings. He moved to Smyrna and became The Bishop of Smyrna. He lived an exciting life performing research and teaching. He emphasized apostolic succession and the correctness of the scriptures. He died a martyr.

CONTENTS

Contents

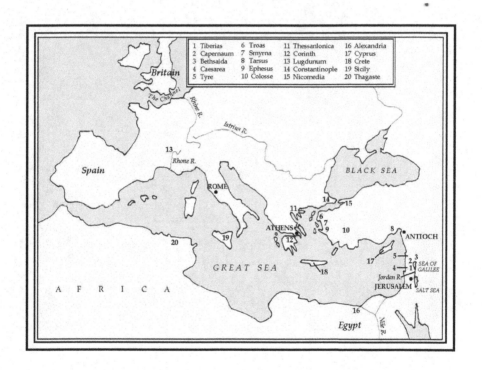

1 Tiberias	6 Troas	11 Thessanlonica	16 Alexandria
2 Capernaum	7 Smyrna	12 Corinth	17 Cyprus
3 Bethsaida	8 Tarsus	13 Lugdunum	18 Crete
4 Caesarea	9 Ephesus	14 Constantinople	19 Sicily
5 Tyre	10 Colosse	15 Nicomedia	20 Thagaste

Britain

The Channel

Rhine R.

Istrius R.

Spain

Rhone R.

13

ROME

BLACK SEA

14

15

11

6

7

9

10

8

ANTIOCH

ATHENS

12

5

3

2

1

SEA OF GALILEE

4

17

Jordan R.

JERUSALEM

SALT SEA

20

19

GREAT SEA

18

A F R I C A

16

Egypt

Nile R.

CHAPTER 1

POLYCARP'S CHILDHOOD

Polycarp was born about forty years after Jesus was crucified. Many of the original followers of Jesus had died, and most of Jesus' original twelve disciples had been killed. The Jewish Rabbis, in Jerusalem, had convinced the administrators of the Roman government that The Way was a threat to their control. The government administrators considered those living in Jerusalem an especially serious threat. Vespasian became emperor and his son, Titus, destroyed the temple and most of the people in Jerusalem. Those that followed Jesus' message had relocated to other cities. Antioch was the unofficial home of the Christian faith. Another city, very important to Christianity and to the Roman government, was Philippi. It was home to many Roman soldiers, because it was situated on a very important Roman highway that connected the East to the West. Polycarp's father, Augustus, served the Roman army for twelve years, but after two years of service he had been sent from Rome to Philippi. The year sixty-nine had been a difficult time for the Roman government. Nero, the emperor, committed suicide and the new emperor, Galba, endured only a few months before he was replaced by Otho. The situation in Jerusalem wasn't any better. The Jewish people planned a revolution. Vespasian, the commander of the Roman military, campaigned very successfully against the Jewish cities, so the senate named him the fourth emperor of the year. His son, Titus, remained in Judah and looked forward to successful completion of his assignment of destroying Jerusalem.

Dianna, Polycarp's mother was born and raised in Philippi. She had been married to Augustus for eight years, bore three daughters, and was pregnant with Polycarp. They lived in a medium size house located on a piece of land that had been in Polycarp's mother's family for many years. She inherited the house, the vineyards, and most of her father's wealth. She was the oldest female child, and no male children were born to her father and mother. When she saw Augustus approach, Dianna noted a frown on his face. They exchanged greeting.

"I have unsettling news," he said. "I was informed today that I am being sent to the Jerusalem area. I will be attached to the legion at Tiberias."

Dianna looked at her husband in disbelief. She hadn't considered his being sent to a dangerous area. She grasped his large hand and focused her sad eyes directly at him.

"Tiberias, I understand that legion is under the command of Titus," Augustus said. "He is going to drive the Jewish faithful out of Jerusalem."

"They won't leave peacefully," Dianna said. "They will fight."

"I am certain I will see some action," he said. "Maybe I will earn a promotion."

"It all started with Nero," she said. "It has been very difficult in Rome. Our government is in turmoil. I wish Rome hadn't burned. Maybe Nero would have been more at peace with those whose religion is based on worshiping one God."

Augustus kissed her hand and looked in her large, dark eyes.

"I am sorry I won't be here when our son is born," he said. "After three girls, you will have a boy this time."

"Do you have to go before our baby is born?" she asked. "Can't you remain with me for a few months?"

"I don't think the army cares when our baby will be born," Augustus said. "They are more interested in destroying Jerusalem."

"I want you to promise me that you will inform your sergeant that I am with child, and you want to remain with me," Dianna said. "He might have a child."

He smiled at her, "I promise I will ask him, but I don't think he is married."

Augustus talked with his sergeant the next day. The sergeant wasn't sympathetic. He explained that if the army wanted Augustus to have a wife they would have issued one to him. When Augustus returned home, he told Dianna that the sergeant was sorry, but he must go to Tiberias.

"Be careful," she said. "We need you."

"If everything goes as planned, I should return in two years," he said. "They could have sent me for a much longer tour of duty."

"That two years will seem like twenty years," she said. "We have never been apart for more than a month."

"I have had a steady assignment since we have been married," he said. "We really can't complain."

"I hope you are correct and our baby is a boy," Dianna said. "You have wanted a boy since we were married."

"I will sail to Caesarea," Augustus said. "We will leave in ten days. I will start packing tomorrow."

"Do you know exactly what you are going to do?" she asked.

"I will probably be given about one week of training concerning our mission," he said. "If I get an early start with the training, I should be prepared before I have to sail."

"Have some wine and bread," she said. "They didn't give you much notice. I guess it is because the situation, in Jerusalem, is changing so quickly."

"I am certain Titus needs more men," he said. "It is a temporary assignment."

She batted her beautiful eyes at him.

"We will all miss you very much," she said. "I don't want you to worry about me. When our child is born, I will have one of my sisters stay with me. It is our good fortune that they all live in Philippi."

He peered deeply into her eyes. He lost concentration for a moment. He paused.

"It is nice to have a choice," he said. "Which sister will be with you?"

Dianna had two sisters. Her sister Mary lived close to her, but she didn't have any children. Her other sister Elizabeth had two children, but she lived on the other side of town in a large home and was busy with her family.

"I will visit with Mary first," Dianna said. "I am certain she will want to help me. My other sister is quite busy with her family, attendants, and house. I will figure that out after you depart."

The time passed quickly, but Dianna and Augustus saw each other every day. When he finished daily training, he was allowed to go home. After ten days, Augustus and several other soldiers from Philippi departed. A melancholy Dianna visited her sister. When she knocked on the door of her house, Mary had just finished her mid-morning tea.

"Hello, Mary," Dianna said. "I will need your help. Augustus has gone to Jerusalem and won't return for two years."

As she looked at Dianna, a startled look appeared on Mary's face.

"Why did he go to Jerusalem," she asked. "I thought he was assigned in Philippi."

"He received a temporary assignment," she said. "We will miss him greatly. I came to see if you could be with me during my birthing time."

"Certainly, I will help you," she said. "I can arrange things, so I can be with you."

Mary paused for a moment, pushed her hair back, and rubbed her forehead.

"Maybe you should consider hiring an attendant to help you with your family," Mary said. "You are going to have three small children and an infant. I am certain you can find a place in your house for an attendant to live."

Dianna thought about her house. As she looked at Mary, a concerned look appeared on her face.

"I don't know if I can afford an attendant, do you know how much an attendant costs?" she asked.

"My neighbor, Elizabeth, has a slave for an attendant, and she doesn't have any more money than you," Mary said. "We should talk to her."

"I didn't know your neighbor has an attendant," Dianna said. "I am certain she appreciates the help."

Mary knew Dianna needed an attendant and wanted to convince her that she could afford one.

"She might know someone who will help attend to your family," she said. "I see her every Sabbath. She attends one of the new churches."

"Is she a Christian?" she asked. "Can slaves belong to a church?"

"Would you like to go to a meeting with us?" Mary asked. "I think you might enjoy the lessons."

"Yes, I would like that very much," Dianna said. "I could ask her a few questions."

Dianna smiled at her sister and indicated it was time for her to take the children home.

"Don't walk too fast," Mary said. "You should be careful."

"I will see you," she said. "When I have to carry Margret, I don't walk very rapidly."

Dianna was certain she couldn't afford a full-time attendant, but she trusted Mary and looked forward to talking with Mary's neighbor at the Sabbath meeting. Taking care of three small girls and an infant required more work than she could handle.

It was a beautiful, sunny, warm Sabbath day, and several people stood outside the neighborhood church. They disapprovingly discussed that army soldiers had been sent to Jerusalem. They interrupted their conservation to greet their friends.

"Welcome to our meeting," she said. "I am your sister's neighbor. She told me that you wanted to discuss the cost of an attendant. I have a slave, and she is a great help. I provide her with a place to stay and food."

"I have room," Dianna said. "My husband has departed."

"A slave attendant will accept almost any amount of money you offer," she said. "My attendant knows a lady named Rachael who would be a good attendant."

"Has she worked with children?" she asked. "I prefer someone with experience."

The neighbor smiled and shook her head in the affirmative.

"She loves children," she said. "She also cleans and keeps her clothing neat. If you are interested, I will have her visit with you tomorrow."

"I would like to talk with her," Dianna said. "I already need help and my family is going to get larger."

When the sisters saw each other, they found a seat and bowed their heads to pray. Then they exchanged greetings.

"Have you discussed having an assistant?" Mary asked.

"Yes, tomorrow I am going to meet with Rachael," Dianna said. "Do you know Rachael?"

"She is a very good worker," she said. "When I need help, she helps me for a day or two. I am sure you will like her."

Dianna enjoyed the lesson very much and planned to return the next Sabbath. She felt much better about having an attendant and looked forward to meeting with Rachael.

Dianna sipped a cup of tea and waited for Rachael. Suddenly, she heard a knock on the door.

"My name is Rachael. I was told you might need an assistant," she said.

Rachael looked around the house and noticed all the dirty clothing.

"It looks to me like you need help," she said. "I will help you feed the children."

"The three young ones are more than I can handle," Dianna said.

"It is important for me to address them properly, what are their names?" she asked. "Are they all girls?"

"Yes, all girls," she said. "I am sorry everything is such a mess."

"One person can only accomplish so much," Rachael said.

She glanced at Dianna.

"I guess I must admit I do need help," Dianna said. "I just don't want to admit it. The oldest one is named after me, Dianna. The two younger ones are Martha and Margret."

Rachael looked at the children and smiled, "They are cute. I love little girls."

"I am certain we can find room for you in our house," Dianna said. "My husband is a Roman soldier and has been sent to Jerusalem for two years. I can only pay you a small amount, can you start today?"

"I will help you for the rest of the day," she said. "I must talk to my employer. He hired me and my brother to pick grapes."

"You work in a vineyard?" she asked. "That is hard work."

"I think I am required to remain with him at least until the end of the week," she said. "I still live with my parents. I don't need much space. I am certain we can find a place for me in your house."

"We will figure something out," Dianna said. "Hand me that cloth."

"Here," she said. "My master told me that if I could find a place to live,

6

he would free me. He prefers to work with men. If I live with you, it would save him money. I am certain he will give you my papers."

A puzzled look appeared on Dianna's face.

"I haven't thought about papers," she said. "I am already looking forward to next week. I should have talked to Mary about an attendant a few years ago."

The week passed slowly for Dianna. Time passed even more slowly for Rachael. Before Rachael arrived at Dianna's house, Dianna had arranged a place for her to sleep and unpack her belongings. When Rachael arrived, Dianna was reading a story to young Dianna.

"Hello, Dianna," Rachael said. "I have my papers."

She handed her ownership papers to Dianna.

"Here take them," she said. "You now own me and are responsible for me."

"That sounds funny," Dianna said. "I own you."

"I really don't like picking grapes," she said. "I do have one problem. My master wants me to work until the harvest is complete or to pay him to hire someone to pick the grapes for him."

"I will put your paper with our other important papers," Dianna said. "I made a place for you to sleep. I'll talk with your old master."

They walked to the area Dianna had prepared for Rachael.

"You can have this area to keep your things," she said. "You can put your bag here and get your other things tomorrow."

"This is all I have," she said. "I have two sets of clothes and an extra pair of sandals."

"I guess that is all you need," she said. "Welcome to our humble home."

"I am lucky to have this much," she said. "I know many people who only have one set of clothes."

"Come in and enjoy your new home," Dianna said. "I am certain you remember the children. After we have cleaned them, we will put them to sleep. Then we can talk."

After Dianna agreed to provide him with a day labor for two weeks, Rachael's old owner was satisfied. He indicated that after the grapes were picked he didn't want anything to do with Rachael. Rachael was now

Dianna's attendant. They quickly learned to live together and cared of the children. Rachael explained that she had helped to birth three babies and looked forward to helping Mary during Dianna's childbirth process. A lifelong relationship ensued.

It was the Sabbath and the family prepared to go to the meeting place. They assembled in the living area of the house. Before they departed, Dianna and Rachael reviewed everything.

"Dianna, you sure are growing," Rachael said. "It will not be very long now."

"I feel well," she said. "It is a little difficult to standup straight."

Rachael worked with the children.

"I have finished preparing the girls for our trip to the meeting place," she said. "I understand we are going to hear another great lesson about Jesus. Do you want me to help you?"

"No, I am fine," Dianna said. "I have to find my head cover."

"I think it is in the drawer," Rachael said. "I shall get it for you."

"When you have the children ready, let me know," Dianna said. "We will walk to the meeting place. You will have to carry Margret. I don't think I will be able to carry her."

The family enjoyed the weekly trips to the meeting place. They socialized and listened to teachings about Jesus' message. Most of the material was new to Dianna, but she was interested and discussed the teachings with Rachael.

"That was a wonderful lesson," Rachael said. "I was glad to see your sister Mary. I thanked her again for introducing us. She is such a nice person."

"Yes, I was glad to see her," Dianna said. "I told her it won't be long, and when we need help, you will inform her."

A few days passed, Rachael heard a knock at the door. She and Dianna were greeted by a Roman soldier. They looked at each other in wonderment.

"I am looking for Augustus' wife," he said. "I have been ordered to deliver this message and talk with her."

Rachael looked at Dianna and said, "This Roman soldier is looking for you."

Dianna and Rachael both sensed the soldier was very nervous.

"I have bad news," he said. "The ship carrying the soldiers encountered a violent storm and sank."

Dianna was greatly shaken by the news and her knees grew weak. Rachael had to catch her before she fell. Rachael guided her to a chair. Dianna was speechless and in shock. Rachael put a damp cloth on her forehead. The soldier looked at Dianna.

"Many of the soldiers survived but many didn't survive," he said. "Your husband couldn't swim. He was lost. He never made it to Caesarea."

Dianna sobbed and experienced trouble breathing. Rachael took her hand and kissed it.

"I have this message from Rome expressing the military's greatest sympathy," he said. "Your husband was a great soldier and will be missed by all. I will try to answer any questions you might have. If necessary, I can return in a few days."

With a glazed look on her face, Dianna looked at him and said, "I don't know what to ask. I think I am in shock."

"If you have no questions today, I will return to my post and allow you to grieve," he said. "We will be in contact with you."

Dianna was so distraught; she didn't ask any questions, so the soldier departed.

While Dianna sobbed uncontrollably, Rachael removed the message from her hand and comforted her until the sunset. Then she lit one candle. Several hours passed before Dianna was able to speak normally.

She motioned to Rachael, "I had a bad feeling. When Augustus boarded that ship, I knew that I might not see him again."

Rachael squeezed her hand, "I will care for you. Don't worry. We will make it."

"I knew it, I just knew it,' she said. "I could feel it."

"You and the children will be fine," she said. "I am sure the Roman government will provide for you."

"You will have to take care of everything for a while," she said. "Please ask my sister Mary to come and visit with me. I will tell her what has happened."

Rachael put the children to bed for a nap and then ran most of the way to Mary's house. She informed Mary that her sister needed help, and they both quickly returned to Dianna's house. They found her seated in her chair crying uncontrollably.

Mary took her hand, "Dianna, we are all very upset about your loss. I will remain with you and grieve with you."

Dianna looked at Mary.

"Thank you," she said. "I feel so alone."

"You are not alone," she said. "You have three children, two sisters and a loving attendant."

The news disrupted Dianna's family. They cried and grieved with each other for many days. Rachael cared for everyone's needs.

Finally, Dianna's time arrived.

"Mary, I think he is coming," Dianna said. "Get Rachael, we will need some cloths."

"I am here, Dianna," Rachael said. "Everything is under control."

Dianna squirmed and looked at Rachael.

"Mary and I will care for you," she said. "He has been born. That was quick."

"She has had practice," Mary said. "Dianna, hold my hand. You have a baby boy. How are you doing?"

"I am fine, how is my baby boy?" she asked.

"He sure is a loud boy," Rachael said. "Someday, he will be a man everyone will hear."

Rachael swaddled the boy and placed him on Dianna stomach. They went to sleep.

Mary looked at Rachael, "I can't believe he was born that quickly. I am very proud of her."

When Dianna woke, she spoke with Rachael, "I am glad you were here to help Mary."

"I will be able to take care of everything for you. Mary said to tell you she had to go home," Rachael said.

"I am sure she will return," Dianna said.

"She told me she will say a prayer for all of us and return in a few days to check on how we are doing," she said.

Mary placed her hand under her baby's head and sat erect.

"I am going to do some cleaning," Rachael said. "I will check on you in a few moments."

Dianna very carefully held Polycarp. She felt his warmth against her stomach. When Rachael checked on Dianna, they were almost asleep.

A few hours later, Rachael noted that Mary was awake.

"I am going to do some shopping tomorrow, do you want me to stop at the shop and purchase some colored cloth?" she asked. "Now, that you have a boy, maybe a blue outfit would be nice."

Mary smiled at Rachael.

"I don't think I will be up to making him an outfit," she said. "Maybe in a few weeks, I will have more strength."

"If you purchase the cloth, I will make Polycarp an outfit," Rachael said. "I like to make clothing."

"We do need a few items from the market," Dianna said. "I guess blue is fine. It is certainly different and can easily be distinguished from white."

"He is too grand for white," she said. "He needs to be different."

"Everyone will know he is not a girl," she said. "When you are at the shop, tell Lydia I say hello."

During the next few years Dianna, her attendant, and her family slowly grew accustomed to their new life style. Polycarp didn't know it, but he was the man of the family. A strong bond developed among the members of the family. It was the Sabbath, the sun shone, and breakfast was finished. Rachael, Dianna, and the family stood in the living area of the house.

"Rachael, are the children ready," Dianna said. "We don't want to be late for our lesson."

"We are on time," Rachael said. "Have we got all of them?"

"I will take Mary and Polycarp by their hands," she said. "I think he can walk most of the way. You take Martha and Margret. I am ready to become a member of the congregation, what do you think?"

"Do they allow slaves to be members?" Rachael asked. "Is Elizabeth's attendant a member of a congregation?"

"I am certain they will allow slaves to become members," Dianna said. "Do you remember the lesson on "One God for All"? That would include you."

"Yes, I think we should join with them," she said. "When will the children be old enough to join?"

"I am not certain," she said. "We will ask the teacher. When they are old enough, they will become members."

Dianna and her family lived in a neighborhood of families. The houses were about the same size and about the same age. The children played outside, with other children, most of the time. Polycarp was a very inquisitive child. He learned to speak at a young age and convinced the teacher, at the meeting place, to help him learn how to read and write. He was fascinated by the scrolls in the church library.

When Dianna saw the priest, she and Polycarp were seated in the library reading. He approached Polycarp.

"I am impressed with how well you read," the priest said. "Most young man can't read until they are much older. How old are you. Are you learning how to write?"

"I am practicing," Polycarp said. "My mother allows me to practice at home. She can write a little bit. I am four years old. I am big for my age."

"I will see you in a few days," he said. "Make certain you continue to practice."

As they walk home, they talk about the scrolls. When they arrived at the house, Rachael fed the children hot bread.

"The priest was happy with how well I can write," Polycarp said. "I think he is going to teach me how to read and write Greek."

"What makes you think that?" Rachael asked. "I can't read or write Greek."

"When I can read Greek, I will be able to read all of the scrolls," he said. "Many scholars write in Greek."

"That is nice," she said. "Your mother and I think you should go fishing with our neighbor and his son."

"Fishing?" he asked. "Does he want me to fish with them?"

"He has said he would be glad to take you along," Rachael said. "He will teach you how to fish. Maybe someday, you will be a fisherman."

"I will enjoy going fishing with them, but I'm not going to be a fisherman," Polycarp said.

"If you caught fish, we could eat them, what do you think you will become?" Rachael asked.

"I am going to be a priest," Polycarp said. "I am listening very carefully to our lessons about Jesus. He was a very great man."

"Yes dear," Dianna said. "He was a man and a spiritual leader of men. I am certain the teacher will tell you anything you want to know about Jesus."

Polycarp enjoyed a day of fishing with his neighbor and the neighbor's son, Daniel. They caught a few small fish. The neighbor taught both boys how to clean fish. Polycarp disliked the cleaning process.

A few days later, Polycarp ate breakfast with his mother and the girls.

"Mother, while we were fishing, our neighbor told me about the theater," Polycarp said. "The Romans use it for games."

"I don't like the theater," Dianna said. "We don't go to it. I wish he hadn't told you about it."

"They have all kind of races," he said. "He asked if I wanted to go to the games. I told him I would check with you."

"I would prefer that you not go to the games," she said. "In Rome and other cities, the Romans treat the one God people, like us, unfairly. They use us as entertainment at their games."

"I was looking forward to the chariot races," he said. "They usually don't kill anyone racing chariots."

"Polycarp, this is important to me," she said. "I don't want you going to the games. Do you understand?"

Polycarp's lower lip protruded from his face. He put his head down and walked outside. He stared at the ground. Dianna watched him pout.

"Rachael, did you feel that?" Dianna asked. "I think the ground shook so violently that the house moved."

The area, in the foothills of the mountains was susceptible to earthquakes. Those that had lived in the region were accustomed to them. Dianna had lived there a long time but had never learned to ignore them.

"Yes, I felt it," Rachael said. "The ground in this area moves around. I hope our house is in a good location. Do you think we are safe?"

"I think my grand-father requested this piece of land because it was safe," Dianna said. "It is not large and only has a partial view of the mountains, but it is ours."

"I hope he did a good job," she said. "We can see the mountains."

"I prefer it here as opposed to being close to the marshland on the other side of town," she said. "When they live near the marshland, some people become sickly."

Polycarp came running and went straight to his mother's arms. He was now aware that Philippi was prone to earthquakes. Dianna was able to assuage his fears. She explained to Polycarp that being near a mountain many times resulted in earthquakes. Their lives quickly returned to normal.

As time passed, the family matured. Polycarp spent many mornings at the library. This day, when he returned home, he found his mother seated in her favorite chair reading to Martha and Margret.

"The priest told me they have found another vein of gold in the mountains," Polycarp said. "I think he is hoping the miners will help fund a larger building for our church."

"They have been taking gold out of that mountain for as long as I can remember," Dianna said. "The mountain is a great asset for our town."

"They spend a lot of that gold," Rachael said. "They could afford to help the priests."

"When they make a large, new find of gold, the miners do get a little generous," Dianna said. "We could use a large building for our meeting place. I noticed a new face on our coins. I guess they have changed the emperor in Rome."

"Yes, Vespasian has been emperor for a few years," Polycarp said. "We finally have new coins with the current emperor's face on them. Vespasian is the father of Domitian and Titus."

"Titus, I have heard that name," she said. "I thought he was a general.

I guess things are different now that they have destroyed the great temple in Jerusalem."

"My teacher told me that most of The Way has gone underground or moved to Antioch," Polycarp said. "Antioch is the new center for the message of Jesus."

"It is the home to many teachers," Dianna said. "I think it is several days north of Jerusalem."

"He also told me that is where Paul taught before he became a missionary," he said. "He started in Antioch and eventually visited Philippi."

Polycarp now studied the Jesus religion every day. He spent most of his time at the libraries reading and talking with the priest. He read and wrote both Latin and Greek. He helped his mother and Rachael with the chores and enjoyed being the man of the family. It was still light but the sun had set. The family sat in the living area of their house.

"I understand the grape crop is large this year," Rachael said. "When I came to work for you, I didn't know you owned vineyards."

"We own a few," Dianna said. "They belonged to my father."

"I know how to pick grapes. If you want me to work in the vineyards this year, I would be glad to help," she said. "Now that the children are older, I have some free time."

"No, that is not necessary," she said. "That is work for a man."

"I don't mind," Rachael said. "I have picked a lot of grapes."

"We women take care of the family and the house," she said. "I have been using the same men for many years."

"That sounds like a good arrangement," she said. "If needed, I can help."

Dianna looked at Rachael.

"They count on working for me," Dianna said. "We have an agreement."

"We also have an agreement," Rachael said. "I like taking care of the children and the house."

"The income from the grapes makes a big difference for us," she said. "If I hadn't inherited the house and vineyards, life would be very difficult."

A large smile appeared on her face as she looked directly at Rachael.

Rachael smiled back at her and said, "Thank you."

"What time do you want to have dinner this evening?" Rachael asked. "Will all the children be eating with us this evening?"

"Serve dinner at six o'clock," Dianna said. "I think everyone will be here this evening. Polycarp should be back from meeting with the priest."

A few hours later, as he entered the house, Polycarp exuded enthusiasm.

"Hello, mother," he said. "I had a good meeting with the priest today. I read several of the scrolls in the church library."

"That is nice," she said. "Which ones did you read?"

"One of the scrolls was particular interesting," he said. "I asked the priest who wrote it. He told me it was written by a man named Luke."

"I have heard of Luke," she said. "He lived here."

"He told me Luke helped the original church which Paul started, in Philippi," he said. "He was here for a long time. I hope I have the opportunity to read more scrolls that Luke wrote."

"I don't know much about Luke. I was told that Paul brought Jesus' message to Philippi. Do you know anything about Luke?" Dianna asked.

"The priest didn't know very much about him," he said. "He thinks he joined Paul as a disciple. Luke was probably from Antioch."

"How did he know about Jesus?" she asked. "Maybe, he heard him speak."

"I doubt it, but he did record many of Peter's and many of Paul's lessons. He knew both of them very well," Polycarp said. "Paul sent him to Philippi to make certain the church understood Jesus' message correctly."

"That was smart of him," she said. "It is necessary to accurately teach what Jesus said."

"Some of the local people, who had been trained when Paul was here, were being confused by false prophets. The false prophets would visit the congregation for a short time," he said. "Many of them told a different Jesus message."

After breakfast, everyone sat in the living area of the house.

"Mother, I have met an honorable man at the meeting place," Dianna's oldest daughter, Dianna, said. "He wants to marry me."

Dianna looked at her daughter through glazed eyes.

"He wants to marry you?" she asked. "Do I know him?"

"He requested permission to talk to my father," she said. "I told him that father had died and you were responsible for me."

"What did he say?" she asked. "Was he surprised?"

"He asked to talk with you," she said. "He was surprised that your name was also Dianna. I hope he doesn't get confused when he talks with you."

"Do you want to get married?" she asked. "I hadn't realized that you were old enough to marry. That is a big step in a young woman's life."

"Yes, mother," she said. "I am seventeen years old. A girl doesn't want to wait too long."

"I would be glad to talk with him," Dianna said. "Where does he work? Do you know how long he has been there?"

"He lives with his parents," she said. "He works on the family farm."

"A farmer, who lives at home," she said. "You can learn many things while being raised on a farm."

"He is the oldest child. He does have one younger sister," she said. "His parents are getting quite old, and he has been running the farm for a few years. I think you will like him. His name is Abraham."

"I look forward to meeting him," she said. "You can have Rachael prepare a dinner for all of us one evening. I am certain your sisters and your brother would like to meet him."

Rachael and Mary spent days planning the meeting. Dianna told young Dianna that everything was arranged, and she should invite Abraham for dinner. Abraham was a little nervous and a lot in love. Everyone liked him. Two months passed before he and young Dianna were married. The ceremony was a simple small event. Dianna moved out of the house and went with Abraham. He had built a house, for them, on the farm. Being a farmer's wife seemed to help Dianna's maturity. The farm was only about a one hour walk from Philippi.

After a few months, the family had adjusted to its reduced number. They had just prepared to start dinner without Polycarp when he entered the house. He went directly to his mother.

"Mother, the priest told me today that I have reached the age of reason and will be allowed to read at the meeting place," Polycarp said. "It won't be very long before I will be able to teach lessons. He is going to tell the congregation at our next meeting."

"We are proud of you," she said. "We will be there with you. I am looking forward to the day when you become a priest."

"I am a little nervous," he said. "I hope the people will like me."

"Polycarp, they know you," she said. "They have watched you grow up. They all love you. Everything will be fine."

Mary, Martha, Margret, and Rachael sat in the front area of the church. They wanted to hear every word the priest said.

"Ladies and gentlemen," he said. "It is my pleasure to introduce you to our newest man. He is no longer a child. He has put away his childish behavior."

The priest looked at Polycarp and smiled.

"He will be working with me," he said. "He hopes to become a priest. Polycarp, say hello to the congregation."

Polycarp slowly stood up. He cleared his throat and looked directly at the congregation. His family watched him.

"It is an honor for me to represent Jesus to you," he said. "I will work diligently to do a good job for him and for you. God's blessing to all of us. Thank you for giving me this opportunity."

While he put his hands together and prayed, Polycarp again looked directly at the congregation.

After the service, Polycarp talked with his mother.

"That was a nice speech," Dianna said. "We are all very proud of you. It is great that the priest has agreed to work with you. Is he charging you any money?"

"No, he is not charging me any money," he said. "I do the chores around the church, and I help write new scrolls. We are trying to keep track of all our lessons. I will be still live with you, probably, for a long time."

Polycarp continued to mature. He taught many lessons at the meeting place and visited other churches in Philippi to teach Jesus' message. He was well liked by everyone and did a great job teaching. His sisters became concerned about Polycarp's plans and how they would influence the long term wellbeing of the family. Martha decided it was time to talk with

Polycarp. One warm summer day, she saw him seated on the porch. She brought a chair and sat next to him. She didn't want anyone to hear their conversation, so she moved close to him.

"Polycarp, are you ever going to marry?" Martha asked. "We need to know who is going to take care of mother."

"No," Polycarp said. "I don't have time for an earthly wife."

"What do you mean?" she asked. "An earthly wife, please explain."

"I plan to marry the church," he said. "I plan to do a great amount of traveling."

"You are going to marry the church," she said. "You mean you are going to spend a lot of time at the church?"

"I want to travel and to learn," he said. "I want to see the world. It would be fine if you would take over the vineyards for mother. I will gladly give you my birthright."

"I think we should tell mother," Martha said. "It will make her life less uncertain."

"I agree with you," Polycarp said. "We will tell her after dinner tonight."

That evening, after the dinner table was cleared, they went into the living area to relax and talk. Martha started the conservation.

"That was a great dinner, Rachael," she said. "Mother, wasn't that a great dinner?"

"Yes, dear," Dianna said. "Rachael always prepares a great dinner."

"Polycarp and I have something we want to discuss with you," she said. "It is time we talk."

"Come and sit with me," Dianna said. "I will ask Margret to join us."

"I am not sure Margret should hear this," Martha said. "If you think it is the proper thing to do, you can tell her later."

Now Dianna was puzzled. She gave Martha a stern look.

"We are all concerned about the future of our family," Martha said. "We want to ensure someone is available to care for you. I have talked with Polycarp and we have come to an understanding."

"What are you in agreement about?" she asked. "I hope I am in agreement. You know I am still the matriarch of the house."

"Polycarp is not interested in living in and maintaining this house," she said. "He wants to study and travel. Polycarp has given me his birthright."

Dianna was startled. She gasped.

"That is a big step," she said. "I hope he knows what he is doing."

"We have this parchment for you," she said. "He won't be with us for long periods of time. I have agreed to be responsible for you and to take care of the vineyards. I hope this arrangement is acceptable to you."

Dianna looked at Martha.

"You two had me worried," she said. "I didn't know what you were going to tell me. It is fine with me. I think we should tell Margret."

Dianna emitted a happy sound and a smile appeared on her face.

"Polycarp, I think this is best for both of us," she said. "I am happy that you gave your birthright to your sister. I am certain she will take good care of me and the vineyards."

She turned and talked with Margret, "Your sister is going to care for me in my old age. Polycarp gave her his birthright. He is going to study and travel."

"I think that is a good idea," Margret said. "I plan to marry and have a house full of children."

Everyone smiled and engaged in conversation.

After a joyous evening, they hugged each other and went to bed.

CHAPTER 2

THE RESEARCH PROJECT – PROFESSOR THOMAS

Dianna, the oldest daughter, was married and Margret planned to be married. Dianna and her husband lived near the family, but Margret and her husband planned to relocate to Corinth. This required an unwanted adjustment for the family. Dianna hated to see her daughter move so far from Philippi. She was pleased that Polycarp and Martha lived at home and Dianna was close to the family. The warm, beautiful day caused her to reflect on her good fortune. She offered a special prayer of thanksgiving. Polycarp's mother was active at the local church and had made many friends. Martha saw a boy occasionally, but she spent most of her time with her mother and helped Rachael care for the house. Polycarp studied, with the head teacher, at their church and read every scroll he could find. He had read all the material in the library and at the church. When he found something new to read, it was not unusual for him to work late.

When Polycarp returned home, it was dinner time.

"Good evening," Dianna said. "Did you have a good day? I have been resting. Martha and Rachael went to the market this afternoon. I believe dinner has been prepared."

"I did have a good day," Polycarp said. "Our teacher told me about a man named John. The new emperor Nerva released him from exile. He is very old and lives in Ephesus."

"Polycarp is home," Dianna announced. "He is hungry."

"John was one of Jesus' disciples," he said. "He wrote many stories about Jesus. I would like very much to visit with him. I will tell you more after dinner."

"Rachael, you may serve dinner," she said. "It looks delicious. After everyone sits down, I will give thanks for our many blessings."

"We were able to find some fresh vegetables at the market today," Martha said. "I hope you enjoy them. We purchased enough for several days."

"I think you will have to go to the market without me," Dianna said. "You always take the time to find the best vegetables."

"Polycarp, are you working tomorrow?" Martha asked. "What time do you think you will be home?"

"Yes, I work tomorrow," Polycarp said. "I will probably be at the university most of the day. One of the professors is preparing to give me some of his notes."

"I will plan supper for just after sunset," she said.

"He wants me to write them in Greek," he said. "He also wants two scrolls. It may take me longer than one day."

"It sounds like you are busy," she said. "It is nice to have enjoyable, steady work."

"If you serve dinner soon after sunset, I will be here," Polycarp said. "They haven't provided me with any candles, so I am expected to leave at sundown."

"How do you like your job?" Dianna asked. "You are lucky to have a job with such flexible hours."

"I love my job," he said. "Writing for the professors is challenging. They are an interesting group of men. They seem to be very pleased with my work."

For the last six months, Polycarp transcribed and wrote for the professors at the local university. He worked with them two long days per week, and on the other days he studied and wrote for himself. He was not paid very much and had to be very frugal with his money. His mother helped him pay his living expenses.

"I think they are going to hire someone to help me," Polycarp said. "I hope he is a good writer."

"Maybe, they will give you a raise," Dianna said. "We could use more money."

One morning while Polycarp worked at the university, a professor approached him. The professor explained that they were going to become much busier and rather than have only one employee transcribing and writing, they wanted two men to do transcribing. The university hired a young man named Papias to work with Polycarp. They expected Polycarp to train Papias and to meet with the professors on a regular basis to ensure their work was being completed. Polycarp decided this was a good time to ask for an increase in pay.

"I appreciate the added responsibility. Would it be possible for me to receive an increase in pay?" Polycarp asked. "I am poor and an increase in pay would help me."

The professor said he would talk with Dean Julius and give Polycarp a good recommendation. The professor asked Polycarp to follow him to his office.

"Polycarp, I want to introduce you to Papias," he said. "He will work directly with you. He will help you complete the work."

Papias looked at Polycarp.

"I will depart and allow you to continue working," the professor said. "I will see you next week, Polycarp."

"Can you write Greek?" Polycarp asked. "We will have to write a lot of Greek."

"I can write a little Greek," Papias said. "I am much better at writing Latin. Maybe, you could write most of the Greek, and I can write the Latin."

"It is important that you become proficient in writing Greek," he said. "I will write the Greek while you increase your writing ability."

"I am willing to learn," he said. "You can help me. I will be a good student, and will ask questions."

"I guess that will keep us current with the professors," he said. "I will expect you to practice your Greek."

"I am ready to get started," Papias said. "Let's go to work."

Polycarp explained the work schedule to Papias. Papias agreed and said he could work at almost any time. They discussed the material that

Polycarp had accumulated and what was expected to be transcribed and written on scrolls. Papias started by creating scrolls in Latin. After he completed a scroll, it was given to Polycarp to proof read before it was given to the professors. Their system worked.

"We have a lot of work to complete," Polycarp said. "The professor must be writing more. I may have to ask if they will allow me to work additional hours."

"I can work longer," Papias said. "I still live at home, and we could use the money."

Papias and Polycarp were a good team.

When Polycarp saw Dean Julius approach, they were at work in the rear of the library.

"Polycarp, I want to talk with you," he said. "I will return to my office. Join me there in one half hour."

The dean never really stopped walking. He just slowed down for a short time. He didn't give Polycarp time to answer before he exited the library. Polycarp turned to Papias and smiled.

"I wonder what he wants," Polycarp said. "I guess I will find out."

"I am certain it will be good news," Papias said. "He seemed in a good mood."

"I might not be back today, keep working on the scroll," he said. "When you finish that one, you can always start another one. I will see you tomorrow."

Polycarp walked slowly to the dean's office. He imagined what the dean wanted to discuss. As he sat outside of the office, thoughts raced through his head. The dean called for him. Polycarp jumped to his feet and entered the dean's office.

"Good afternoon, dean," he said. "I have never been in your office."

"The university is growing rapidly," he said. "We are doing more research, and the student population is growing rapidly. I have talked with the professors. We want to hire you fulltime."

Polycarp tried not to act overly excited. He paused for a few moments.

"I will have to discuss this with my mother," he said. "I still live at home."

"You are a man, you don't need your mother's approval," Julius said.

"We plan to pay you a nice salary."

Polycarp became very interested and smiled at the dean.

"That would be great," he said. "The family could use more income. I will work diligently."

"What about your father?" he asked.

"He was a soldier," Polycarp said. "He died many years ago."

The dean sensed Polycarp's sad mood.

"Let's go outside and enjoy the sun," he said. "The fresh air will do us good."

Polycarp stood and followed the dean.

They sat on a bench on the campus green. The dean stroked his beard.

"You will be assigned an office and given the title of assistant professor," he said. "We will expect you to continue what you are doing and perform research for one of the professors."

"Assistant professor," he said. "Doing research sounds very interesting."

"He is interested in Jesus' message and indicated you were also interested in that topic," Dean Julius said. "Maybe you can help him teach."

"I am very interested in Jesus' message," Polycarp said. "I want to be exact about what he said."

"Papias will continue to work for you," he said. "We plan to hire several more faculty members, and you will probably be allowed to hire another employee to help you."

"I will need help," he said. "Preparing lessons can be very time consuming. I am looking forward to teaching."

"Do you have any questions?" Dean Julius asked. "I don't suppose you do. Consider what we have discussed and see me tomorrow."

"Thank you, dean," he said. "I can't wait to tell the family."

Dianna and Martha were excited for Polycarp, but they knew he would no longer be at home every evening. They asked Polycarp how often he would have to travel. He indicated he would travel for a month at a time. The dean said that the professor, he was going to work for, expected him to find and visit with anyone that had been with Jesus. Polycarp was expected to interview them and to take voluminous notes. He couldn't imagine a research project that better suited his interests.

The next day, Polycarp visited with the dean.

"You can call me Dean Julius; I'll call you Professor Polycarp," he said.

"I talked with my mother," Polycarp said. "We are both excited. She was concerned about the travel."

"You will have to travel," he said. "It is part of doing research."

"I look forward to traveling," he said. "Mother is accustomed to having dinner with me every evening."

"You might be interested in what we are going to pay you," he said. "We decided you have two jobs, so we will pay you two salaries."

Polycarp was very surprised. He looked at the dean.

"A full-time job with two salaries," he asked. "That is wonderful."

"One salary, as an assistant professor, which is fixed for all beginning assistant professors and another salary to manage the transcribing and scroll production process," he said. "Money will no longer be a problem for you."

"I would like to know how much I will have to travel," he said. "Do I know the professor, for whom you want me to work?"

"No, I will introduce him to you," he said. "He has been around for a long time."

"His experience should help me learn," Polycarp said. "When will I meet him?"

"He is rather old and is not very outgoing," Dean Julius said. "You will have to do all the traveling necessary for his research project. He is too old to travel."

A few moments passed and then there was a knock on the Dean's office door. The dean stood up and went to the door. An elderly man, escorted by a student, entered the office and saw Polycarp.

"Come in, Professor Thomas," the dean said. "I want you to meet your new assistant, Professor Polycarp."

"I was expecting you to visit me before you decided to join us," Professor Thomas said.

"I have been working at the university for a while," Polycarp said. "Before I accepted the position, I planned to talk to you."

"That is a good idea," the dean said. "You two talk. When you are finished, you can tell my assistant on what date you will start full-time."

"Come to my office," Thomas said. "I think the office next to mine is the one they plan to give to you. As you can see, I am quite old and can't travel. Getting home is a journey for me."

He smiled at Polycarp and wiped his hand over his gray hair.

"I like to travel," Polycarp said. "I will travel for you."

"I want to interview everyone who is alive that was with Jesus," Thomas said. "I can't do it, so I want to hire you."

"Do you know who you want me to visit?" he asked. "Is it a lot of people?"

"You will do a lot of traveling," he said. "The university will pay your expenses and provide a scribe to travel with you."

"I was worried about traveling without someone accompanying me," Polycarp said.

"I think traveling, interviewing, studying, writing and teaching will take all of your time," he said. "It has kept me busy for a lifetime."

"I am looking forward to teaching," Polycarp said. "I have read many scrolls about Jesus."

"You might like the life of a professor," he said. "I hope you are interested. I know you work for the university, and I have seen much of your work."

"I am interested," he said. "You have been looking at my work?"

"That is why, I requested you," he said. "Don't be excited by Dean Julius. His attitude is why I asked him to join the university twenty years ago."

Polycarp liked Professor Thomas and started to work fulltime the following week. Papias became his fulltime scribe and they hired a new member to transcribe the professor's research. When he wasn't traveling with Polycarp, Papias was the daily supervisor of the transcription department.

The morning of the first day of the week was generally busy at the university. Professor Thomas waited, in his office, for Polycarp to arrive.

"Good morning," Thomas said. "I have a list for you to consider. It is everyone that I think might be alive that was with Jesus."

"That should be interesting," Polycarp said. "Let me see it."

"The most important person still alive is John," he said.

He handed the list to Polycarp.

"John was one of Jesus' original disciples," he said. "I believe he is the only original disciple still alive."

"I will study the list," Polycarp said. "I have been told a little about John, by our teacher at the church. Do you know where he is located?"

"John lives in Ephesus," he said. "He has been there since Nerva freed him from his exile on Patmos. I think you should make plans to visit him as soon as possible."

Polycarp went to the library and looked at a parchment map of the Great Sea. He and Papias studied the map and discussed their research trip. The next day, they walked to Neapolis and checked the schedule of ships that departed the Philippi area and sailed to Ephesus. They arranged passage on a cargo ship that departed the following week. The ship transported ingots of metal and only stopped twice before reaching Ephesus. They walked back to Philippi and returned to the university. Polycarp sent the schedule for their trip to Professor Thomas. The sun set low in the sky and the lighted candles cast a warm glow.

Polycarp was excited about the trip and walked home at an increased pace. When he arrived, Dianna greeted him. She sensed joy in his voice and guessed that he had planned his first research trip.

"Papias and I are going to Ephesus," he said. "We will depart next week."

"Next week," she said. "It didn't take them long to give you an assignment that required traveling."

"Traveling is a large part of my new job," he said. "Before I go, I will need to purchase a few things. Professor Thomas told me the university would pay for anything I need."

"How long will you be gone?" Martha asked. "We will need to change our habits."

"I will probably be gone at least a month," he said. "When I return home, I should remain here for a few weeks. When they are fresh on my mind, I have to organize my notes about the trip.

On a warm, bright, sunny day, Polycarp and Papias were taken by carriage from the university to the local port. They found the ship, The Markus, loaded with metal removed from the mountains. They saw iron bars and ingots of copper. They carried their bags aboard and were shown to their small quarters. The dock workers struggled to load the ship. It wasn't prepared to sail on schedule.

The captain didn't allow his ship to venture too far from shore, and he didn't like to sail in the dark, so he decided to wait until early the next morning to depart. A cabin on a ship was a new experience for Polycarp. He spent the evening inspecting the ship. Early the next morning, Polycarp felt the ship move.

"Well, we are finally underway," he said. "You look a little pale."

"I feel weak," Papias said. "I have never sailed before."

Two days later the ship reached Troas. Papias had spent most of his time bent over the ship's rail on the main deck. Polycarp dined and talked with the other ten passengers. This vessel was primarily a merchant cargo ship, with a few cabins for passengers. Papias was glad to sit on the ground while material was delivered from the port of Troas. Early the morning of the fourth day, they continued to sail to Ephesus.

Papias spoke with Polycarp, "I think I will stand on the deck and watch the sea. I just can't remain in our cabin."

The next two day passed very slowly for Papias. He learned to know every inch of the ship's rail. They finally arrived at Ephesus. They stood on the ship's main deck and gazed at a great street while the ramp was put in position. They grabbed their bags and disembarked. The ship's crew made a few remarks to Papias. He ignored them and hurried into Ephesus.

Polycarp reread the directions the professor had given to him. They were to walk south to Curetes Street. The instructions said to ask any of the merchants, in the area, where John lived.

Polycarp talked with a shopkeeper, "We are new in town. We have come to visit John, the disciple of Jesus; can you tell us where he lives?"

"If you mean the old fellow who teaches, go straight on this street."

After they walked a few blocks, they found someone who knew exactly where John lived. They knocked on his door.

"Hello, can I help you?" Abraham said. "I don't believe I know you."

"My name is Polycarp and this pale fellow is my scribe, Papias," he said. "We have come to see John. We work at the university in Philippi. Will John talk with us?"

"Just one moment," he said. "I will check."

Polycarp hadn't considered that they might have traveled all this distance and John wouldn't talk with them. Abraham returned in a moment and escorted them to see John.

"Come in," John said. "I didn't know they had a university in Philippi. Sit down."

"Our university is not nearly as large as your university," Polycarp said. "I work for Professor Thomas. I am trying to speak with everyone who knew Jesus. Professor Thomas is compiling a journal about Jesus."

"I have heard of Professor Thomas," John said. "I didn't know he was in Philippi. He must be quite old."

Polycarp saw John smile.

"You are correct. He is quite old," he said. "How long did you spend with Jesus?"

"It is a good story," John said. "I traveled with him for about three years. My brother and I were with John the Baptist, and when he told us Jesus was our Messiah, we started to travel with Jesus."

They remained with John for two weeks. They listened to him teach and they listened to all his stories. He explained that no one could tell a story like Jesus. They carefully took copious notes and asked many questions. When they asked John, about Timothy, he replied that he knew Timothy and that Timothy had lived the last few years of his life in Ephesus. They visited Timothy's grave and prayed.

On another day, they visited the university, where Paul had lectured, and the Temple of Artemis. John recommended they try to find Titus in Crete, he was not certain if he knew Jesus. He also recommended Jesus brother's son Menahem. Polycarp and Papias thanked John and started their journey home.

When they walked to the ship, it was a sunny warm morning.

"Polycarp, I will carry the extra bag," Papias said. "When we return home, we have a lot of work. You will have to do without me for a while."

"Without you, where will you be?" Polycarp asked.

"I will be standing at the railing on the main deck," he said. "I like traveling with you, but this is my first and last sailing adventure. When we get home, we will find someone to travel with you."

"Are you sure you don't want to do research with me?" he asked. "You will get accustomed to the sea."

"I am certain," he said. "I will never become accustomed to being sick."

"You will lose part of your pay," he said. "I like the extra travel money."

"I don't care if I am discharged," Papias said. "I am not traveling by ship again."

"I don't think anyone will discharge you," he said. "We need you to manage the transcribing."

"Having traveled once was an education for me," he said.

"I understand not everyone can be a sailor," Polycarp said. "While we sail home, I will read your notes and make a few notes. I am sorry you are so sick."

A week passed, before they arrived in Neapolis. Professor Thomas and a driver met them. When Papias told Professor Thomas that he was no longer going to sail, Thomas laughed and explained that not everyone made a good sailor. The professor said Polycarp could pick his own traveling companion from those in the transcribing section, and that Papias could return to transcribing. After they had stored their notes, they went home for a few days.

As he walked home, Polycarp visualized his family. He had purchased his sister and his mother presents. He was surprised how much he missed them. When he approached the house, Polycarp smelled the aroma of a freshly home-cooked dinner.

"I hope you cooked enough for me," Polycarp said. "I haven't had a really good meal while I was away."

Dianna hugged him and said, "Sit down and Rachael will prepare something for you. Tell us about your trip."

"One thing was determined," he said. "Papias is not a sailor. Before we sailed, he was sea sick."

"Some people just can't sail," Rachael said. "I like to sail."

"I will talk to those at the university and determine if any of them want to travel with me," he said. "I am sure I will find a new traveling companion."

After dinner, they relaxed in the living room. Polycarp sat in his favorite chair and sipped a cup of hot tea. He told this family all about John and Abraham. He also explained how many notes they had accumulated and how busy he was going to be rewriting the notes.

"I am glad you will be with us for a while," Dianna said. "Your clothes don't look very clean. Put them in a pile in your room. Rachael will clean them."

"I cleaned them occasionally," Polycarp said. "I must not have done a good job."

"You have clean clothes in your box," she said. "Do you have to get up early tomorrow?"

"I want to rise with the sun," he said. "I will have one of your wonderful breakfasts, and then I will spend the day at the university with Professor Thomas."

"We will be waiting for you to return," she said. "We can talk tomorrow evening."

"I have presents for you and Martha," he said. "This one is for you. The other one is for Martha. You can open them. I had them wrapped so they would be secure while I travel home."

"Thank you," she said. "Mine looks like a silver cross."

"They are different," he said. "I brought each of you, a silver cross. The silversmiths in Ephesus are very good craftsmen. I hope you like them. I will get chains."

The women had never seen a silver cross. They were very surprised and pleased. They said their evening prayer and went to bed.

The next morning, when Rachael served breakfast Polycarp gave her a present. He had brought her a small bottle of perfume. Dianna wore her new cross. She had found an old chain and explained that she didn't need another chain. After they enjoyed their breakfast, Polycarp walked to the university. It was a bright sunny day with no clouds in the sky. When he arrived at his office, Papias greeted him.

"I have found you a new traveling companion," he said. "I felt very badly, because I was always sick. I talked with those doing transcribing and Assaf would like to talk with you."

Assaf entered Polycarp's office and was seated. He started the conversation.

"I have sailed many times," he said. "My father's brother lives in Tyre. I have made the trip with father several times to visit with him. When the seas were quite rough, I never got sick. I write Greek, and I would like to travel with you."

Polycarp hesitated for a moment. He allowed Assaf to relax.

"I would like to see a sample of your writing," he said. "Have Papias give you some of our notes. When you have transcribed them into Greek, come back and visit me."

"I will start on them at once," he said. "I will see you later today."

"I will probably be in my office working," he said. "Just talk with my student assistant or knock on the door."

Polycarp talked with Professor Thomas almost every day. The professor showed great interest in what John had discussed with Polycarp. Polycarp explained that John had read all the scrolls in Ephesus, and he was currently writing a series of scrolls that would emphasize Jesus' most important stories. John's discourse would contain many stories the other writers had not included. John indicated he and Abraham had been working on recording his recollection for several months, and he thought it would take them another year to complete their task. Polycarp then explained that it would take two months to transcribe all their notes without getting behind with their normal work. Professor Thomas understood and congratulated Polycarp on his interview with John.

After a month passed, Professor Thomas visited Polycarp. Polycarp noticed that Professor Thomas was not steady. When he stood, he braced himself against the wall. The professor was absent from the university for many days. Dean Julius entered Polycarp's office.

"I visited with Professor Thomas," he said. "He is ill and won't be able to continue to come into the university."

"I am sorry," Polycarp said. "I didn't know he was that sick."

"I want you to visit with him at least once a week," he said. "I will need you to teach the professor's classes."

"I will be glad to do it," he said. "Papias would probably like to teach his class."

"Can Papias teach?" he asked. "After you have had time to think about our situation, visit with me tomorrow morning."

Polycarp went to the room where the transcription was completed. He asked Papias to come to his office. They had a long discussion about the situation. If someone was hired to help with the transcribing, Papias agreed to teach. Polycarp explained to Papias they would know more tomorrow. They planned to talk again.

As Polycarp walked home, he thought about Professor Thomas. When he arrived, his mother greeted him.

"You look concerned," she said. "You must have had a busy day."

"We are very busy," Polycarp said. "We are going to make some changes."

"Sit down and let's talk," she said. "I will tell Rachael you are home. She will serve dinner."

"Dean Julius told me that Professor Thomas is quite ill," he said. "He can't continue to work full-time at the university."

"Are you going to have to do his job?" Dianna asked. "You can't do three jobs."

"I am going to visit the professor's house once a week and talk with him about his research," Polycarp said. "I need to learn a great amount of information in a short time."

"That is admirable," she said. "I know you like the research."

"The dean wants to see me tomorrow morning," he said. "Papias and I are going to have to teach the professor's classes for a while. When I come home tomorrow evening, I will have additional information."

"Clean the ink from your hands and have a seat at the table," she said.

They enjoyed dinner and retired to the living area. After talking with Martha and Rachael, Polycarp went to bed. He was tired and needed a good night of rest. Sometimes what you need is not what you get. He tossed and turned all night. He was concerned about Professor Thomas.

The next morning, he ate his breakfast and slowly walked to the university. He met with the dean.

"I talked with Papias, and we will teach Professor Thomas' classes," he said. "We will need help in the transcription department."

"Yes, I am sure of that," Julius said. "That is not my major concern."

"What is your major concern?" he asked.

"When I visited with Professor Thomas last evening, he had problems talking with me. He was very short of breath," he said. "I did understand that he wants you to visit someone named Menahem as soon as you can arrange your schedule to allow it to happen."

"I know who Menahem is," Polycarp said. "Menahem is the son of Jude, one of Jesus' brothers."

"We need your help," he said. "I have talked with the other professors. We want you to complete Professor Thomas' research and be responsible for his classes."

"I will need some assistance," Polycarp said. "I will be glad to help."

"We will make Papias your assistant and you can hire all the help you need with transcribing," he said. "After you review our offer, I will change your status to full professor."

The dean handed Polycarp several manuscripts. He went to his office. The manuscripts said exactly what the dean had described. Polycarp hated that Professor Thomas was ill, but he was pleased with the promotion. After he read the offer the second time, he went to the dean's office to consummate it. It was a short discussion.

"All you have to do is tell me you want the position," Julius said. "I will take care of all the necessary paper work. After you have had time to think about it, you can tell me how you are going to handle your new position. Good day, Professor Polycarp."

The title, Professor Polycarp, sounded good. As he walked to his office, a large smile appeared on his face.

Polycarp found Papias working in the transcribing area. He asked him to come to his house for dinner that evening. He told him they had a great many details to consider. He challenged him to formulate a plan concerning how to perform Professor Thomas's job and the transcribing position. On his walk home, he planned what he would discuss with Papias.

"Papias is going to join us for dinner," he said.

"This evening?" she asked. "We will have to go to the market."

"That is fine," he said. "Have Rachael prepare something special."

Dianna stared at him.

"I am sorry I didn't give you more time," Polycarp said.

"That is fine," Dianna said. "It might require a little time for us to prepare dinner."

"Papias and I have several things to discuss," he said. "We will be in the living area."

"I am sure Rachael will prepare a nice dinner for us," she said. "I will bring you some hot tea."

After they enjoyed the dinner, Polycarp and Papias thanked the women for the wonderful dinner and went outside and sat on the porch. Papias told Polycarp the he would teach Professor Thomas' classes and manage the transcription department. He also indicated that he would expect a raise. Polycarp said that was satisfactory, and that he would continue with Professor Thomas' research and writing. He would have Assaf promoted to be his assistant. They agreed it would be best to hire two additional men to transcribe. When they finished their discussion, they went inside and talked with the women. Eventually, Papias excused himself and went home. Polycarp and the women relaxed and discussed his plans.

Early in the morning Martha cooked breakfast for Polycarp. When he went to the university, he felt great. Shortly after sunrise, Polycarp was in his office. He planned his discussion with the dean. A few moments after the dean arrived at the university, Polycarp went to his office.

"Papias and I talked for a long time last evening," he said. "We think we can handle the situation."

"We know you can," Julius said. "Papias will need you to mentor him."

Polycarp sensed he was in a good position. He requested a long list of items that he might need.

"When he starts teaching and managing full-time, Papias would like a pay raise," he said. "We want to hire at least two additional new employees for transcribing."

"That will not be a problem," he said. "We can hire one person now and maybe another one later."

"I think we need two now," he said. "I don't want to get behind with our transcribing."

"I will have to check with the treasurer to make certain we can afford two additional transcribers," he said. "What else do you need?"

"I would like Assaf promoted to be my assistant," he said. "When I travel, he will be my scribe. When I am at the university, he will transcribe my notes from traveling and work with those doing the transcribing for the professors."

"That is a lot of change," Julius said. "We need to be mindful of our budget."

"We need to be mindful of our research and our students," Polycarp said. "Tell me when you want me to make the changes."

"Hire one person to transcribe," he said. "Before you leave on your next trip, if everything goes as planned, you can hire the second employee and promote Assaf to your assistant."

Polycarp went to Professor Thomas' old office. Papias had moved into that office and was busy working. Polycarp instructed Papias to have all the research material in Professor's Thomas' old office, taken to his office. He explained that the dean had approved the hiring of one new man to do transcribing and another one before the next research trip. He related that Assaf agreed to help with transcribing.

Polycarp returned to his office and started reading his notes. He saw Assaf approach.

"How did your meeting with the dean go?" Assaf asked. "When do I get my raise?"

"I want you to work transcribing and helping Papias and me," he said. "When we leave on my next trip, you will be promoted and receive a raise. We have to make this work within our budget."

"I have bills now," he said. "When are we leaving for a trip?"

"Before I make that decision, I will see Professor Thomas," Polycarp said.

"I want the job," he said. "But I don't like doing the work now and getting a raise later."

"I am sorry," he said. "That is the offer. Being patient is not always pleasant."

During the next two weeks, Polycarp spent several days with Professor Thomas. He recorded everything the professor could remember about his research. Again, Professor Thomas suggested that he visit Menahem on the next research trip. Menahem was currently the bishop of Smyrna. Polycarp explained Professor Thomas' request to Dean Julius. The dean instructed him to make plans for the trip, but to wait thirty days before departing. That was fine with Polycarp. He had a lot of changes and planning to complete during the next month. Assaf was informed of their journey. He spent many hours with Polycarp. Smyrna was a little closer than Ephesus. The schedule, for the ships, indicated two ships from Philippi to Smyrna and back each week. Each ship transported ten passengers. Polycarp made reservations on a ship that departed in thirty-five days.

When Polycarp walked home, the sun set and the stars became visible. As he approached Dianna's house, he watched a candle flicker.

"I had a productive day at the university, what's for dinner tonight?" he asked.

"We are having fresh vegetables," Dianna said.

"I will be going to Smyrna," he said. "I will be leaving in thirty-five days. I have already scheduled passage for Assaf and me. It is a ship that carries metal. It is owned by the same company as the last ship. I think they are getting to know me."

"How does Papias like teaching?" she asked.

"I think he is happy," he said. "The classes are full and the students like his lectures. I believe he will do fine."

"I see Rachael," she said. "She and Martha have served our dinner."

The aroma of the food filled the air. Polycarp enjoyed a vegetable dinner with his family. The next thirty-five days passed quickly for him, but they passed very slowly for Assaf. Polycarp remained busy with his notes from the last trip and helped Papias with his lesson plans. Two days before the trip, Assaf was allowed time to make arrangements to become Polycarp's scribe and traveling partner.

The moon shone brightly. When they arrived at the dock, the sun peeked over the horizon. It was early in the morning.

"Good morning, Polycarp," Assaf said. "After I saw you yesterday, I saw the dean."

"Why did you do that?" Polycarp asked. "Did he say anything about our trip?"

"He informed me that I was promoted to your assistant, and that he expects me to do a good job for you and the university," he said. "I didn't tell him you had explained the plan to me."

Assaf looked at Polycarp.

"Where should I put our packs?" he asked.

"The mate will help you," he said. "We will just stand here for a few minutes. The captain will see us and have someone show us to our quarters. Did you bring plenty of writing supplies?"

"Yes, I am well prepared," he said. "I even brought a drawing that shows the streets of Smyrna. I am certain we will be able to find the church."

"We will find it," Polycarp said. "I am good at finding churches."

"It is large enough to have a bishop," he said. "I wonder how long Menahem has been in Smyrna."

"I think he has been there for many years," Polycarp said. "The captain is motioning for us to board. Get you pack and the supplies."

"Good morning, professor," the captain said. "I have cabin number one for you and your scribe."

"It is good to see you," Polycarp said. "We are ready to travel."

"The university is becoming one of our best customers," he said. "They tell me you probably will be doing more traveling."

"Yes," he said. "My research will require travel to many distant locations."

"We will do our best to accommodate your needs," he said. "My mate is Jason. He will check with you on a regular basis. If you need anything, ask for him."

The ship had been loaded the previous day. As soon as all the passengers were aboard, the ship sailed. Two days later, they arrived at the harbor in Smyrna. Polycarp was relieved that Assaf hadn't been sick and had planned their trip quite thoroughly. When the ship docked, the sun was bright and the harbor was filled with the sounds of sailors unloading ships. The gang plank was lowered and they disembarked.

"When we get there, I will ask for Menahem. He is expecting us. I sent him a message," Polycarp said.

They found the church and sat in a pew. The local priest greeted them. Polycarp explained who he was and his mission. The priest escorted him to the bishop.

"This is bishop Menahem's office," the priest said. "He expects you. I will knock on his door. I always check before entering."

"Come in," Menahem said. "You must be Polycarp. I see you have your scribe with you. We have prepared a place for you to stay and a place for your scribe to work."

"Thank you," Polycarp said. "It is a pleasure to meet you."

"I can keep your scribe busy for some time," he said. "As you know, my father Jude was Jesus' brother."

"I am hoping to talk to you about Jesus," he said. "You said you could keep Assaf busy?"

"I have scrolls Jude and Salome wrote with the help of Thomas," he said. "Paul taught Thomas how to write Greek. How was your trip?"

"Our trip was pleasant," he said. "Did you speak with Jesus? You must have been quite young."

"No I didn't speak with him," he said. "My father told me all about him. I have some notes for you."

"You didn't talk with him," he said. "I thought you had spoken with him."

"I am told I did meet with him," he said. "I was one of the children Jesus blessed. I feel like he gave me the spirit of God."

"You are very lucky," he said. "Jesus gave you his blessing."

"You will like Smyrna, the people here are great. Polycarp, I want you to teach a lesson for us and explain your research," he said. "Your research is very interesting."

"I will be honored to teach a lesson," he said. "I can talk almost endlessly about my research. When would you like me to teach?"

"We have a meeting tomorrow evening," he said. "Is that enough time for you to gather your thoughts?"

"We will be prepared," he said. "I am looking forward to meeting your members."

The next evening, Polycarp taught a lesson about John's writings. After he taught, he explained his research and his travels. After the meeting, Menahem talked with him.

"I enjoyed your lesson," he said. "I didn't know you knew John. John and I have a friendly rivalry."

"I visited with John," he said. "I consider myself a disciple of John's."

"I send him my best lessons and he sends me his best lessons," he said. "If you would send me some lessons, I would appreciate it."

"I would be glad to send you some of my lessons," Polycarp said. "That will keep John writing for a while longer."

"I will provide a city tour for you next week," Menahem said. "You and Assaf need a day off. I will have one of the priests show you our city."

"We would enjoy a tour of the city," he said. "I have only visited a few buildings."

"We have a great university. It specializes in science and medicine. I think you will also like the circle of beautiful public structures."

As Assaf copied scrolls and made notes, a few days passed. Menahem appeared in the room with his arms loaded with scrolls. He told Polycarp they were the personal scrolls his father had given to him. They were written by Jude and Thomas. He indicated that Assaf could stay as long as necessary, if he wanted to make a copy of them. Polycarp instructed Assaf to stay until everything was copied before he returned home. Polycarp stayed another five days.

After he thanked Menahem and returned to the dock, he sailed home on the same ship. When he talked with the captain, he explained that it would be about another month before Assaf would be returning. The trip home was uneventful.

When Polycarp arrived in Philippi, he went straight to the university. He gave a messenger a note for his mother, telling her he would be home for dinner. He walked to the dean's office.

"Hello, Dean Julius," he said. "I have news for you."

He sternly looked at Polycarp.

"While you were gone, Professor Thomas died," he said,

Polycarp became very weak. Tears filled his eyes. He bent forward and put his head in his hands. He was silent for a long moment. The dean sensed his grief. He stood and walked to Polycarp's chair. He put his hand on his shoulder.

"The gentleman that was paying for Professor Thomas' research came to see me, and I told him about you," Julius said. "We had a long talk."

"When did Professor Thomas die?" he asked. "He was a great mentor."

Julius didn't answer Polycarp's question. He wanted to focus Polycarp on the positive and not on death.

"He agreed to endow your teaching and research," he said. "He has been a great help to the university. He will come and visit with you. Tell me your news."

Julius patted Polycarp's shoulder and smiled at him.

"He has endowed my research?" he asked. "The last time I saw Professor Thomas, he told me, he would probably not be alive when I returned. He told me to talk with you about my research."

"He had faith in you," Julius said. "Now it is up to you."

CHAPTER 3

THE RESEARCH PROJECT - POLYCARP

When Dean Julius located Polycarp, he sat in his office entrenched by the scrolls recently obtained from Menahem. The dean inquired about his latest research trip.

"We were able to find and interview Menahem," Polycarp said. "He didn't really know Jesus personally, but his father was Jesus' brother."

"I hoped he had talked with Jesus," Julius said. "He must have been very interesting."

"Bishop Menahem had many scrolls that his father or Thomas wrote," he said. "Assaf remained with him to copy the scrolls. He probably won't return for a month."

"Do you know where you plan to visit next and when you will depart the university?" he asked. "I need to have you make a verbal report to the professors."

"No, I will look at the material Professor Thomas gave me. After I have analyzed it, I will talk with you," he said. "I won't see Assaf for several weeks."

"Can you talk with the professors tomorrow?" he asked. "They are very interested."

"Yes," he said. "You might be interested to know I taught a few lessons in Smyrna. I am going to send Menahem's church a few of my lessons."

"I know, they sent me a message," he said. "They made you an honorary member of their church. They expect you to return often and teach them about Jesus."

"They sent you a message?" he asked. "That was quick."

"Go home and have dinner with your family," Julius said. "I won't be here tomorrow. I will see you next week."

Polycarp perused a few parchments that had accumulated on his desk and then stored the material from his trip. He stood up, rubbed his face, and walked home. His sea legs disappeared. The ground wasn't moving like a ship, and his only meeting tomorrow was with his peers.

When he approached the house, he saw his mother waiting for him.

"I got your message," Dianna said. "Thank you for sending the messenger to me."

"I didn't want to surprise you again," Polycarp said. "I thought I might give you a little notice."

He smiled at her. She gave him a hug.

"We are preparing a very special meal for you," she said. "Martha found some game birds at the market. Come in and sit in the living area with me. I want you to tell me about Smyrna."

"It is great to be home," he said. "Bishop Menahem was very hospitable. They had rooms prepared for us to live at the church, and one day they provided a tour guide. I especially enjoyed the great array of buildings. They are arranged in an ellipse."

Polycarp noticed Martha standing in the room.

"Hello, Polycarp, welcome home," she said. "Rachael prepared a special meal for you, are you going to be home for a while?"

"Yes," he said. "I am not exactly certain for how long. Assaf is still in Smyrna."

"Your scribe stayed in Smyrna?" she asked. "What is he doing?"

"He probably has another month's work copying scrolls," he said. "While I was there, I made a friend. Bishop Menahem and I are going to communicate. I am going send him lessons and, when possible, teach in Smyrna."

"Dinner is ready," Rachael said. "Please bless the food for us."

Polycarp enjoyed his special dinner. After dinner, he gave each of the women a small gift from Smyrna. It had been a long day, so he went to bed early.

The next morning before he walked to the university, he ate breakfast with his mother and prayed for a peaceful, productive day.

Papias visited Polycarp in his office.

"How was your trip?" he asked.

"It was fine," Polycarp said. "Assaf is still copying scrolls written by Menahem's father. He remained in Smyrna. I love the people I met, and I hope to return many times. The university is unbelievable and the city is great."

He looked at Polycarp.

"If you aren't too busy tomorrow, I would like you to lecture to my students," he said. "They often ask when you will return, and if you will lecture to them. The class became so large, I teach in a lecture hall instead of the old classroom."

"I am going to be busy tomorrow," Polycarp said. "I am working on some data for the dean. Ask your students if the middle of next week would be satisfactory. I am going to meet with the dean early next week."

"They will be very disappointed," he said. "They were hoping to see you tomorrow."

Polycarp didn't want to disappoint Papias, but he was very busy.

"I am scheduled to see the dean and must prepare to update him about the research project" he said.

"I hope everything is copacetic," Papias replied. "We all know Professor Thomas died."

"I think his programs will continue," Polycarp said. "I will be told the details during a meeting next week."

Papias sensed concern in Polycarp's manner.

"I will inform my students," he said. "I am certain next week will be satisfactory."

"Maybe, I will have some news for them," he said. "A mixture of news and history can be very interesting."

"While you are home, I would appreciate it if you lectured once a week for my students and me," he said. "I have a surprise for you. You will meet him tomorrow."

When Polycarp arrived at his office the next morning, he was surprised to see Joel. Papias had assigned him to work for Polycarp and for a small stipend he agreed to complete anything Polycarp needed. His first assignment involved organization of Polycarp's office and his scrolls. After they greeted each other, Polycarp sat at his desk and created a list of destinations and a schedule for the dean.

When Dean Julius returned the following week, his first visit was to Polycarp's office.

He looked into to Polycarp's office and said, "Give me a few moments and then come to my office."

By the time Polycarp looked up from his work, the dean had departed. He made some notes to ensure he discussed all the pertinent items with the dean, filled his tea cup, and walked to the dean's office.

"I hope you enjoyed a beneficial few days," he said. "I have a new student assigned to me."

"Yes, I know," Julius said. "Papias and I talked about which student would work best with you. He introduced the student to me. While I was gone, I did have a few beneficial meetings. Tell me your plans."

"I want to take one more trip similar to what I have been taking. I would like to go to Crete and locate Titus," he said. No one knows for certain if he is still alive. I plan to leave about two weeks after Assaf returns."

"Crete, Titus?" he questioned. "Remember I told you about your research being endowed? I met with our benefactor."

Polycarp became mildly concerned, "Yes, I remember. He has been very generous. I hope he likes what we are doing."

The dean stroked his beard and smiled at Polycarp, "You could say he is pleased. He is going to arrange for us to have a new large building, and he requested we teach religion."

Polycarp sighed in relief.

"That is great," he said. "Papias informed me his classes have become quite large."

"He had a few other surprises that concern you," he said.

"Does he know me?" he asked. "I don't know him."

"When you were in Smyrna, he listened to you teach," he said. "He was very impressed."

"He was in Smyrna?" he asked. "What was he doing in Smyrna?"

"He lives not far from Smyrna," the dean said. "He knows you are going to send Bishop Menahem lessons and knows Assaf is still copying scrolls."

"He seems to know everything," he said. "I guess he is involved with the church."

"He wants you to visit Smyrna and teach on each trip you make," he said. "It will make it easier for you. You can schedule a ship from Smyrna to anywhere you want to visit."

Polycarp visualized Smyrna for a moment, and then he looked at the dean.

"The dock seems to be quite busy," he said. "They must ship grain and ore to many different areas."

The dean continued to talk. He exuded enthusiasm.

"He purchased a house and gave it to the church. It is exclusively for your use," he said. "It is a very nice house."

"He gave the church a house, so I would have a place to stay?" Polycarp asked.

The dean had gained his undivided attention.

"An attendant, James, will live in the house at all times. When you are in Smyrna, he will care for you and Assaf," Julius said. "I know this is a lot to comprehend. I hope I have remembered all the details. After a few days, we will talk again."

When he walked to his office, Polycarp had a smile on his face, but his head ached. His attention was focused on his trip to Crete. He would go to Smyrna to teach, and then he would go to Crete. His attendant in Smyrna, James, would schedule and reserve his ship to and from Smyrna.

A few weeks passed, Polycarp became accustomed to regularly sending messages to his attendant in Smyrna. He received a message from Assaf that indicated he was coming home. He requested a carriage, because he had several extra bags full of scrolls.

Polycarp met him at the port.

"I have a student with me," he said. "He will carry your extra bags."

Assaf smiled at him.

"I am glad to be home," he said. "Is there anything new at the university?"

"What we have obtained from Menahem should be very interesting reading," Polycarp said. "I had never read anything Jesus' brothers wrote."

"Thomas is a very good writer," Assaf said. "I didn't study his writings, but they contain some very poignant sayings. I am sure you will like many of them."

Assaf smiled at Polycarp.

"I am glad someone in that family was proficient with Greek," Polycarp said. "The words of Jesus' brother should give us some insight to the family."

"I think Thomas was very different than Jude," Assaf said. "His writings are really interesting reading. They are not a story. They are written as poignant one line messages."

During the next week, Polycarp and Assaf planned their trip to Crete. Many of the arrangements were handled through messages sent to James. Assaf was allowed a few days away from the university, and then they packed for their journey to Crete.

While the rode a carriage to the dock, the sun partially appeared above the horizon. They discussed their last trip and anticipated their current venture. The morning clouds disappeared and the sun shone brightly. The carriage stopped at the dock. They unloaded their packs, and finally they located their ship. They greeted the captain.

"We will be with you again," Assaf said. "It appears we will be making many trips to Smyrna with you."

"We have cabin number one prepared for you," the captain said. "My mate will show you to your cabin."

The captain greeted Polycarp with a large smile.

The ship slowly moved away from the dock. The sea was choppy and the ship couldn't maintain its normal speed. Eerie, creaky sounds from the ship filled the air. Polycarp heard a knock on the door.

"Sir, the captain asked me to inform you that we will make a stop in Troas," a mate said. "We are going to remain in port until the storm subsides."

Polycarp wasn't pleased with the delay, but he didn't want the ship to be in danger. While in Troas, he and Assaf visited a church which Paul had started. The local members told Polycarp a story about Paul bringing a young man back to life. Assaf compiled copious notes and asked to hear the story several times.

After two days had passed, they boarded their ship and sailed to Smyrna.

When they arrived, James met them.

"We were informed you had been delayed. My name is James," he said. I will care for you and the house."

"The church is going to care for the house," Polycarp said. "That is nice."

"I am a priest at the church. You and the church's house are just a few of my duties," he said. "If you need anything, please ask me."

"You must be a busy man," Polycarp said. "We are pleased to meet you. This is Assaf my scribe. Do you work for Bishop Menahem?"

"Yes, we all work for the bishop," he said. "I have arranged for you to teach tomorrow in the church's lecture hall."

"Thank you, James," he said. "Did you say the lecture hall?"

"I think you can expect a large crowd," he said. "I will take your bag, follow me. It isn't far to the house."

That evening, the three of them ate dinner at the church with the other priests. After they reviewed their lessons, James informed them they would be sailing to Crete in two days and return two weeks later. The next day, James took them to the lecture hall. It was already full of members, professors, and students. Polycarp surveyed his audience and greeted them. He then lectured for one hour. Everyone seemed to enjoy Polycarp's lesson. He gave James his notes and asked that they be delivered to the bishop.

After they ate, Polycarp asked James about Paul and the church in Smyrna. James knew that Paul started the church during one of his journeys, but not many of the details.

The next day, they boarded a large ship that sailed to Rome with a stop in Crete. James introduced them to the captain and showed them to their cabin. The sea was calm and they arrived on schedule. The ship remained in port overnight. Many of the passengers enjoyed an evening in Knossos. Polycarp and Assaf located the local church. They were informed that the church had been founded by Paul and Titus. They ascertained that the last time anyone heard of Titus, he lived in Gortyn.

They walked south across the island to Gortyn and found a church and spoke with the priest.

"Hello, I understand you are asking about Titus," he said. "I am Abraham. I am the teacher at this church. What is your name and what do you want with Titus. I have been his guardian for several years."

"My name is Polycarp," he said. "This is my scribe Assaf. I perform research as part of my duties for the university in Philippi."

"A university professor?" he asked. "He will probably see you."

"I hope to interview everyone that talked with or knows details of Jesus," he said. "May we please meet with him?"

"I will ask him if he would like to talk with you," he said. "Have a seat. A church is a good place to pray. I will return in a few moments."

Polycarp and Assaf became worried that they would not be allowed to interview Titus. The priest finally returned. He indicated he would take them to Titus and then escorted them to Titus' house.

"It is an honor to meet you, Titus," Polycarp said. "How much time did you spend with Jesus?"

In a very low and worn out voice, Titus replied, "My parents took me to listen to Jesus on two occasions. The last time I saw Jesus, I was about eight years old. I did spend several years with Paul. I have an epistle he wrote to me. I will show it to you."

Polycarp became excited. Assaf gained permission to copy the scrolls. Titus became quite tired and the priest took him away. When he returned, he spoke with Polycarp and indicated that Titus wouldn't be available for many days.

They returned to Knossos and reread the scrolls. Their return trip to Smyrna was pleasant. The weather was warm and the breeze was steady. They disembarked the ship and walked to the house. They found James seated at a table studiously reading.

"We were able to talk with Titus," Polycarp said.

James looked at Polycarp and said, "I am glad you located him. He must be very old."

"He thought he was the only one alive that had been with Jesus" he said. "I told him about John. It won't be long before all those that knew Jesus will have died."

"I will make arrangements for you to teach tomorrow," he said. "I know the schedule for ships, and I will purchase passage for you."

"That is fine," he said. "When will we sail?"

"You will remain with us for two days," he said. "We will eat with the other priests this evening. Give me your clothes. I will have them cleaned."

That evening they enjoyed a dinner with the priests of Smyrna.

The next morning after breakfast, Polycarp lectured to a standing room only crowd of priests, professors, and students. In the afternoon, they relaxed and talked with James.

When James took them to the ship, the sun was still below the horizon. They greeted the captain.

"You are becoming like family," he said. "Your cabin is prepared, and this time I don't plan on stopping in Troas."

A smile appeared on the captain's face. Polycarp grinned and walked to his cabin.

While sailing, Polycarp and Assaf spent the days on deck. They enjoyed the sun and the breeze. They constantly talked about their visit with Titus. Polycarp realized his good fortune of being able to talk with both John and Titus. The trip seemed shorter than normal.

When they arrived at the dock, they located a man with a carriage and paid him to take them to the university. Polycarp and Assaf walked to Dean Julius' office and greeted him.

"We had a really successful visit in Crete," Polycarp said.

"Great," Julius said. "How was Smyrna?"

"We were able to find Titus in Gortyn and interviewed him," he said. "We will organize our notes. If you are available later in the week, I will talk with you."

The dean stared at Polycarp.

"Did you lecture in Smyrna?" he asked. "Did a great many people attend your lectures?"

Polycarp sensed the dean's great desire to satisfy their benefactor.

"Yes, I lectured to large audiences," he said. "It is good to be back to work."

The dean appeared satisfied.

The next day was the Sabbath, so Polycarp and his family went to church and rested most of the day. His mother was glad to have him home and only asked a few questions. Polycarp informed Dianna that he planned to be home for a month. Rachael purchased more food and prepared an additional place at the table. Dianna asked for breakfast to be served a little earlier. She wanted to eat with Polycarp. Polycarp and his research became very well known throughout Philippi and the church.

Early in the morning on the first day of the following week, Polycarp walked to the university and discussed his plans with Assaf.

"I have decided to change our focus," he said. "Instead of visiting with those who might have talked with Jesus, I plan to visit people who might have old original scrolls written about Jesus."

"That will include many more people," Assaf said. "That will keep us busy for a while."

"I will have to get approval from Dean Julius," he said.

"Why change the focus?" he asked. "We have been quite successful."

"Yes, I am certain," he said. "I have prayed about it many times. John was the only person who has been able to tell me any detail about Jesus."

"John was very helpful," Assaf said. "I hope we can find original scrolls."

Polycarp looked at Assaf.

"By locating scrolls, we will be locating the keepers of the scrolls," Polycarp said. "Their ancestors probably knew Jesus. They will provide scrolls for us to copy and stories for us to record. Think about it, and we can talk tomorrow."

When Assaf went to the university, it was very early. He prayed for many hours and asked for sound reasoning. He didn't come to a firm conclusion. He saw Polycarp approach.

"Did you consider what we talked about?" Polycarp asked. "We need to create an itinerary. I am certain that the material that Paul and Luke wrote is more accurate than seventy year old memories."

"Yes, I thought about it," Assaf said. "What I have concluded is that you are the boss, and it is your research project. I will be happy looking for scrolls."

"You gained great understanding," he said. "I will visit with the dean today."

When Dean Julius arrived, Polycarp explained his idea to him. The dean liked the idea, but told Polycarp not to change what he was doing until he gained approval from their benefactor. Polycarp was surprised and went back to his office and worked with his notes.

Papias greeted Polycarp and asked, "Will you lecture to my class tomorrow?"

"Certainly," Polycarp said. "I have many concerns to ponder."

"I will make the arrangements," he said. "Would you like me to assign you a student helper? We always have students looking for a job."

"I would enjoy lecturing to your class," he said. "I don't really have a schedule. I will probably make additional plans with the dean next week."

"I am certain the dean will give you a fixed schedule," Papias said. "Enjoy this week."

Polycarp smiled at Papias.

"Yes, I would like a student to help me," he said. "He can organize my notes. I want them written in Greek. If he needs help, he can work with Assaf."

"Did you hear I read an original scroll written by Paul?" Polycarp asked. "Titus showed it to me and allowed Assaf to copy it. I am glad we found Titus. He is very old and feeble."

Polycarp taught a large group in the lecture hall. After he finished, many waited to speak with him. He spent most of the day discussing his research with them. The next day, his routine retuned to a normal pace. He prepared a list of those who might have original scrolls. His new student assistant arranged his office and answered his messages. Polycarp wrote a lesson and had it sent to the Bishop Menahem.

The following week as he approached his office, Polycarp saw the dean.
"I have been with our benefactor," Julius said. "He was interested in your idea and your reasoning. He asked that I send him a list of places you plan to visit."
"I will send you the list as soon as it is compiled," Polycarp said. "I want to discuss it with Assaf."

Polycarp and Assaf met each day and discussed the possible location of scrolls. They agreed that Luke and Paul were the most accurate writers. They also agreed that each of them had written many scrolls concerning Jesus' message. Eventually they completed their list and sent it to the dean. The dean didn't respond immediately.

Many months went by before he asked Polycarp to come into his office and to explain the list.
"I have been very busy, but I am now ready to try and understand your list. Before we get into the detail, give me a short explanation," he said.
"I want to read all of the very old original scrolls about Jesus," Polycarp said. "I am interested in scrolls and parchments. The scrolls will be found mostly in churches. The parchments will be found with descendants. This is a mammoth undertaking, and I may need more help. It will require long periods of time away from the university."
"I think I am getting the picture," Julius said. "Give me another month, and I promise I will have an answer for you."

Polycarp went back to his office. He had sufficient work to keep him busy for many months. He wasn't certain what was taking the dean such a long time, but he kept his concerns out of his mind by focusing on his work.

Finally, Polycarp saw the dean approach his office.

"I am still analyzing the proposed direction you want to take with your research," Julius said. "I have a question for you. Why do you consider the parchments so important? How will they benefit your research?"

"They are very important," Polycarp said. "By studying the parchments, I will gain a much better understanding of the writer."

"Please explain what you mean?" he asked. "I need specifics."

"The parchments are less formal," he said. "The writer is communicating with someone he knows. It might contain personal information."

"That is what I thought," he said. "How is the writer's personal life going to help us?"

"It will allow me to understand their more formal books," he said. "Personal opinions are often not included in the more formal writings. It is the manner of trained writers to be impartial concerning what they write."

"By studying their informal writing, you will better understand their formal writings," Julius said. "That makes sense."

"For instance, Peter spent many years with Jesus, but every scroll I have seen concerning Peter and Jesus was written by either Luke or Mark," he said. "Luke wrote many of them, and he never traveled with Jesus. He was a disciple of Paul. If I can understand Luke, I will have a much better chance of understanding Jesus, Paul, Peter and Mark."

The dean smiled as he looked at him. Polycarp realized the dean was really trying to understand every detail of what he had proposed. He wondered how many questions the benefactor had given the dean to ask him.

When the sun started to go down, it was time for Polycarp to go home. He thought of a hot dinner and enjoyed the sunset. His walks, to and from the university, became very therapeutic. While he walked, he looked forward to quite time. As Polycarp approached Dianna's house, he thought he saw an extra person.

"We have a guest for dinner," Martha said. "I want you to meet my friend Daniel."

Polycarp greeted Daniel.

"He knows more about your research than I know," she said. "He has attended many of your lectures at the university."

Polycarp stared at Daniel.

"We have become very good friends, and he has asked me to marry him," Martha said. "He has already spoken with mother, but I wanted you to meet him."

"I will be honored to talk to him," Polycarp said. "This is a big step. Is he willing to live here and help you with mother?"

"Yes," she said. "We have talked for about a year. You are so busy; I didn't want to bother you."

"Fine, feed me," he said. "I will talk with him after dinner."

As soon as Martha stopped talking, she escorted Daniel to the dinner table and was seated. Rachael served the dinner. Martha asked Daniel to bless the food. Calm hung over dinner. No one wanted to speak.

After dinner, they relocated to the living area. When Rachael served hot tea, the mood became more relaxed. Polycarp broke the silence.

"Good evening, Daniel. I am very happy for you and Martha, where do you work?" he asked.

"I work at the university," Daniel said. "I work for Papias. He is an assistant professor. I think he is your friend."

"Yes, I know Papias," he said. "You must be one of his student assistants."

"You occasionally lecture to our class," he said. "I hope to be a teacher. Maybe, I could do research. I am learning Greek."

"That is a good start," he said. "Greek is still the formal language of education."

Polycarp was impressed. He instantly acknowledged Daniel, and they became great friends. Martha's wedding was set for two weeks.

The next morning, Polycarp ate breakfast with his mother. He then walked to the university, and he looked for Papias. He found him at work in his office.

"Papias, do you know Daniel?" he asked. "He is going to marry my sister. I didn't know he worked for you."

"I know a good student named Daniel," he said. "I had no idea he was in love with your sister. He seems like a good young man. He is quite spiritual."

"I want you to come to the wedding," Polycarp said.

"I will plan on it," Papias said. "I enjoy weddings."

That afternoon, the dean found Polycarp seated in his office.

"I have news for you," he said. "We are going to open our new building next week."

"That is nice," he said. "I haven't been watching the construction very closely."

"Our benefactor is coming to the university and will make a speech at the dedication," he said. "After the ceremony, he wants to meet with you."

"Great," Polycarp said. "I would like to meet him."

"He desires to discuss your research," Julius said. "I will introduce him."

They walked to the new building.

"It certainly is a large building," he said. "I hope we have enough students."

"We have plenty of students," the dean said. "I have been telling many students they couldn't enroll until we open the new building."

Polycarp expressed his surprise and smiled at the dean.

"I have hired two new teachers. They will work for Papias," the dean said. "We have over two hundred students studying about Jesus and his followers. Your research is becoming quite famous."

"Two hundred!" he exclaimed. "That is a lot of students. Did you say they are interested in my research?"

"Yes, many came to our university because of your research," he said. "They want to read and study the scrolls you are preparing."

"We will have to prepare more scrolls," he said. "It is a time consuming process."

Polycarp faced two very important events during the next two weeks, a wedding and a building dedication. He spent time with his mother planning Martha's wedding. Several professors and students were invited to attend the wedding. Polycarp occasionally thought about the new building.

When the day arrived for the opening of the new building, he was mildly surprised. Dean Julius discussed the building with him.

"This is a great day for our university," he said. "Now we will be one of the largest universities teaching about Jesus. I want to thank you for continuing with Professor Thomas' research. You have taken it to a new level. Be at the new building with your family at ten o'clock this morning."

"With my family?" he asked. "Should I bring all of them?"

"Sure," he said. "I would like to meet your family."

At ten o'clock, Polycarp, Dianna, Rachael, Martha, Papias, Assaf, and Daniel were seated in the new building waiting for the ceremony to start. The dean greeted everyone and explained the new building. He detailed how the university had grown. He then introduced the university's benefactor.

"It is my great pleasure to introduce a very important man to you," Julius said. "Without him we would not have this new building or our great research program. Mr. Philemon is the grandson of the Philemon who started three churches in Asia Minor."

Polycarp looked at his mother.

"I knew I heard that name," Polycarp said. "No wonder he is interested."

"He is associated with the church in Smyrna," he said. "He is very interested in any information we can discover about Jesus. He is also interested in obtaining original or copies of scrolls written by Paul."

"We have a lot in common," Polycarp said. "We will be good friends."

"Mr. Philemon is the owner of most of the ships in the harbor in Smyrna and Neapolis," he said. "His shipping business empire reaches throughout the Roman Empire. Please greet Mr. Philemon."

"I am honored to be able to support your great university by providing this new building, The Polycarp Hall for Religious Studies," he said. "I am also honored to be part of the research Professor Polycarp is undertaking. It is my intentions to expand his research program."

Dianna grabbed Polycarp's hand and tears formed in her eyes. She looked at him.

"He named the building after you," she said. "I am so proud of you."

The ceremony lasted for several hours. Six different professors and business men thanked Mr. Philemon for his interest in the university. After the ceremony, Dianna went home and talked with Martha and Rachael about the ceremony.

The dean escorted Mr. Philemon to Polycarp's office.

"May we come in?" Julius asked. "Mr. Philemon is going to remain with you. I am going to my office."

"Before you go, I have a question," Polycarp said. "Did Papias know you were going to name the building after me? We need him."

"Yes, I talked with him," he said. "We decided it should be named after you and your research. Your name will draw many more students than his name. We expect you to teach one class per year."

"Good, I want Professor Papias to be my friend," he said. "He is a good professor."

"Professor Papias has been named, the director of religious studies," the dean said. "He will administer the program, with your and Mr. Philemon's approval."

Mr. Philemon looked at Polycarp.

"It is good to finally talk with you," he said. "I like your idea about obtaining scrolls. I have several other ideas."

Polycarp and Philemon spent several days discussing the new Roman Emperor, Trajan, and Polycarp's research. Philemon had obtained approval from Pope Evaristus for Polycarp to be concreated a bishop in Smyrna. His plan included building another facility in Smyrna which would house their new school of religious studies. The building would be named the Menahem Building of Religious Studies at The Polycarp Research Center.

Polycarp was expected to spend eight months per year working in Smyrna. A department of transcription was to be included in the school of religion. When in Smyrna, Polycarp would teach. The offer was such that Polycarp felt obligated to agree with it. After they formalized the details, Dean Julius was informed.

Mr. Philemon was aware of Emperor Trajan's great building program, in Rome, and his popularity. Philemon reasoned that if construction was good for the people in Rome, it would benefit his people in Philippi and Smyrna.

Polycarp would now switch his attention to his sister's wedding. He didn't divulge his plans until after the wedding. He knew his mother wouldn't like his spending most of his time in Smyrna.

That evening after dinner they continued to plan Martha's wedding.

"The cloth, you purchased for Martha's gown was delivered today," Dianna said. "It is the most beautiful cloth I have ever seen."

"I am glad you like it," Polycarp said. "I ordered it for you."

"The seamstress started to make the gown today. It will be finished in time for the wedding," Dianna said. "Did you know the cloth came from Egypt?"

"Yes, I knew," he said. "The shop provides cloth to the University for our Robes."

"I wondered how you knew about the cloth," she said. "We are very thankful for it."

"I hope she likes the gown," he said. "One day, when I was down town, I visited the shop. After I told them what I wanted, they ordered the cloth for you."

The wedding was grand. Polycarp gave Daniel and Martha a trip to Smyrna as a wedding gift. Martha had never traveled far from home. They would live in his house for five days. James would attend to them and be their tour guide.

After they sailed to Smyrna, Polycarp spoke with his mother.

"I have something to tell you," Polycarp said. "I have been named a Bishop at the Smyrna church. Mr. Philemon and I are going to start a school of religion and a research center."

"In Smyrna, you live in Philippi," she said.

Polycarp looked at his mother.

"I will live in Smyrna for eight months a year," he said. "I will be with you here in Philippi four months a year."

She sadly looked at her son.

"Oh, Polycarp," she said. "I have been dreading this day. Martha and I knew it was coming. I am relieved that you will be with us four months per year."

Polycarp noted tears in her eyes. He kissed her wrinkled forehead.

"A mother knows that when her son matures, he might move away from home," Dianna said. "It doesn't make it any easier."

"I will be here in Philippi with you part of the year," Polycarp said. "We will still spend quality time with each other."

Polycarp was relieved. He anticipated a stronger reaction from his mother. Now, he had to talk with Assaf.

The next morning, Polycarp slowly walked to the university. He found Assaf in the transcribing area.

"Come into my office," he said.

"I hope you have good news," Assaf said.

He followed Polycarp to his office.

"I plan to spend most of my time in Smyrna," he said. "I will complete most of my research from Smyrna. I want you to relocate to Smyrna."

"You want me to move to Smyrna?" he asked. "Philippi is my home."

"You can help me get established in Smyrna," he said. "I think we will like Smyrna."

Assaf hesitated for a moment.

"I am not moving to Smyrna," he said. "I am a homebody."

"The opportunities for you will be greater, in Smyrna," Polycarp said. "We can start a new program from the very beginning."

"That might be great for you, but I am not willing to move away from Philippi," he said.

"I really think you are making a mistake," he said. "Smyrna is the place to be."

"I will be happier here," he said. "I will help Papias."

Polycarp hadn't considered the possibility that Assaf wouldn't move to Smyrna. His decision caused him to reflect about his own position. He felt compelled to continue with the research project. Assaf agreed to prepare two copies of every scroll in Philippi for Polycarp and his new research center. Polycarp felt anxious. He hated to lose such a skilled helper. He planned how he would inform the dean of Assaf decision. He slowly walked to the dean's office.

"We have a problem," Polycarp announced. "Assaf has refused to relocate."

The dean looked at Polycarp.

"That doesn't surprise me," Julius said.

"He wants to remain here with Papias," he said. "Philippi is his home. He plans to spend his life here."

"He is a good employee," Julius said. "He will have a job with us."

"I am certain Papias needs him," Polycarp said. "I will need copies of many of the scrolls."

"Yes, we can use Assaf," he said. "It is nice of you to keep me informed."

"I feel comfortable talking with you," he said. "I will miss you."

"Don't forget Philemon is your new boss," Julius said. "He will expect you to solve these small problems by yourself."

"I guess, I will learn to work with him," he said. "He seems like he is always busy."

"Mr. Philemon is busy with one of his engineers concerning the new building," Julius said. "He also spends time each week with the man who runs his shipping business. He is a very busy man."

"It is considerate that he takes time to work with the universities," Polycarp said. "When he wants to know what you are doing, he will contact you," Julius said.

"I guess you know him much better than I know him," he said. "I will eventually adapt to my new environment."

"You have the full authority of a bishop and a full professor," Julius said. "Mr. Philemon's backing is better than both of those. Do it your way."

"I understand," he said. "Thank you. I am going to my office. I need to pray."

Polycarp sent a message to James. The message contained a lesson for Menahem. He also requested James to make arrangement for him to come to Smyrna the following week and to remain two weeks. The second thing he did was find Assaf.

"Assaf, I talked with the dean,' he said. "Everything is fine. You have a long term position here at the university. How would you like to do some teaching?"

"Thank you Polycarp," he said. "I was a little worried. I would like to teach."

"Come with me and help find Papias," he said. "We will tell him what happened and that when I am in Smyrna, you will teach."

They walk from the transcribing area to Papias office.

"Papias, we would like to talk with you," Polycarp said. "I need your help to complete a few changes."

"What can I do for you?" Papias asked.

"I have obtained you an excellent transcriber and a beginning teacher," he said. "His name is Assaf. I will be spending eight months a year in Smyrna."

"A few changes!" he said. "Slow down, allow me time to understand."

"I plan to spend most of my time in Smyrna," he said. "I will be in Philippi, four months per year."

"You are relocating to Smyrna?" he asked. "What about your research?"

"I will continue with my research," he said. "Traveling will be easier from Smyrna."

Papias stared at Polycarp.

"When I am in Smyrna Assaf will teach for you," he said. "When I am in Philippi he will assist me. Dean Julius approved the arrangement."

Papias hesitated for a moment. He didn't want to believe what he had heard.

"If it is fine with the dean, it is fine with me," he said. "When is your next trip? I have a lecture time for you tomorrow."

"My next trip is next week," he said. "I will see you tomorrow."

Polycarp and Assaf walked back to his office. He agreed to teach Assaf how to write a detailed lesson plan. He also agreed to review a few of his lessons.

When the day ended, Polycarp walked home. He was so preoccupied he almost walked past his house. That evening, he enjoyed dinner with his mother and Rachael. After a few days, Daniel and Martha arrived home. They told stories all evening about their journey and how they enjoyed Smyrna. They were totally delighted with James and Polycarp's house. Everyone retired to a long night of sleep.

The following morning, Polycarp ate breakfast with his mother. He told her, he was going to Smyrna for two week. They embraced, then his driver packed Polycarp's bag and they went to the dock.

"Hello, Bishop Polycarp," the captain said. "It is a pleasure for us to take you to Smyrna."

"You have been talking with someone," Polycarp said. "I am happy to see you."

"All the captains received a message, from Mr. Philemon," he said. "He expects us to extend you every courtesy. Your cabin is ready, sir"

"You have been doing fine, captain," he said. "You even provided a side trip to Troas on one of my journeys."

He looked at the captain and smiled.

"I don't have any side trips planned," he said. "The seas are calm and the wind is good. Will you dine with me this evening?"

That evening, Polycarp ate with the captain. The cook served a fish that had just been caught. Later, the captain showed Polycarp his maps. Polycarp requested a tour of the ship. The captain was surprised at his interest and personally directed a tour of the entire vessel. Polycarp noted the closeness of the crew's quarters. He also noted, the ship carried oars in case of a no wind condition.

"How often do you use them?" Polycarp asked.

"We never plan to use them," he said. "If the wind is completely silent, you might have no choice but to row."

It was a pleasant journey. When they arrived in Smyrna, James met Polycarp.

They exchanged greetings and Polycarp boarded the carriage. He asked James if he knew Mr. Philemon.

"No, I don't know him," he said. "Have you heard we are going to get a new building? I don't know much about it."

"Yes, a new building," he said. "That has something to do with what I want to talk about. Where is your home?"

"I am from Smyrna," he said. "I have done a little traveling. I have been to Jerusalem."

"The new building is going to be The Menahem Building of Religions Studies at The Polycarp Research Center," he said.

He looked at James.

"It was a surprise to me," he said. "They also ordained me a bishop."

"That I knew," he said. "I guess you will be spending more time in Smyrna."

"Soon this will become my home," he said. "Philippi will be my home for four months per year. Have you been to Philippi?"

"No," he answered. "I think I would like to visit Philippi."

CHAPTER 4

RELOCATION TO SMYRNA

Polycarp spoke with James for a long time and explained Mr. Philemon's plans. He projected the new building would be completed in a year. James seemed very interested in the new School of Religion.

"James, how would you like to work for me?" Polycarp asked. "I mean all year."

"I do work for you," he said. "You and this house are a major portion of my job."

"I mean, would you like to be my research assistant?" he said. "Assaf won't be moving to Smyrna."

"I am assigned to the church," he said. "I am a parish priest."

"I need someone to travel with me and to transcribe my notes into Greek," he said. "You would also be expected to transcribe many other things."

"I would like it very much," he said. "I will have to ask my bishop. I will walk to the church and speak with him."

James wasn't certain what he should do concerning Polycarp's offer, but he was certain he needed to talk with Bishop Menahem. After a long discussion with Menahem, he returned to the house.

"I talked with the bishop," James said. "He wished me good luck and reminded me that you are a bishop, and I am already working for you."

"That was very understanding of him," Polycarp said. "He is a gracious man."

"When we aren't here, he will assign a priest to maintain the house," he said. "Please explain your plans to me."

Polycarp provided James with an abbreviated copy of the parchment he had given to Dean Julius. He asked James to make arrangements for him to return to Philippi. He wanted to arrive to Philippi as soon as possible. He wasn't sure when he would return to Smyrna.

Two days later, James took Polycarp to the dock. He sailed to Philippi and began to make plans for his new assistant. He and Papias agreed it would be good if Polycarp spent the late summer through fall in Philippi. The remainder of the year, Polycarp would work in or from Smyrna. It was fall when Polycarp explained his plans to his mother.

After two weeks, James arrived. He lived and worked at the university. Polycarp informed his mother he had invited James to dinner. After they completed their day's work at the university, they walked to Polycarp's home.

Polycarp introduced James to his mother.

"James is a priest and has agreed to be my assistant," he said. "It is a full-time position for him. He writes Greek and understands our religion."

Dianna smiled at James. She wanted him to relax.

"Is this your first trip to Philippi?" she asked. "I think you and Polycarp will make a good team."

"I have worked with your son for a while," he said. "I was his attendant."

"I want you to meet my daughter Martha and her husband Daniel," Dianna said. "My other children married and moved away."

James hesitated for a moment. He returned Dianna's smile.

"I have met Martha and Daniel," he said. "I had the pleasure of touring them around Smyrna."

"James, will you bless the food for us," Martha asked. "It is an honor to have a friend of Polycarp's with us."

"Martha and Rachael's food is much better than the institutional food we eat," James said. "Maybe they can teach me how to cook. I would like to learn how to make a meal this good."

Soon they retired to the living area. They talked for several hours. Then James returned to the university.

The next morning, Polycarp walked to the university. He located James at work in his office.

"Good morning, Bishop Polycarp," James said. "I have been arranging your notes."

"Once a day," Polycarp said. "After that, call me professor. We will work in Philippi for several months."

"After the building opens, we will spend late summer through fall in Philippi and the remainder of the year we will work from Smyrna," he said.

Polycarp paused and looked at James.

"This week I would like you to discuss the church in Smyrna with our students," he said. "I will help you prepare a lecture."

"Thank you," James said. "I should know that topic."

The next day, Polycarp and James discussed a trip to Corinth. James contacted the shipping company and obtained a schedule that indicated ships departed from Smyrna to Athens every two weeks. After James had obtained a parchment map of Corinth, they agreed to depart in one month.

"After we return to Phillipi, I would like you to teach," Polycarp said. "You need to prepare to lecture on a regular basis."

James looked at him.

"You may have to help me with topics," he said. "It will take me a while to get used to lecturing on a regular schedule."

"When in Corinth, we will go to a local church," he said. "We will seek members whose ancestors might have known Paul. He was in Corinth on several occasions and assigned one of his disciples to remain. I am certain he must have written to him"

During the trip to Smyrna, the sea was very rough. The wind gusted and the waves became quite high. They weren't able to be on the main deck. They heard the captain shout instructions to the crew on several occasions. It took three days to reach Smyrna. The captain apologized to them. James tried to assuage his feelings.

"Captain, you did a fine job sailing the ship through those choppy seas," he said. "When we return to Phillipi, I hope we sail with you."

"Thank you," he said. "I hate that it took longer that a normal trip. Somedays the sea doesn't cooperate."

They collected their bags and disembarked.

"I see John," James said. "John is your new attendant in Smyrna. He is also a priest. He will do a good job for you."

"Hello, James," John said. "Good evening Bishop Polycarp, I am pleased to see you. I have the house prepared for you."

Polycarp looked at him.

"I plan to deliver a lecture," he said. "Please contact Bishop Menahem and establish a time. We will unpack and rest for a while."

"I am sorry to inform you that Bishop Menahem is quite ill," he said. "He has named a priest to perform his functions. I will inform Priest Mark you are prepared to lecture."

"James, please determine the bishop's illness," Polycarp said. "I will say a prayer and try to relax. I hope it is nothing serious."

Several hours passed before Polycarp heard a knock on the door. When he answered the door, Mark greeted him. They sat and discussed Menahem's illness. Mark informed Polycarp that when he was in Smyrna he was the senior representative for God. Polycarp responded that he understood, but would expect Mark to operate the churches and to keep him informed.

"I will introduce you to your class tomorrow at ten in the morning," he said.

James and John entered the house and where seated. The bishop invited them to dine with him. They walked to the church and enjoyed dinner.

The next morning, Polycarp arose and found John seated in the kitchen. He had prepared their breakfasts. When ten o'clock arrived, they went to the lecture hall. Mark introduced Bishop Polycarp.

"Priests, gentlemen, and students," he said. "I would like to introduce our lecturer for today. We are honored to have with us Bishop Polycarp."

Polycarp explained the new building which was under construction. He then introduced James and explained his new position and how they would spend their time in Philippi, Smyrna, and traveling. He gave them a quick overview of his research and trip to Corinth. He promised to update them when they returned. After the class, he talked with the students in an informal setting for two hours.

Soon, the ship was loaded for its trip to Corinth via Athens; John escorted them to the dock. The captain greeted them. He advised they would sail in one hour. Polycarp went to his cabin to pray and then explained to James, "The ships that sail to Athens are larger than the ships that traveled between Philippi and Smyrna. These ships always carry a large load of grain to Rome and sail across about fifty miles of open sea. The sea is generally choppy and with a heavy wind. On previous shorter trips, I normally looked at the shore. Open seas will be a new experience for me."

They arrived in Athens on the second day and disembarked.

"It is not far to Corinth," James said. "All we have to do is walk along the canal they have been digging. If you want to ride, I can rent some horses."

"No, walking is fine with me," Polycarp said. "I have been told about this canal."

After a ten mile walk, they reached Corinth. They were covered with dust and thirsty. They purchased lodging at the Corinth Inn on Lachaion Road.

The next morning they sought a church.

"Excuse me, sir," Polycarp said. "Can you direct us to your largest church?"

"Certainly, it is south and west of the great temple," the Corinthian said.

"Thank you," James said. "I am sure we will find it."

After a short walk, they stood before a large building with a belfry.

"Come in and sit down," a priest said. "I am the local teacher. My name is Jude."

He brushed a speck from his robe.

"This is a beautiful church," Polycarp said.

"We have a beautiful bell, but we are only allowed to use it once a week on the Sabbath," he said. "The local Roman officials don't like popular churches. Would you like a drink?"

"Yes, Jude, that would be nice," James said. "This is Bishop Polycarp from Smyrna. I am James, his scribe."

Jude greeted James.

"We are in Corinth concerning our research at the university," James said. "Do you have time to tell us about your church?"

"Certainly, this is the largest church in Corinth," he said. "Paul started it about seventy years ago."

"We hoped to find the church founded by Paul," Polycarp said. "You weren't hard to locate."

"We have some of his scrolls that contain his lessons," he said. "I am certain you will want to copy of them. You should also talk with the Chloe family."

James placed his hands together in a prayerful attitude. He then smiled at Polycarp.

"You can live with me," the priest said. "Bishop, will you explain your research to our members?"

Polycarp hesitated for a moment. He looked at James.

"I am certain our members will appreciate hearing from you," he said. "I have been told of the new building in Smyrna. After the Sabbath service, I will introduce you to the Chloe family."

"We will certainly visit the Chloe family," Polycarp said. "I look forward to meeting them."

For the next few days Polycarp and James were very busy. They carefully copied all the available scrolls. James noted that some of the scrolls were written by Apollos. Polycarp explained that Apollo was a learned man, who traveled with Paul. On the Sabbath, Polycarp addressed the members. After the service the local teacher introduced Polycarp to the Chloe family. The Chloe's invited Polycarp to visit the following day and indicated they had a parchment Paul had written.

The next morning, Polycarp and James went to the house of the Chloe family.

"Professor Polycarp," Mr. Chloe said. "After we came home yesterday, I searched and finally located these parchments. You can have them for your research. This one was sent to my grandmother."

Polycarp graciously accepted the parchments. As he analyzed the first parchment, he stroked his beard and smiled.

"She and Paul communicated on several occasions," Mr. Chloe said. "The other two parchments are from Paul. The family didn't keep any of the other parchments."

"That is too bad," he said. "Anything Paul wrote would be helpful."

"I think my grandmother was very impressed by Paul," he said. "She wanted everyone to do exactly as Paul requested."

"I will keep the parchments as part of my research in the new building in Smyrna," he said. "We hope to open the new building in the fall."

"I am so glad you can use them," Mr. Chloe said. "Will you say a prayer for us?"

Polycarp placed his hand on Mr. Chloe's shoulder and prayed with them. Then he and James returned to the church.

The next day, they visited with Polycarp's sister Margret.

"We got your message and are so pleased to see you," Margret said. "How are mother and Martha? I see you have someone with you."

"This is my scribe, James," he said. "We came to Corinth to perform research, and I wanted to visit with you."

Polycarp felt melancholy and hugged his sister.

"Mother and Martha are well," he said.

She greeted James, and then looked at Polycarp.

"Tell me about Martha," she said.

"I am certain they sent you a message about Martha's wedding," he said. "Daniel works at the university. He is a fine young man."

"I did receive a message," she said. "The message wasn't very long."

"They have agreed to live with mother," he said. "Martha will continue to care for her."

"That is wonderful," she said. "I am pleased she found a husband."

"We can't stay long, but I wanted to see you," he said. "Mother will want to know all about you. If you give me a message, I will deliver it to her."

"That is a great idea," she said. "Sit for a moment and drink some water."

She wiped her face and scurried to find writing material.

After a short visit, they returned to the church and continued transcribing.

After twelve days, they returned to Athens and waited for their ship. Early the next morning, they walked to the dock. It was a beautiful, sunny morning. The sunshine reflected from the sea, and the sound of birds filled the air. Polycarp paused for a few moments and said a silent prayer. He looked at the blue sky and then at James.

"This has been a very rewarding trip," he said. "Our next journey will be a short excursion to Thessalonica. Assaf visited there for me and copied all the scrolls at the church, but I didn't tell him to check for parchments."

"I have always wanted to visit, Thessalonica," James said. I will look forward to our trip."

"The parchments have opened my eyes," he said. "This will add a great amount to our understanding of the large scrolls. One of the parchments Mr. Chloe gave to me was written by Paul concerning the church in Thessalonica."

"I see our ship," James said. "The captain is waving for us. Follow me; I will carry the extra bags."

They exchanged greetings with the captain and went to their cabin. The captain indicated they might reach Smyrna ahead of schedule. The trip to Smyrna was uneventful. James and Polycarp didn't think about the open sea. They were now "old salts". John met them at the dock.

"I see you gained a few bags," John said. "I will carry them for you. You must have copied quite a few scrolls."

"Yes, we had a good trip," Polycarp said. "How is Bishop Menahem?"

"He is a little better," he said. "Mark is doing a fine job for him. Everyone is very pleased."

"I am happy he feels better," he said. "I was worried about him."

"If it is acceptable with you, we will eat with the priest this evening," John said. "I know they will want to talk with you."

"Certainly that is fine," Polycarp said. "First, we will relax for a while. When it time for us to leave, call me. You may inform me of my lecture schedule and our return trip schedule tonight."

Polycarp had just gone to sleep, when John appeared and explained that a Mr. Philemon was on the porch. He wanted to talk with him. Polycarp arose and went to the door. He greeted Mr. Philemon. Polycarp exuded enthusiasm about how successful their trip had been and explained they would now always seek parchments to accompany the larger scrolls. Mr. Philemon was impressed. He wasn't able to eat dinner with the priests and excused himself. The dinner was pleasant, but Polycarp told the priest that they would have to attend his ten o'clock lecture to hear the details.

After dinner he revealed the details to Mark and informed him that he had already seen Mr. Philemon. He knew the building construction was ahead of schedule. Before his lecture, Bishop Mark introduced Polycarp.

"It is my pleasure to inform you that we obtained some very interesting scrolls," Polycarp said. "We also were given several original parchments that will help us understand the scrolls."

"Will students be allowed to read the scrolls?" A priest asked. "I would like to read them."

"Copies of all our material will be available to our students in the new building," Polycarp said. "The original material we gather will be kept in a vault. It will only be accessed by James and me until my research is completed."

"That was a great lecture," James said. "They already have students signing up to take classes next year. We are scheduled to leave for Philippi in two days. That will allow us time to arrange our notes."

The following morning, several priests visited with Polycarp. They requested to read the parchments. Polycarp made one of the parchments, written by Paul to the Thessalonica church, available to them. It was a busy day, they accomplished very little work. Polycarp told John they would be available by appointment only for everyone except the bishop and Mr. Philemon. They looked forward to sailing to Philippi.

The following morning as the sun glistened on the water, they walked to the ship.

"I will have my mate stow all your bags," the captain said. "Welcome aboard. We will sail as soon as everything is loaded."

"I think I will watch the sailors work," Polycarp said. "It is such a beautiful day. The sun invigorates me."

"It looks like we have a full load of passengers," James said. "I will return topside in a few moments."

"Cast off, stand clear, starboard around," the sailor said. "Man the masts."

"It's like a foreign language," James said. "I think it might be a rewarding job. Do you think you might like to be a sailor?"

"Not me," Polycarp said. "I like being a bishop and a professor. It is much safer, and my office doesn't roll with the waves."

Late that afternoon, the ship made an unscheduled stop. One of the other passengers had become ill and was taken to receive medical attention.

"They are lowering the large sail," James said.

"We must be stopping at Troas," Polycarp said. "We did this on one other trip. I am certain the captain will explain the problem."

The next morning, the ship set sail for Philippi. The captain apologized to Polycarp for the delay. The breeze was strong and the ship sliced through the water. Polycarp and James didn't expect anyone to meet them, so they hired a carriage to take them to the university. By the time Polycarp had finished at the university and walked home, it was very dark. He couldn't see a star. He knocked on the door.

"Don't be alarmed," Polycarp said. "It is I."

"Have a seat and relax," Dianna said. "How was your trip? Would you like a cup of tea?"

"I would enjoy a cup of tea," he said. "It was a very successful trip. I will remain at home for a while."

"The tea is hot,' she said. "Be careful."

"My next trip is to Thessalonica, it won't be a long trip," he said. "If you want to go along, I might take you. I brought you a present from Corinth."

She smiled at Polycarp.

"You are spoiling me," she said. "I am not used to receiving so many presents. I don't want to go to Thessalonica. I really don't like to travel. I like staying close to home. Rachael and I are fine and you have work to do. I would just be in the way. You can tell me about your trip. Martha and Daniel are visiting his mother this evening. They will be home tomorrow."

He smiled at his mother.

"I have another present for you," he said. "I have this message from Margret. She is doing fine. She misses you."

"Oh, Polycarp," she said. "Thank you, I was afraid you didn't have time to see her."

She clutched the message to her breast and a tear appeared in her eye. She wiped her face with her long gray hair. They talked for a while, and then Dianna went to sleep.

In the morning, they ate an early breakfast and Polycarp walked to the university. When he arrived, he located James.

"I want to read the parchments we obtained," Polycarp said.

"I have them organized and on the table," James said. "I am still working with the scrolls."

"It is amazing how much they tell us about the necessity for the large scrolls," he said. "I want a copy of each parchment for my office. Check on my lecture schedule for me."

"I have your schedule," he said. "Lecture tomorrow, and then see Dean Julius the next day. I will be busy transcribing."

Polycarp was very thankful for James. He smiled at him.

"Good, I am thinking about what we might find in Thessalonica," he said. "Now that we know what to look for, thing are different. We might locate many parchments."

After a few months passed, they were on their way to Thessalonica. They traveled in a carriage. When they arrived at Thessalonica, they went to the largest church and put the horses in the stable. Polycarp had sent a message and informed the local priest of his visit. The church provided quarters for them.

"Come in, Polycarp," the priest said. "I am Paul. I have been here a few years. After I have taken you to your room and you are ready for visitors, our senior priest will see you."

"You can tell Joseph I will see him," Polycarp said. "I will be ready before he gets here. I want to meet him."

The priest informed Joseph that Polycarp had arrived. It was not long before Joseph went to Polycarp's room.

"It is good to finally meet you," Joseph said. "I hope you like the accommodations. If you would teach us a lesson, we would appreciate it."

"Certainly, I will be glad to lecture about my research," he said. "I would like to see all your scrolls."

"I will make them available to you," he said. "We have several scrolls."

"James will make copies of them," he said. "Do you have any parchments or know anyone who might have any? I am also interested in reading parchments that might have been written by Paul, Timothy, or Silas."

"I am certain we have several," he said. "The church members might have parchments."

"That is a good idea," Polycarp said. "On our last trip, a member gave us a few parchments."

"We have a member whose grandfather knew Timothy quite well," he said. "I believe Timothy lived with them and used their house as a church."

"I hope they kept any notes Paul wrote to them," he said. "I would like to read them."

"I am certain he has several parchments," he said. "I will introduce you at the meeting tomorrow evening."

The next day, James was busy coping scrolls and Polycarp was busy reading scrolls and parchments. Polycarp insisted that James copy everything. Polycarp saw the priest approach.

"Good evening bishop," Joseph said. "Would you and James have dinner with me and my staff? It is served in our dining hall. We have a large selection of fresh roots."

"Yes, we will," he said. "We both like roots."

"I contacted the member I told you about," he said. "His name is Mark and he will be with us this evening."

They enjoyed dinner and were escorted to the church. After Polycarp had finished his lecture, Mark approached him.

"The priest told me you would like to read the parchments that were given to me by my father," Mark said. "Father inherited them from his father."

"Yes, I would like to see them," Polycarp said. "How many do you have?"

"I am not certain," he said. "If you visit with us tomorrow, I will show them to you. I want to keep them, but you may copy them."

The next day, James and Polycarp visited with Mark. He had five parchments. After he read the parchments, Polycarp became excited. James copied all of them. Mark changed his mind and gave Polycarp one parchment. He didn't know Secundus and didn't know why he had the parchment. They thanked Mark for dinner and for allowing them to copy the parchments.

Later that evening, they returned to the church.

"Did you read the parchments?" Polycarp asked.

"I had to read them to copy them," James said. "I haven't had time to study them. It takes all my efforts to ensure I produce an exact copy."

"I plan to send Mr. Philemon a message," he said.

James scratched his head and then looked at Polycarp.

"What is so interesting?" he asked. "What did the parchment say?"

"The one parchment was from Paul," Polycarp said. "He explained to Timothy how to use the scrolls in the church. He wanted to ensure Timothy's understanding of the scrolls was accurate."

"I think Paul would be surprised to know, his instructions to Timothy are instructions to us," James said. "If Timothy could understand Paul's message, we should be able to understand it."

"We are making progress," he said. "This will be a great body of knowledge. The parchment he gave us was written by Secundus, do you know who he was?"

A puzzled look appeared on James' face.

"No I don't think I have heard of him," he said. "Do you know who he was?"

"Yes, I have heard of him," Polycarp said. "I know he was one of the people, from Thessalonica, who traveled with Paul."

When they returned to Philippi, Polycarp explained their success to the dean. Julius was pleased and envisioned many additional students.

"I think, you should include your explanation of the parchments and the scrolls, as part of your research," Julius said. "Many people will not dedicate enough time to understand what they are reading. Your explanation of the material will help everyone."

Polycarp ran his fingers through his beard to untangle a knot. He paused and then spoke softly.

"It will involve a great amount of work," he said. "I am certain you are correct. James and I will carefully document each of our finds and write explanations."

"Where do you plan to visit next?" the dean asked. "The weather will be turning cold."

"I haven't discussed it with James," he said. "I would like to go to Jerusalem and the surrounding area. It is farther south."

Julius smiled at Polycarp.

"Just send me a schedule ahead of your departure," he said. "Jerusalem could be quite exciting."

When Polycarp discussed going to Jerusalem with James, he was not thrilled.

"I want to go to Jerusalem," James said. "But not next."

"Where do you think we should visit?" Polycarp asked. "It is warmer in the south."

"We could go somewhere close to Smyrna," he said. "I think we will find a great amount of material in and around Jerusalem but it is a long way from Philippi. If we only have to ship the material to Smyrna, less will be lost and damaged."

"That makes sense," he said. "Let me think about it for a few days. Sometimes my mind is stubborn."

After thinking about James' suggestion for a few days, Polycarp agreed

"James, I think you are correct," Polycarp said. "Our next trip will be to Troas and Mitylene. When Paul taught about Jesus, he was very successful and started churches in both towns."

"That is much closer to Smyrna," James said.

"We might be able to find something," he said. "You can make plans for us to be in Smyrna for a month. I will tell the dean of our plans."

"I like living in the house," he said. "We can sail to Smyrna and take a carriage from Smyrna. This time we will have a chance to see all of the very old parts of cities."

Polycarp informed the dean why he had changed his mind, and that he would be absent for a month. James arranged for their travel.

When they arrived at the dock, John met them.

"It is good to see you," he said. "I have everything prepared for you. Your lecture is tomorrow."

"How is Bishop Menahem?" Polycarp asked. "I want to see him."

"He is not well," he said. "I am certain Mark will take you to see him. You must visit the building. The walls for the building are very large."

"I would like to see the bishop first," he said. "I am sorry to hear he is not doing well."

"I will carry your bag," John said. "Was it cold in Philippi?"

"Yes," he said. "That is one reason we came to visit you."

"I have plenty of wood for our fireplaces," he said. "We won't be cold."

They spent a few days in Smyrna. Polycarp lectured to a large crowd of prospective students. Later in the week, they prepared to leave for Troas. Polycarp and James visited the church's stables and surveyed the horses and carriages.

"That is a fine looking horse," James said. "They must comb him every day."

"I have packed plenty of food in the carriage" John said. "The extra bag is full of writing supplies and blank scrolls."

Two days later, they arrived at a church in Troas. The priest was prepared for them and had arranged a stable for the horse.

"Welcome Bishop Polycarp," he said. "My name is Michael, this is our church."

"You have a very fine looking church," Polycarp said. "It is quite large."

"It will take you a while to absorb all the Greek history in our city," he said. "When you want a guide, I will have one of the local young men at the church show you our town. We have several men studying to be priests."

"Research first," he said. "Then Greek history."

"I will show you to the room we have prepared for you," he said. "Dinner is at sunset. You will have time to unpack and clean."

James looked at Polycarp.

"He seems like a nice fellow," he said. "Our room is fine. While you rest, I will go and visit with the other priest."

"Thank you, James," he said. "It has been a long day."

They dined with the priests and then sat at a long table in an area normally used for reading. Polycarp explained his research, and that he would try to locate any information about Eutychus. The priest said that a descendant of Eutychus was a member of the church. James indicated they would visit with him the next day.

They arose early and walked to the house.

"We are looking for a descendant of Eutychus," James said. "We would like to talk with them."

"Come in," he said. "I am a son of Eutychus. May I help you?"

"We understand your father was healed by Paul," James said. "We would like to discuss the incident with you. If you have any parchments about it, we would like to see them."

"I was very young at the time," he said. "I don't remember anything, but I have been told plenty."

"Tell us what you know," Polycarp said. "James will record your recollection and we will study what you were told."

"I was told father generally worked at the shipyard warehouse. After work, he went to listen to Paul," he said. "He was seated, in a third story window, when he fell asleep and plummeted to the street. Luke looked at him, but Paul prayed for him and he was restored."

Polycarp looked at James.

"Do you know about Luke?" he asked. "He was a friend of Paul's."

"Luke was a doctor," Polycarp said. "What did Luke say?"

"Luke was certain he was dead," he said. "He also said, his faith in God had allowed him to be restored."

"It is an amazing story," Polycarp said. "It was witnessed by a large crowd of people."

"I do have a few parchments, one from father to Luke, one from father to Paul, and one from Luke," Mr. Eutychus said. "They are getting worn. I think Luke returned them to us."

After a few moments, Eutychus' son returned with the parchments. He handed them to Polycarp. He quickly perused them.

"This one from Luke is quite extraordinary," he said. "Can I keep them for my research?"

"I don't want to give them to you, they are my inheritance from father," he said. "They were his prize possession."

Polycarp was disappointed but understood his feelings.

"If you decide to part with them, please contact me," Polycarp said. "The university would probably purchase the parchments."

"May I make copies of them?" James asked. "That would help our research."

"That is fine with me," he said.

He looked at James.

"Where will you keep the copies?" he asked.

"There will be in the new building at the church in Smyrna," he said. "We will house our research there starting next fall. We will also retain a copy of our research at the university in Philippi."

After James copied the parchments, they returned to the church and spent a few days copying the scrolls Paul had given to the church. One scroll included the lesson he taught of Eutychus' faithful day. They relaxed by touring the many great Greek buildings and the more modern Roman buildings.

James pointed at a building.

"The Obion was used for music and singing performances," he said. "Next we will visit the theater, and then we will go to the stadium where they raced."

"I am ready for the Roman baths," Polycarp said. "Can you find them?"

"That is our last stop," he said. "First, I want to see the remainder of the wall."

After a few days enjoying Troas, they boarded a ship and sailed to Mitylene. It was a very small ship and a very short trip. After they disembarked, they looked for a church. Polycarp wasn't having any success. Finally, a person was able to provide directions.

"Go to the second block turn left and ask at the third house," he said.

When they reached the house, they were greeted and given a seat. The gentleman told them that his house was used as a church.

"We only have a few members," he said. "We meet occasionally and review Jesus's message. We used to have one old man who heard Paul teach. He died about a year ago. Since then, we have to go to Troas to learn new messages."

"Do you have any scrolls or parchments?" Polycarp asked. "We are trying to locate material Paul might have written."

"No we don't have anything," he said. "Most of us can't read or write. We just work in the fields or on the dock."

James and Polycarp went back to the dock and sailed on the next ship to Smyrna.

After they disembarked they walked home. John was seated reading in the living area of house. He heard a knock on the door. When he opened it and saw James and Polycarp, he was surprised. They stayed in Smyrna long enough to make copies of everything they had found in Troas. Polycarp spent the next morning with Mr. Philemon discussing the new building. He sought Polycarp's advice concerning the library and size of the lecture halls. Polycarp explained that the library should have two sections. The main section would contain all the scrolls available to the students and an area for them to study. The second section would contain all the other scrolls and an area for the researchers to work. The second area would be secure and controlled by Polycarp. After the details were finalized, Mr. Philemon went back to work, and Polycarp returned to the house.

Later in the week, John arranged for them to sail to Philippi. He made certain Polycarp and James arrived at the dock before the ship was ready to sail.

"I hope you don't make any unscheduled stops in Troas," John said. "Before you return, send me a message."

"Thank you," Polycarp said. "We will contact you before we return. I have a great amount of work to accomplish, and I want to teach a class. I know James will be busy preparing for our relocation."

They sailed to Philippi. The waves were small and the breeze was steady. They smiled when they saw the dock in Neapolis. They found their friend and hired him to take them to the university.

When the dean appeared, Polycarp was seated in his office.

"Did you have a successful trip?" Julius asked.

"Yes, we did," Polycarp replied. "We copied many scrolls and some very interesting parchments. James will provide a copy of everything for the university."

"When and where do you plan to visit next?" he asked. "The more you find, the more students become interested in your research."

A student assistant brought them tea.

"I haven't decided where I will go next," he said. "James and I are prepared to spend most of our time in Smyrna helping to open the new building."

"Have you seen the new building?" Julius asked.

"The building looks great," Polycarp said. "I spent several hours with Philemon finalizing the plans for the library and the lecture halls."

"We are very fortunate to be opening a new building," Julius said. "It is a great structure."

"I must ensure the library is large enough to accommodate five hundred students," he said. "It will take us a few years to attract that many students."

The dean returned to his office and Polycarp went to find James. Polycarp's student assistant went and informed Dianna that Polycarp was home and would dine with her that evening. James carefully sorted their new scrolls and parchments.

"I will put the copies with your research, and I will put all the originals and parchments on the table in your office," James said. "If it is acceptable to you, I will use the table in your office to transcribe the parchments. The room designated for those transcribing text is full of students."

Papias saw James and Polycarp and stopped to talk with them.

"Are you going to be available for a while?" Papias asked. "My students are very interested in your research."

"Yes," Polycarp said. "We must be prepared for our move to Smyrna and the new building."

"It sounds like you will be busy," he said. "Do you have time for my students?"

"I have learned a lot about students in the last few years. I always have time for students," Polycarp said. "I am going to ensure the new building has two large rooms available for transcription and large lecture halls."

"We will be looking forward to your lecture," Papias said. "Bring James along."

After a brief stop in his office, he walked home. When he thought about not being able to have dinner with his mother for eight months, he became sad and frowned. As he approached Dianna's house, he quickened his pace.

"I am home and plan to be with you for many months," he announced.

She was very elated to hear his voice.

"Sit down and let's talk," she said. "I have something to tell you."

Polycarp detected a worried tone in her voice. He went to her and held her hand.

"It is your sister, Martha," she said. "We are having some problems. She wants everything exactly her way. She has forgotten this is my house. Before I said anything to her, I wanted to talk with you."

His worst fears dissipated.

"Where is she?" he asked. "Will she be here for dinner?"

"I don't know where she is," she said. "She usually is here for dinner. Sometimes, Rachael and I eat alone."

Polycarp was surprised how distraught his mother had become.

"I will talk with her this evening," he said. "I am certain we can resolve the situation."

That evening Martha and Polycarp had a very long discussion. Martha's dissatisfaction was that she and Daniel were never given any privacy. Daniel insisted things had to change or he would find another house in which to live. She indicated he claimed to work late, so he had time to look for a house. Polycarp heard Daniel walk across the porch.

"We have waited for you," he said. "Rachael will serve dinner."

"I guess Martha told you that we are moving," he said. "I have found a house for us. It is on the other side of town. It is small, but we will be alone."

"Martha, get your things packed," Daniel said. "You can come back tomorrow for your other things."

It was a tense situation. Rachael didn't serve the dinner. They sat and watched as Martha and Daniel packed a few items in a bag and departed. Then Dianna asked Rachael to serve dinner.

After dinner Polycarp and Dianna went to the living area. They didn't say much. Polycarp assured his mother everything would be resolved. He explained it would take some time.

The next morning at breakfast, Polycarp asked Dianna to be patient and relaxed when Martha came for her other belongings. He said, he would be home at sunset and discuss the situation. He thought it was best to allow a little time to pass before having a discussion. He walked to the university. The day passed slowly.

When he arrived home, Dianna met him.

"Did you have a good day?" Dianna asked. "Martha and I had a long talk. We decided it was best for them to be by themselves for a time. They will visit and will have dinner with me occasionally."

"That sounds like a starting point," Polycarp said. "I am sure the two of you will remain best of friends. Continue to talk with each other."

"Dinner is served," Rachael said. "We have fresh vegetables and hot bread."

Polycarp smiled at his mother.

During the next month, Martha visited Dianna at lunch on several occasions. Satisfied, she and Rachael assumed their old routine.

One evening after dinner, Polycarp decided he would discuss his relocation with his mother.

"I want you and Rachael to visit with me in Smyrna," he said.

"We can't do that," she said. "We have a house."

"Your house isn't going anywhere," he said. "The house at the church is plenty large enough and I have a house keeper. He is a priest and will take good care of you."

"I don't know," she said. "I have never traveled very far, and Rachael has never traveled at all."

"I want you to think about it," he said. "You could stay a month and then return home."

The building in Smyrna was almost completed. The library was completed and scrolls were being catalogued and stored. The research center started receiving material from Philippi. John made a trip to Philippi to help James transport ten packs of copied scrolls. A month later, they made a second trip.

Polycarp thought about how being the dean of a school would be a new experience. The contractors concentrated on the library and research areas. They were a little behind schedule with the office and classroom areas. Mr. Philemon instructed them to continue what they were doing but to ensure the classrooms were completed. The delays in construction meant the professors wouldn't have private offices when they started teaching. Polycarp talked with the new professors.

"Gentlemen, this will be a temporary inconvenience," he said. "Our offices will be completed one month after classes start. I will be working on a long table on the fourth floor. Our new offices will be very nice and well worth a short delay."

"I don't like the idea of starting before the building is complete," Patmost said. "We were promised private offices with security when we started. Having our belonging lying on a long table unprotected is not acceptable. We should delay the opening."

"I will talk to my boss about your concerns," Polycarp said. "I will talk with you tomorrow."

When Polycarp discussed the situation with Mr. Philemon that evening, Mr. Philemon was furious with the professor.

"If he is going to cause problems, we don't need him," he said. "You can apologize to him and then dismiss him. If he tries to cause problems, I will have the situation handled."

"I understand," he said. "I will take care of it."

Polycarp now understood that it was in his best interest to handle as many situations as possible. He decided to only involve Mr. Philemon with the most serious of situations.

The next day Polycarp met with Professor Patmost and apologized to him.

"I am sorry for your displeasure," he said. "If you don't want to continue with us, I will understand."

Professor Patmost hesitated. He finally spoke.

"That is fine with me," he said. "I have a better position waiting for me. Good luck."

He exited the room. His departure was only a minor inconvenience.

The next day, Polycarp interviewed a professor who wasn't hired during their first round of interviews. Polycarp and James agreed to hire him. James and John continued their trips between Philippi and Smyrna. Polycarp moved his personal belongings out of Dianna's house and shipped them to Smyrna. His materials from the university were his last items delivered to Smyrna. Just before they arrived, he was informed that his office was ready.

"After you move, we will start the other offices," the builder said.

Polycarp was pleased about the situation.

"I will put my material in my office," he said. "I will be working from the table, on the forth level, until all the offices are completed. I hope you understand."

The contractor became worried. He stared at Polycarp.

"Yes, sir," he said. "I will inform Mr. Philemon of your decision."

The builder eventually informed Mr. Philemon of Polycarp's decision. Mr. Philemon replied that he was not surprised and that the other offices should be finished as soon as possible. The first day of classes approached. The professors worked at the tables and the student assistants worked with them.

"I want to thank you," Professor Alexander said. "Having so many students to help us has made our lives much easier. When our offices are completed, I will be glad."

"Thank you," Polycarp said. "James has hired many student assistants for us. We hoped it would help everyone be ready for the first day of classes. Have you looked at your classroom?"

"Yes, I hope we can fill it with students," he said. "It is quite large. I think it will hold fifty students."

"The rooms are a little large, but we have many students," he said.

As the first day of class approached, Polycarp talked with James.

"I have moved and unpacked all of our materials," he said. I think we are ready. Do you know how many students we will have in our classes?"

"No, I haven't counted them," he said. "I have assigned a priest the duty of being the head administrator for the school. Mark assured me he would do a good job. If we have any problems, he will solve them. His name is Thomas."

Thomas stayed busy completing all the last minute adjustments. He reported to Polycarp twice a day.

CHAPTER 5

THE NEW BUILDING
AT SMYRNA

The new building was four stories of glimmering marble and granite. It reflected the sunshine like a new gold coin. The first level was a library that would house scrolls and the research material. The plan was to eventually copy every scroll and make all of them available to the students. The second floor provided offices, two large lecture halls, and the third floor classrooms. The fourth floor was built to allow future expansion. When Polycarp visited the fourth floor, he paused and prayed for an increase in student enrollment.

After the beginning of the New Year, the building would be designated the college of religion. About two months before the building officially opened, James and Polycarp had started working full-time in Smyrna. James supervised the unpacking and placement of the scrolls and parchments into the new cabinets. The cabinets were a special design by a company in Tarsus. Polycarp learned about the cabinets from a professor at the university in Tarsus. He stayed busy interviewing prospective professors. Mr. Philemon planned to open the college of religion with three professors to assist Polycarp and James. James interviewed and hired several student assistants. A few students already worked for Polycarp and James, and the new hires would transcribe and help the other professors. The dedication ceremony for the building was scheduled for Monday morning. A large number of people had been invited, and the priesthood was scheduled to attend. Classes were scheduled to start at one o'clock.

The entire town came to the dedication of the building. Many took time to thank Mr. Philemon for his generosity. He was very pleased and smiled as he gazed over the large number of people.

"This is a great crowd," he said. "I might as well start planning for our next building."

As Polycarp sensed Mr. Philemon's joy, he said a silent prayer.

"Yes, we have a lot of interested people," he said. "I hope they all want to be students or have children who want to be students."

The dedication ceremony lasted two hours. Mr. Philemon took the necessary time to explain his intentions and Polycarp's research to the crowd. The building's name was carved in the marble above the front door. "The Menahem School of Religion at The Polycarp Research Center" was now officially carved in stone. After the ceremony, Mr. Philemon provided food and drink for all who attended.

The classes commenced as scheduled. Three professors taught at one o'clock and the other two taught at three o'clock. That afternoon, everyone seemed filled with the Holy Spirit. The students found the proper classrooms and located a place to sit at the tables to take notes. The professors greeted the students and checked their enrollment parchments. There were about forty five students in each of the three classrooms. After classes were completed on the first day, Polycarp and James sat at a table and discussed how to improve the first day of class procedures before the next study period. They thought it had been necessary to help too many confused students.

After a very rewarding first day, James looked at Polycarp.

"My classroom was completely full," he said. "We had a great turnout of students."

"Yes, I was in one of the lecture halls," Polycarp said. "My student assistant told me that he had to turn a few students away. We had seats for one hundred. Mr. Philemon will be elated."

He paused and smiled at James.

As Polycarp mentioned Mr. Philemon, he appeared. He indicated that as soon as the professors moved into their offices, he was going to have additional classrooms and one very large lecture hall built on the fourth floor. He was in a very joyous mood. Everyone exhibited a smile as they went home for the evening.

When Polycarp approached his house, he saw John.

"We are expected to have dinner at the church this evening," he said. "When you are ready, please tell me. I think Mark may have something to tell us."

"It will take me a few minutes," Polycarp said. "I wonder what he knows that we don't know. Please pour me a glass of wine. I need to pray and relax for a moment, and then I will be ready."

After Polycarp drank wine and prepared for dinner, they walked to the church and joined the already seated priests. Mark welcomed them and dinner was served. After dinner was completed, they adjourned to a sitting room and relaxed. As soon as they were seated, Mark addressed them.

"I met with Mr. Philemon today," he said. "He inquired about doubling the size of the university. He wanted to know if the priesthood could manage the administration of a much larger university. I told him that we could."

The priests were perplexed and looked at one another. They didn't comprehend why this fantastic idea was so important to Mark. Polycarp looked at him.

"Do you really think he was seriously considering doubling the size of our school?" he asked.

"I have no doubt," Mark said. "He wants to share his good fortune with the people of Smyrna."

"I am certain we have a sufficient number of priests," Polycarp said. "If more are required, we can train more priests."

Mark looked at Polycarp and smiled.

"He was pleased with my answer," he said. "He informed me that he planned to purchase all the properties near the church. He will build a new larger school building and places for students to live."

"Double the size of the school," John said. "He must have been really pleased."

"He is going to pattern the student living quarters after what the Roman military uses for permanent quarters for the troops," Mark said. "The facilities are relatively inexpensive and can be built very quickly."

"You told him we could manage a school twice the size of the existing school?" Polycarp asked. "I hope you were correct. Did he tell you what would be taught in the new building?"

"He told me he would have several additional meetings with you," he said. "He wants to increase the number of fields of studies, so we can become recognized as a university."

Polycarp looked at Mark. He wasn't aware that Mr. Philemon had spoken with him.

"This is a large undertaking," he said. "Our church will own and provide administration for the expanded university."

John looked at Polycarp.

"Bishop, what has he discussed with you?" John asked.

"Nothing in great detail," Polycarp said. "He did ask if I thought a larger school was a good idea. Just because something can be accomplished, doesn't always make it a good idea."

Polycarp paused. Mark looked at him.

"It is a great idea," he said. "I am very excited. I hope he is obtaining information about other universities."

"I can tell you that the fourth floor of our existing building will be outfitted as soon as possible," Polycarp said. "It will open to students next learning period. I must locate additional professors. If any of you are interested, please make an appointment to see me."

Over the next two months, Mr. Philemon and Polycarp met many times. They agreed the new university would offer medicine, science, languages and mathematics. Two new professors would be hired before the new building was opened and three additional would eventually be hired. Mr. Philemon didn't discuss building size with Polycarp. He did inform Polycarp he planned to provide living quarters for one hundred and fifty students. He was certain students from the surrounding areas would attend the university. Land was cleared and construction of the new buildings started. Polycarp watched the construction of the new building from his office, as he interviewed additional professors. His assistant appeared at his door.

"Bishop, I have an interviewee to see you," the student assistant said. "His name is John."

"Show him in," he said.

Polycarp was surprised.

"John, I didn't expect to see you. Do you want to teach?"

"Yes Bishop," he said. "I would like to teach Latin and Greek. Until the new building is opened, I could help with religion. I will continue to maintain your house."

Polycarp smiled at John.

"You have earned one of the openings," he said. "However, I will expect you to dedicate all your time to teaching and writing."

"Thank you," he said. "I am looking forward to being a professor."

"You can inform Mark that you are an instructor. He will assign a priest to care for me and the house," he said.

Mark and Polycarp met and discussed John. Mark wanted John to continue managing the house until the new building opened. He did agree to relieve John of all his duties as a priest, except the house, so he could teach one religion course. Polycarp agreed to the arrangement and agreed to mentor John with the religion course.

After a few days passed, Polycarp sat down to dinner with John.

"It appears that you are going to take care of the house for about eight months," he said. "I will help you with your religion course. I would like you to teach about my research, I am sure that will fill a classroom."

John was speechless. His prayers had been answered. He was now an instructor and the bishop was going to help him get started in the classroom.

After dinner, Polycarp sent a message to his mother and provided her with the schedule of the ships. He asked her to pick a time to travel and that he would make all the arrangements."

John took the message to the dock and sent it to Polycarp's mother.

The next day, Polycarp sent a message to James and asked him to come to his office. That afternoon, James knocked on Polycarp's office door.

"You wanted to see me?" he asked. "I needed a break. Transcribing can be tedious."

"Yes, James," Polycarp said. "I want to be certain you want to continue traveling with me. I have hired John as an instructor, and he is going to start teaching on a limited schedule."

"I am looking forward to helping you with your research," he said. "To where will we travel next?"

"John will meet with you and arrange to teach for you during the next study period," he said. "I want to go to Galilee. You can start planning."

The next week as Polycarp sat in his office, a priest hurried to see him.

"While I was in the church praying, two Roman soldiers brought a man to pray," he said. "He was tightly bound and wore the robe of a bishop."

Polycarp became very curious.

"Take me to them," he said.

The priest escorted Polycarp to the prayer rail. The man was on his hands and knees praying. He looked at Polycarp.

"These men have been assigned the duty of delivering me to Rome," he said. "I am Ignatius. We have traveled from Antioch."

Polycarp helped him to his feet. He kissed the back of his bound hands.

"May we assist you," he asked.

"No," he said. "If necessary I am prepared to die for my God."

Polycarp knew about Ignatius, The Bishop of Antioch. He looked at the soldiers.

"Would you dine with us?" he asked.

They went to the dining area and were served a meal.

"Thank you," a soldier said. "We must continue our journey."

Polycarp and the priest escorted Ignatius and the two soldiers to the carriage. Two mounted soldiers rode before the carriage as it headed north.

The next week, the priest brought Polycarp a message.

"It is from Ignatius," he said. "They are in Troas."

Polycarp read the message.

> Polycarp
> Bishop of Smyrna
>
> God bless you, your priests and our church.
> While being transported to Rome, I have been
> allowed to write to several churches.
> The church in Smyrna is the only church I have
> visited.
> The messages I write today maybe my last.
> Things have become more difficult.
> It was a blessing to meet you and your priesthood.
> Pray for me and my guards.
>
> Ignatius
> Bishop of Antioch

After dinner, Polycarp read Ignatius' message to the priests. They paused and prayed for his wellbeing.

During the next few months, John taught about Polycarp's research and learned how to teach James' religion course. The new buildings became visible to all who attended church. The school building looked very much like the existing building. The area where the living quarters would be built was marked for construction. James and Polycarp planned their trip to Galilee.

Polycarp continued interviewing prospective professors. His student assistant appeared at the door to his office.

"Sir, I have a priest to see you about a teaching position," the student assistant said. "His name is Simon."

"Come in Simon," Polycarp said. "How long have you been at the church?"

"I have been here for five years," he said. "My duties have included taking care of our scrolls. I have talked with Mark, and we think I would make a good teacher. He instructed me to see you."

"I want you to teach a lesson," he said. "See Professor James and arrange to teach a class. He and I will listen to your lesson. When you are prepared to teach, tell my student assistant."

After a few days, the student assistant informed Polycarp that Simon was scheduled to teach for James, and he was invited to attend the class. Polycarp smiled as he remembered the beginning of his teaching career. Simon was informed by Polycarp's student assistant that his lesson would be evaluated by the faculty. Simon's lesson was well prepared and the students appreciated his presentation. Mark was asked to release Simon from his duties as a priest, so he could become an instructor.

The following day, Simon visited with Polycarp.

"What would you like to teach?" Polycarp asked. "You have a lot of choices. The more professors that are hired, the more restricted the choice will become."

"I would like to teach religion," Simon said. "I am interested in your research. Would you provide me with details about your studies?"

"Certainly," he said. "I have read material written by or for Mark, Luke, Matthew, John, and Paul. I have read many other scrolls, but I consider those the most important."

"That must have been very interesting," he said. "I hope to be able to compare their writings."

"Mark, Matthew, Luke, and what John added give us many different perspectives of the same story," Polycarp said. "Maybe, you could teach about how the four stories are the same and how they differ."

"I think I would like to do that," Simon said. "I will have to do a lot of reading."

"Reading and research will make you a better informed teacher," he said. You can start, part time, the next study period. When the building is completed, you will become a full-time instructor."

"Thank you," he said. "I will be reading."

James scheduled a meeting with Polycarp, so they could discuss their research trip. Near the end of the week, they ate lunch at James' favorite restaurant. James suggested sailing to Tyre, going to Galilee, and sailing from Tyre on their return trip. They would visit Tyre, the Sea of Galilee area, and Nazareth. Polycarp liked James' plan and asked him to prepare a schedule. James indicated he would need at least a week to complete a schedule.

"When you prepare our schedule, don't make it to aggressive," Polycarp said. "If we have extra time, we will look at some buildings. I think we should visit Cana."

"I will put Cana in the schedule," James said. "I have heard a lot of stories about that wedding."

"The miracle of the wine is well known," he said. "I would like to hear it as told by a Cainite."

"Maybe you will find a wine jar," he said. "If you do, we will purchase it and have it shipped back to the university."

"Wine jars at the university?" Polycarp asked. "We will have to fill them with water."

Polycarp saw James smile and pointed at him.

"You will have to keep it in your office," James said. "No one will question you."

"We will travel between towns via carriage," Polycarp said. "We should take a student and allow him earn some money. I will talk with Mark and find someone to travel with us."

Polycarp sent a message and asked John to arrange dinner at the church with Mark. When Polycarp arrived home that evening, John said Mark would be glad to have dinner with them and would wait at the church. He also handed Polycarp a message from his mother. After Polycarp washed and rested, they walked to the church.

"I want to talk to you," Polycarp said. "I have an idea. Neither James nor I are very good at driving a carriage, but we want to travel on our next trip by carriage."

"You must be planning on covering a lot of area." Mark said. "How can I help?"

"Our research could pay for a student priest to drive us." he said. "I thought you might have one who would like to travel and earn some money."

"I am certain I can find someone," he said. "What other duties will you want him to perform?"

"If he could read and write Greek, it would be great," Polycarp said. "We will have two long sections of our trip by ship. He must be sea worthy. We will sail from Smyrna to Tyre and return from Tyre."

"I will locate a priest to travel with you," he said. "If I can't find anyone, maybe the Bishop will allow me to travel."

He flashed a large simile in Polycarp's direction.

Two day passed, Polycarp was reading at his desk when his student assistant appeared.

"Excuse me, sir. I have a student named Joazar to see you."

"Record his name," Polycarp said. "Then show him in."

"Good day, Bishop," Joazar said. "I would like to discuss working for you concerning your next research trip."

"Have a seat," he said. "Can you drive a carriage and read Greek?"

"Yes sir," he said. "I am also sea worthy and can write Greek. I have been at this church for many years. I am studying to become a priest."

"You have a job," Polycarp said. "The research will pay you a small stipend and pay your expenses at the university for a year."

"Thank you, sir," he said. "When will we depart?"

"Please call me Bishop or Professor, sir makes me uneasy," he said. "I don't know when we will depart."

"Professor James is compiling our schedule and itinerary," he said. "You should introduce yourself to him. You will be working with both of us."

A very enthused Joazar exited, at a very rapid pace, and headed to Professor James' office. He spoke with his student assistant.

"I am here to see Professor James," he said. "Bishop Polycarp sent me."

"I am sorry Professor James isn't available," his student helper said. "You could return tomorrow."

A disappointed Joazar asked, "When will he be in his office, may I make an appointment?"

"He has not told me his schedule for tomorrow," he said. "You could come before or after he teaches his class."

"I will see you tomorrow," he said. "I will arrive before his class."

The next day, before it was time for Professor James to teach, Joazar was seated at his office. Professor James didn't visit his office before his class, so Joazar waited outside his classroom. After the class, he introduced himself to Professor James and asked about the schedule for the research trip. Professor James was pleased to make his acquaintance. He informed Joazar he would send the schedule to Polycarp when it was completed. Joazar smiled at him and returned to the church.

Polycarp decided he would again invite his mother to visit before he went on his research trip.

"John, I would really like mother to visit with me," he said. "I have sent her the ship schedules. She hasn't answered my messages."

"She might be intimidated by travel," John said.

"Check the ship schedules," he said. "I am going to write to mother and invite her and her attendant to visit with us."

"That sounds good," John said. "We have plenty of room for guests. I will have it for you tomorrow."

"I have to convince her to travel," he said.

The next day, Polycarp wrote a message to his mother and included a ship schedule. When Dianna and Rachael received the message, they studied the schedule of the available ships and replied. They realized it was important to Polycarp that they visit.

After Polycarp returned, from his work at the university, John gave him the message.

"I hope she has sent you good news," John said. "I am certain she would enjoy Smyrna."

He opened and read it.

Dear Son

May God always be with you.
Rachael and I have studied the
schedule concerning available ships.
We would like to visit with you
for three weeks.
I miss you very much and have

decided it is time for me to travel.

We will arrive in ten days.

I look forward to seeing you.

I hope the seas are calm.

Your Mother

Dianna

Polycarp informed John that they would be having house guests. He said his mother and her attendant would arrive in two weeks and remain about three weeks.

"I will make all the arrangements," John said.

"I would like you to arrange two things for them," Polycarp said. "First, I want you to show them around Smyrna. Second, I want you to arrange a dinner at the church. I want mother to meet Priest Mark."

The next few days, John spent his free time making all the necessary arrangements. He planned a leisurely paced walking tour of the city, the new school building, and the church.

Polycarp was busy working. The day approached for their arrival.

"Your mother will be here the day after tomorrow," John said. "I plan to meet her ship."

"Thanks for reminding me," Polycarp said. "I have arranged to be off for a day. When she arrives, I will go with you to greet her."

It was a beautiful day. The sun shone brightly and the weather was warm. John talked and Polycarp smiled as they rode in a carriage to the dock.

"I see her ship," John said. "It is docking. Soon, she will disembark."

As he waved to her, Polycarp said, "I see her."

With the help of a mate, Dianna and Rachael make their way to Polycarp and John.

"We had a pleasant trip," Dianna said. "The sailors took very good care of us."

"Welcome to Smyrna," John said.

As they walked to the carriage, Polycarp gave his mother a hug and gripped her hand.

"John will put your packs into the carriage," he said. "It is good to see you."

John drove them to the house and then showed them to their rooms. He unloaded the carriage and took their bags to their rooms. When everyone gathered in the living area, he served water.

"I have prepared dinner," John said. "Would you like me to serve it?"

"May we wait a while?" Dianna asked. "We are not hungry yet. Could we eat in an hour?"

"Yes, I will serve the food in an hour," he said. "Would you like another cup of tea?"

"Bring us all a glass of wine," she said. "We will talk for a while."

Dianna smiled at Polycarp and told him about their trip. The hour passed quickly and John served the dinner. The dinner was quite good. After dinner, Dianna and Rachael excused themselves and went to bed. Polycarp told John not to wake them, at his normal breakfast time.

The next morning, Polycarp arose early, ate his breakfast with John, and then walked to the school.

A few hours later, the women arose and smelled the odor of hot food.

"Good morning, ladies," John said. "I shall serve your breakfast."

"Thank you," Dianna said. "I think Rachael and I will rest today. Maybe you could take us to the market later."

John went to the market by himself. Dianna and Rachael rested all day. When Polycarp came home, they sat in the living room and talked.

"Did you enjoy your walk in town," Polycarp asked. "John has several walks planned for you."

"We didn't want to walk today," Dianna said. "Tomorrow we can walk."

"I want you to look at the new buildings," he said. "When they are completed, we will be a university. John will show them to you tomorrow."

The next day, John showed Dianna and Rachael the new classroom building and the new living quarters. They didn't go in. Dianna was tired and wanted to rest. John could see it would be necessary to reduce the length of the trips he had planned. He explained to Polycarp that they wouldn't go anywhere the day of the dinner with the priests.

A few days passed, they enjoyed several short walks and carriage rides. When Polycarp arrived home, they went to the church for dinner.

"Mother, this is Mark," Polycarp said. "He is responsible for the church."

Dianna looked at Mark.

"You have a beautiful church," she said. "We go to pray every day."

"Those seated with us are the priests of the church," Mark said. "We are pleased you like our church."

"This is Rachael," she said. "She helps me."

"It is very important that each of us has a care giver," Mark said. "God provides for all of us."

He smiled at Dianna.

When Dianna had finished her dinner, she told Polycarp that she wanted to go home and sleep. Polycarp excused them, and they returned home.

Polycarp discussed his mother's weak condition with John. They decided to allow her to rest as much as she desired. It wasn't long until it was time for her to return to Philippi. Polycarp took the morning off from his duties at the university and went with John, Rachael, and Dianna to the ship.

"Hello, Bishop," the captain said. "We have quarters ready for your mother and her attendant."

"Please take good care of her," Polycarp said. "She seems tired all the time."

"I will assign a mate to be at their cabin door at all times." he said. "They should have a good trip."

John helped the mate with the packs, and the ladies walked to their quarters.

After the ship sailed, John and Polycarp rode back to the house.

"Mother sure has slowed," Polycarp said. "I am glad I got to spend a little time with her. Thank you for being so understanding."

By the time the building was sixty percent completed, Polycarp had hired two more instructors. John had prepared to teach full-time the next study period. John and Mark decided to assign two priests, in training, to take care of the house. One needed three more academic courses before he would become a priest. The other priest, in training, had just arrived at the church. He would be assigned to do menial tasks at the house and to take courses at the university. He lived at the church.

When James appeared, Polycarp was at work in his office.

"I have a proposed itinerary," he said. "I would like to review it with you."

Polycarp greeted him. A student assistant brought them tea.

"We will sail to Tyre," he said. "The entire trip will take about forty days, and we will sail home from Tyre. I was able to schedule the trip as we planned it."

"That is good," Polycarp said. "Leave the itinerary with me, and I will discuss it with Mr. Philemon."

"I hope he approves it," James said. "I have put a lot of work into it."

"I am certain he will approve it," he said. "Giving him our itinerary is a courtesy."

Polycarp scheduled a meeting with Mr. Philemon. He liked their plans and advised Polycarp to send some unique items back to the university. The trip was finalized; they would depart in two weeks. Polycarp sent a schedule to Joazar. After he received the message, he hurried to visit Polycarp.

"Good morning," Joazar said. "I have been practicing writing Greek."

"Make certain you have plenty of writing materials," Polycarp said. "Professor James has a very detailed plan for us. Before we sail, I will meet with you."

"I will be ready," he said. "I am excited."

Polycarp visited with Professor James and acknowledged his good work on the schedule. He told James they would try to find unique items to purchase for the university. The day before they sailed, the three men met and discussed last moment details concerning the schedule for the ship.

When Polycarp arrived, Joazar and Professor James were at the dock.

"Our ship is large," James said. "They are just about finished transferring goods."

"Good morning Bishop Polycarp," the captain said. "My name is Ontimeamus."

"That is an interesting name," he said. "I like the looks of our ship."

"It is Mr. Philemon's largest and newest ship," he said. "We travel from Rome to Caesarea and back about every forty days."

"What type of cargo do you transport?" he asked. "Soldiers I guess."

"Yes, we take soldiers from Rome to their posts," he said. "We are almost always loaded with grain on our return trip. I see you will also be sailing back with us on our next trip."

"We will probably have a few items for you to transport to the university," James said. "We will also have a few extra packs."

"That is no problem," he said. "I have your quarters prepared. The Bishop is in cabin number one and you and your scribe are in cabin number two. If you need anything, please just ask the mate I have assigned to you."

The captain went about preparing the ship to sail.

Soon, they were underway. The ship seemed to cut its way through the seas. They heard the waves, but the ship didn't rock. It was much smoother than the smaller ships on which Polycarp had sailed.

On the second day, the captain invited Polycarp and his traveling companions to dine with him.

"We have a special dinner, thanks to Mr. Philemon," he said. Mr. Philemon ensured we had shell fish and fresh sea bass for our dinner. My table is at the end of the mess-hall, please be seated."

"I didn't know sailors ate so well," Polycarp said. "This fish is very tasty."

"We don't usually eat this well," Ontimeamus said. "Mr. Philemon provided the food as a special treat for you. My mates eat a lot of hardtack and usually drink grog."

"When do you expect to dock in Tyre?" Polycarp asked. "Do we have a good wind?"

"We are doing fine," he said. "Our sails will catch almost any wind. We will enter port the morning of our fourth day. We will wait at anchor until our slip is ready."

Soon after sunrise on the fourth day, they enjoyed breakfast as the ship entered the slip in the port of Tyre. They thanked the captain for the special service and they disembarked.

"Joazar, rent us a carriage," Polycarp said. "We will need it for thirty days. James, have we located all our packs? We don't want to forget anything."

"Yes we have all of them," he said. "I will help Joazar load them into the carriage."

"I want to visit the large tent making facility," Polycarp said. "Paul's father owned it. I am certain it is probably still in the family."

They located a man who explained which highway would take them to the plant. After they arrived, they entered the facility.

"Hello," Professor James said. "Is anyone a descendant of Omar?"

"Our owner is Omar's grandson," he said. "I will get Mr. David for you."

He disappeared into the large building.

After a few moments, a middle aged man appeared and introduced himself as Omar's grandson.

"My name is Polycarp," he said. "I am trying to locate scrolls written by Paul or any other things related to Paul."

"Most of Paul's things are at the university here and in Tarsus," David said. "He was a great man."

"Do you have any of his letters?" he asked. "I would like personal letters."

"Yes, I have been given a few," he said. "They are at my house."

"Could we make copies of them?" he asked. "We could come back tomorrow."

"That will be fine," he said. "I will bring them tomorrow and show them to you."

The next day, they were given ten messages, from Paul. They were allowed to copy them and keep one of the messages. Polycarp sent a message to Mr. Philemon. They experienced a great start to their journey.

Their next stop was to be in Bethsaida. It would take two days by carriage. When they arrived, they stayed overnight at the Inn. They arose early, ate breakfast, and then headed to the home of John, Jesus' disciple. When they found the home, an elderly man approached them.

"May I help you," he said. "We have two boats for sale."

"We are not looking for a boat," Polycarp said. "We are looking for anyone who might have known John."

"I knew John," he said. "He was my father's brother. My name is Joseph."

Polycarp greeted Joseph.

"Do you have anything that John wrote?" he asked. "We are trying to locate any parchments written by those that traveled with Jesus."

"I am not sure," he said. "We have a box full of stuff. John didn't write much, but his brother James did write, and we have many messages and a diary of his."

"Could we see them?" James asked. "Joazar will copy them for us."

"Have a seat on the porch," he said. "I will have my wife bring them. Would you like a glass of water?"

As they sat on the porch and enjoyed the sea breeze, they drank a glass of water.

"We have a very large piece of property," he said. "We are the only business on the lake that repairs large boats."

Joseph's wife brought them a box of parchments. They were excited by what they saw. Joazar started to copy them.

"We don't need them," Joseph said. "You can have most of them. I am certain the university will make good use of them."

Polycarp thanked Joseph and Joazar finished copying a few parchments.

They departed for Capernaum. They looked for Phillip's house, but could not find any trace of him or where he lived. That evening, they stayed at the Inn in Capernaum.

The following day, they visited the local synagogue. The priest said they didn't have anything of Peter's or Andrew's and was quite short with them. They travel through Capernaum, but found nothing for their research. Polycarp had the parchments from Bethsaida sent to Mark in Smyrna. They traveled to Magdala.

The next morning, they stopped people and asked about Mary of Magdala. The second person they stopped was a descendant of hers and invited them to her home.

"My grandmother was Mary's sister," Bathsheba said. "I have a few scrolls she wrote. None of us can read them."

"I would love to read them," Polycarp said. "We are grateful for your hospitality."

As they sat in the living room of her house, she retrieved the scrolls. Polycarp took the scrolls and explained his research to her.

"These scrolls are very interesting," he said. "They are a story of her time with Jesus."

"If you want them, you can have them," she said. "I was thinking of burning them for heat this winter."

"The university will purchase enough wood for you to heat you house this winter," Polycarp said. "Tell Joazar where he can get the wood. We will have it delivered to you."

"These scrolls will help our students," Professor James said. "We thank you very much."

"I am pleased someone will benefit from them," she said. "I am certain she learned a lot from Jesus."

Bathsheba requested that Polycarp send her a message explaining to her what the scrolls said. Polycarp agreed to have James communicate with her.

The researchers moved to their next destination in Tiberias. They were unable to find anything of interest.

Next, they went to Nazareth. They were told by an inhabitant that Judah's grandson lived in Mary's house.

"Do you have any thing that belonged to Jesus?" James asked.

"No, my father was given all of it," Zoker said. "He was certain that someday it would be important."

"I have met with your father, Menahem," Polycarp said. "I just wanted to visit Nazareth."

"Jesus was not very popular here." Zoker said. "However, Menahem did keep everything he could find. It is in the church at Smyrna."

The group thanked Zoker and departed

They traveled to Cana and entered the synagogue.

"I would like to see the senior priest," James said. "You can tell him Bishop Polycarp is calling on him."

Soon, a priest approached them.

"Hello, which one of you is a bishop?" the senior priest asked. "We have to travel to Jerusalem to speak with a Bishop."

"I am Bishop Polycarp," he said. "We are here on a research mission."

"You are The Bishop Polycarp of Smyrna?" he asked. "It is an honor to have you visit us. What can we do for you?"

"I want to see the jars that held the water Jesus turned to wine," Polycarp said. "Do you still have them?"

"We've had the same water jars forever," he said. "Would you like to see them?"

"Sure," James said. "Which ones are they?"

The priest showed them ten jars full of water. The jars were located in the hallway of the synagogue.

"If you would part with a few of the jars, our university could make a nice contribution to your synagogue," Polycarp said.

"You may have half of them," the priest said. "I will expect twice the cost of new jars to replace the five you take."

"Thank you," Polycarp said. "I will have Joazar pay you and make the necessary arrangements to have the jars transported to Tyre."

"Come back anytime," he said. "It is a pleasure doing business with you. I am certain most people will not even notice our new water jars."

That afternoon, Joazar packed the jars unto a wagon. They hired a driver to follow them, with the jars, as they traveled to Tyre.

Dock workers loaded the ship for its return trip, and the wagon returned to Cana.

The captain saw and then greeted Polycarp.

"We have everything ready for you," he said. "I see you have some extra items for us to transport back to Smyrna. I will have a mate stow them and secure them in one of our holes."

"Thank you," Polycarp said. "I am ready to get home. I think I will go to my cabin and sleep."

After a few hours, the ship was fully loaded, and they sailed. When a mate knocked on the door of his cabin, Polycarp was asleep.

"Bishop," he said. "I am the mate who is responsible for your material. I wanted to tell you that one of your jars arrived at the dock broken."

"Did you save all they pieces?" Polycarp asked. "We can probably reassemble it."

"It is not severely damaged," he said. "I wrapped the two pieces and put them into the jar."

"That is fine, mate," he said. "When we get home, I will inspect the jar. Thank you for informing me."

Polycarp went to the cabin occupied by James and Joazar. He explained the problem with the jar to them.

"It is my fault," Joazar said. "I packed it as carefully as possible."

"Joazar, you have done a fine job for us," James said. "When we return to the university, you and I will look at it."

"I hope the other jars survive the return trip without damage," he said. "We still have four good jars."

"They are all good jars," Polycarp said. "One of them has a few extra pieces."

The ship stopped at Crete to deliver a group of soldiers from Caesarea. Their next stop was Smyrna. Polycarp stood on the main deck and enjoyed the sunshine and warm, mild sea breeze. They noted that the ship was moving slowly. Polycarp visualized preparing the scrolls to be copied.

"I am very pleased with what we have found," he said. "We have a lot of work ahead of us."

"What are your favorite items?" James asks. "We will work on them first."

"The scrolls Mary wrote," he said. "They should be very interesting. Second would be the jars from Cana. They were a pleasant surprise."

"We will make copies of the scrolls and send the originals to you," he said. "I agree they could provide a great amount of information."

"Joazar, I want you to work with James until he doesn't need you," he said. "I think he plans to assign you to the transcribing section."

After the stop in Crete, the ship found very little wind, and the wind that was located blew from the wrong direction. It took the ship an extra day to arrive in Smyrna.

When the ship arrived, John met them at the dock. He took them home and returned to the ship to collect the jars. A mate helped him load them into a wagon.

When they arrived at the house, Mark met them. He was very excited. He explained that the scrolls he received from Bethsaida included several scrolls John had created especially for the priesthood. The scrolls included special instructions for priests and other "secrets" not found in John's other writings. Polycarp was interested and indicated they would be the first scrolls he would study.

CHAPTER 6

THE UNIVERSITY AT SMYRNA

After Joazar, James, and Polycarp returned home from their research trip, it required a week to sort and organize all the scrolls and material they had gathered. The new building was mostly completed and Mr. Philemon looked forward to the opening ceremony. Polycarp finalized the curriculum for the next study period. All the construction was completed on time, so it wasn't necessary for the professors to occupy temporary offices.

Polycarp requested a meeting with Mr. Philemon.

"Your meeting with Mr. Philemon is after lunch," Polycarp's student assistant said. "Do you need me to do anything extra?"

"We will be fine," Polycarp said. "Find Joazar and bring him to my office. I have something I would like him to do for me."

After only a few moments elapsed, Joazar appeared at his office, Polycarp was reading at a scroll.

"What may I do for you?" Joazar asked. "You were correct. When I am not working directly for Professor James, I am working in the department transcribing for the professors."

"I would like you to have the broken jar delivered to my office as soon as possible," Polycarp said. "Mr. Philemon will be here after lunch. I want to show it to him."

Joazar quickly departed to retrieve the jar. Later, he delivered it to Polycarp's office. The two pieces were still wrapped and stored at the bottom of the jar.

After lunch, Mr. Philemon arrived. He greeted the student assistant and asked for Polycarp.

"I will inform him you are here," the student said.

Polycarp greeted Mr. Philemon. He smiled at Polycarp.

"I looked at the material you had sent back," Mr. Philemon said. "It appears to me that you had a very successful trip."

He smiled as he noted the jar in Polycarp's office.

"What is that jar?" he asked. "I can't wait to hear the story."

He grinned at Polycarp.

"When I visited John a few years ago, he told me about Jesus changing water into wine at a wedding in Cana," Polycarp said. "When we visited Cana, I went to the synagogue and purchased these jars."

"You mean a miracle might have been performed in that jar?" he asked. "That is what I call a great story and a real find."

"I am certain it is one of the original jars," Polycarp said. "We purchased half of the old jars from the synagogue."

"How many did you purchase?" he asked. "Are they all alike?"

"We purchased five jars similar to this one," Polycarp said as he pointed to the jar.

"A large old jar would be great conservation piece for my office, may I have one?" he asked.

Polycarp paused and smiled at him.

"I guess we can survive with four," he said. "The two broken pieces are wrapped and in the bottom of the jar."

A grin appeared on his work stressed face.

"Could you survive with three?" he asked.

Polycarp stared at him.

"I want to send one of the jars to our new Pope Alexander," he said. "I like how he standardized the communion service."

Before Polycarp could answer him, he continued, "I will have one of my men come for the jars. Keep up the good work. If you need anything send for me. I will visit with you before we open the building."

Mr. Philemon quickly departed Polycarp's office.

Later that afternoon, one of Mr. Philemon's men arrived for the jars.

"I am here to obtain a magic jar," he said with a smirk on his face.

"The jar isn't magic," Polycarp said. "Jesus performed a miracle using these jars."

The worker sensed Polycarp's mood and became very serious. He carefully delivered one to Mr. Philemon's office, where he had prepared a special platform for it. It became the center piece for his very large office. He shipped the other jar to the Pope.

Polycarp talked with Professor James.

"I know one thing we must do on our next research trip," Polycarp said. "It shouldn't be very difficult."

"What is that?" James asked. "Do we need anything special?"

"No, we need to bring something back for Mr. Philemon," he said. "I gave him the broken jar we purchased. I think it funded anything we will need next year. He is going to display the jar in his office."

Polycarp displayed a large grin. After a moment, James returned the smile.

"I'll put it on our itinerary," he said. "Find something for Mr. Philemon's office. One never knows what can be really important!"

"Have you made a copy of the scrolls from Mary?" he asked. "I am interested in reading them."

"Joazar has been busy with other things," he said. "I will have him make a copy for you. He can probably do it tomorrow."

"I want the originals protected," he said. "Tell me where they will be stored. I don't want anyone except you and me to have access to the original scrolls."

James left Polycarp's office. He understood how important the scrolls had become to Polycarp.

The next afternoon copies of Mary of Magdala scrolls were written and delivered to Polycarp's office. Polycarp read them several times.

A few days later, Polycarp met with James about the next study period.

"I want you to try something a little different," Polycarp said. "I have an idea."

"What is that?" James asked. "Do you want me to do it personally?"

"Yes," he said. "You are the only one I trust to do it the first time. I want you to teach about the travels of Jesus."

"I do that almost every period," he said. "What is different about that?"

"I want you to tell the story from four perspectives," he said. "Simon tried it, but he never mastered the approach."

"All four?" he asked. "Teach all four at the same time. That will be a challenge for me and the students."

Polycarp explained to James that he shouldn't use the last scroll they found in Bethsaida.

Polycarp continued to study the scrolls John wrote especially for the priesthood. Those scrolls would only be made available to the bishops, and he would teach the bishops about John's instructional writings. James asked questions about a few scrolls that were originally written by Mark. Polycarp agreed the last few verses of one scroll were probably not written by Mark, but stated that the verses were not important to understanding the message contained in the story. James was allowed to teach from either writings.

"I think that is the way they should be taught," Polycarp said. "Think about it. We will be the first to do it."

"We will give it a try," James said. "I might ask John to help me."

"That is fine," he said. "I am going to teach about Mary of Magdala. Her scrolls are very interesting."

"Is there anything else?" he asked. "I must go to work."

"Yes, there is one other thing," he said. "I want a course developed on the sayings of Thomas. We need to put all our research to work. When it comes to gaining new students, our research will give us a competitive edge."

"We will probably need another building," James said. "Before the new building is open, we are already at maximum enrollment."

"That is a problem, I will enjoy explaining to Mr. Philemon," he said.

The day ended, and Polycarp went home to rest. The new head

housekeeper's name was David and his helper was Jeb. That evening, they walked to the church and dined with the other priests.

"Good evening, Bishop Polycarp," Mark said. "Please be seated with us."

"It has been a busy week," Polycarp said. "I am certain you are busy planning for the opening of our new buildings."

"Yes," he said. "I have talked to Professor James. He told me about your idea of teaching Matthew, Mark, Luke, and John as one story."

"I think it is one story," Polycarp said. "It is just four perspectives written years after the events happened."

"We will try it," Mark said. "I am going to lecture the first day to impress the idea of "one story" to the students. James will then teach the remainder of the course."

"I didn't expect you to have to teach," he said. "It will do the student good to meet you."

"I have been studying," he said. "It is quite an idea you have. I just want to get the students started on the proper foundation."

"Thank you," Polycarp said. "What is for dinner tonight?"

Many prayers were offered at dinner that evening. It was unusually quiet.

After dinner, Polycarp retuned home and relaxed in his favorite chair.

The next morning, he had an early breakfast and went to the university to visit with James.

"I had dinner with Mark last evening," Polycarp said. "He told me you discussed our new course with him."

"Yes," he said. "I wanted to make sure we get off to a good start."

"I am pleased that you are so interested in the success of this course," he said. "You can send me a report every week and keep me up-to-date."

"I will have Joazar send you a report," James said. "He is a big help."

"I would prefer that you take time and do it personally," Polycarp said as he stared at James.

"I will prepare you a report," he said. "I will keep you informed."

James now understood, to a better extent, Polycarp's interest in the new course.

Polycarp returned to his office and scheduled a meeting with the new faculty. Each new faculty member was instructed concerning his duties and the first day of class.

Mr. Philemon planned a meeting with Polycarp. When he visited Mr. Philemon's office, he received a special greeting.

"The jar you gave me is quite the deal," Mr. Philemon said. "I have never had so many comments about a furnishing. I think people are coming and giving me their shipping business just so they can see the jar."

"I hope our students are that excited," Polycarp said. "We have a lot of new material and many new students."

"That is great," he said. "I have started planning our next new building and living areas. I also talked with Mark."

"Our new building?" he asked. "The second one opens tomorrow."

"If you aren't going forward," Mr. Philemon said. "You are going backward. We are moving forward. You know I am a busy man."

"We are very thankful for your support," he said. "We all want to move forward."

"I have made two decisions," he said. "First we are going to grow the university, and second I am only going to meet only with you. You can keep Mark and the others informed."

"Have you discussed this with Mark," he asked. "I am sure he likes meeting with you."

"No, but I will inform him today." he said. "Too many cooks can ruin the stew. By the way, I love your idea of one story and four perspectives. We will be the largest and the greatest university."

Mr. Philemon departed Polycarp's office. He stopped at the church and spoke with Mark.

The next morning, the day of the ceremony, the priests gathered in the dining area of the church. Their religious regalia glittered in the bright sunlight as they processed through the crowd to the new building. Polycarp, outfitted in his grandest robe, was seated with Mr. Philemon on the temporary raised platform. After everyone arrived, the crowd became quiet. Mr. Philemon stood up. He talked about a new day in education. The day of student research, and that Polycarp and the faculty would provide the best education available. He spoke about the new building that was being planned. He then officially named the entire complex, The University at Smyrna. The reception, that followed, provided food for everyone. The students discussed the classes that started the next day.

After the ceremony, Polycarp returned to his office. A line of professors formed outside his office.

"Bishop Polycarp, are we going to have more buildings?" Mark asked.

"Yes, we are," Polycarp said. "Mr. Philemon plans to open two more buildings, the year after next. One will be a classroom building and the other new living quarters for students."

"He must really like what you are doing with your research," he said. "Where do you plan to visit during your next research trip?"

"We haven't decided yet," he said. "I have been working with Mr. Philemon concerning our new building and our future buildings."

"He must be a very busy man," he said. "I hate that he doesn't have time to meet with me. You will have to keep me informed of his plans for the church and the university."

Polycarp departed and Me. Philemon visited the church and talked with Mark.

After a few weeks, Professor James came to see Polycarp.

"We are doing well with the new courses," he said. "I am looking forward to teaching next study period."

"Are you planning our trip to Judea and Samaria?" Polycarp asked. "I would like to see the details."

"I have decided I want to teach and stay at the university to manage the transcribing department and the storage of what is being collected," he said. "I don't think both of us should be away from the university for long periods of time. I understand you have the final say."

"I am sorry to hear that," Polycarp said. "I will think about it and get back to you. Do you have someone in mind to travel with me?"

"No, I don't," he said. "We have many students and young priest who would enjoy the travel and research. You could ask Mark."

"I will see you tomorrow," he said. "I want to pray about your decision."

That evening, Polycarp prayed about James' concerns. He had to agree, the university needed one of them present at all times. He arose early, ate breakfast, and walked to the university. James was working, in his office.

"I have thought about your concerns," Polycarp said. "I agree with you, one of us should be here at the university. Is John doing a good job for you?"

"Yes, he is doing fine," James said. "I came to the same conclusion. He would make you a great assistant. I will ask him see you."

Polycarp remained with James. He wanted James to understand, how much he appreciated his efforts.

That afternoon, John came to Polycarp's office."

"Hello, bishop," John said. "James said you wanted to see me."

"Yes, come in and have a seat," Polycarp said. "How do you like teaching?"

"I like it fine," he said. "I enjoy reading the scrolls you are locating for us."

"How would you like to be my research assistant?" he asked. "While I travel, James is going to stay at the university. He will answer any questions that might arise. He is going to be doing more teaching."

John didn't hesitate.

"That is fine with me," he said. "I guess I should ask Mark. I am currently still assigned to him."

"Yes, you are correct," he said. "Ask Mark if you can become a full-time instructor and research assistant. After he approves the change, come back tomorrow and talk with me."

Later that evening John ate dinner with Mark, who was very happy for him and relieved him of the primary duties of being a church priest.

He would now be an instructor and a priest.

The next day, John went to Polycarp's office.

"I talked with Mark and he gave me his blessings," he said. "He is happy for me."

"That is good," Polycarp said. "I will change your title to instructor and research assistant. You will get a small increase in pay. Your first job is to make an itinerary for our next research trip."

"May I have a copy of your last itinerary?" he asked. "I can learn from it."

"Yes, you may obtain one," he said. "You should learn to know Joazar. He will be a great help to us."

John found Joazar transcribing a scroll.

"I am the newest member of the research team," he said.

"What happened to James?" he asked. "What is he going to do?"

"He wants to teach full-time," he said. "He told Polycarp one of them should always be at the university."

"That makes sense," Joazar said. "What did you say your name is?"

"I am John," he said. "I have known Polycarp for several years."

"Welcome to our team," he said. "I look forward to working with you."

"Polycarp asked me to produce an itinerary for our next trip," he said. "I would appreciate a copy of your last itinerary. I want to use the same format."

John departed to teach his class. Polycarp returned to studying his new course about Mary.

A few days later, John visited Polycarp and they discussed the research trip. They determined they would sail to Caesarea and return from Joppa. Polycarp added a visit to Jericho and Bethany to the list John had presented. Now John's job was to determine the schedule for the ships and the time needed to visit each of the sites.

After a few peaceful routine weeks, Polycarp decided it was time for him to have a meeting with Mr. Philemon, so he walked to his office and asked to see him.

"He is out of town," his aid replied. "Could I have him contact you?"

"When do you expect him to return?" Polycarp asked. "I can return."

"We are not allowed to divulge that information," he said. "Give us your name, and we will have him contact you."

Two weeks elapsed before Polycarp was contacted by Mr. Philemon. He invited Polycarp to visit him the following day.

Polycarp arrived before noon and said. "I hope you had a nice trip."

Mr. Philemon looked at him.

"It was not much fun. My mother died, and I went home to straighten out a few things," he said.

Polycarp bowed his head.

"I am sorry," he said. "I will say a prayer for her. Is there anything we can do?"

"No, the people of Colosse were helpful," he said. "I am ready to go back to work. How do you like my jar? I had the two broken pieces attached, and you must look quite closely to locate the repair."

Mr. Philemon exhibited a smile of satisfaction.

"It looks great," Polycarp said. "I am planning a research trip, and I wanted to discuss it with you. I am planning to visit Samaria and Judea."

"When are you going to leave?" he asked. "I have a home in Jerusalem. I will send a message to the servants and inform them to prepare it for your use."

"That would be a help," he said. "While staying in Jerusalem, we could visit several sites. There will be three of us. When I have the dates and a complete itinerary, I will send it to you."

"Good luck," he said. "Don't forget my office."

As he left Mr. Philemon's office, Polycarp saw him smile.

When John inquired about passage, he was invited to visit with the shipping company's dispatcher. They wanted to insure he had the best available ships for their journey. They were able to solidify the departure and return dates. The trip would take forty days. John returned to the university and shared the information with Polycarp. They decided to start the journey ten days after the study period ended. That would allow time for James to become familiar with Polycarp's plans for the next period. Joazar was informed and indicated he would be prepared. He started to gather his materials. Mr. Philemon wasn't the only one building great buildings in Smyrna. The Roman government was building a great number of government building. The local government had built a great temple to honor Emperor Tiberius and made certain none of Mr. Philemon's building were larger than the temple. In an effort to appease the Roman government, Mr. Philemon asked Polycarp to have the university offer a course in pagan religions. The land for the next group of building was cleared. Student enrollment was only limited by the number of classrooms available and the number of available places for student to live. The church had a waiting list for priest candidates.

Soon after the end of the study period, Polycarp was ready to leave on his research trip. He advised Mr. Philemon of his imminent departure.

"John, I am ready to travel," he said. "Send me your updated itinerary. It took a while for me to get ready. My responsibilities at the university have grown."

"I will prepare everything," John said. "I will advise Joazar. We are glad you are able to travel with us. We have noticed how busy you have become and how everyone depends on your judgement."

The two weeks passed quickly. The trio went to the dock. They were greeted by the captain of the ship. Captain Ropus explained their sailing schedule and assigned a mate to them. The mate and Joazar took the packs to their cabins. Polycarp bunked in cabin number one and his team was in cabin two.

The ship slowly maneuvered to open water. The sails were raised and the ship was soon underway. Polycarp was invited to dine with the captain.

"Mr. Philemon has provided our dinner this evening," Ropus said. "The cook is preparing us fresh fish and vegetables. I hope you and your team will enjoy it."

"Thank you for your extra effort," Polycarp said. "I am certain we will enjoy it. Do you sail to Caesarea regularly?"

"Yes, I do," he replied. "However, I don't go to Joppa. You will be returning on a different ship. Mr. Philemon has taken care of everything. The captain will be expecting you. He is planning to transport cargo for you."

"I hope we don't disappoint anyone," he said. "Often, the number of items we ship back is related to our success."

On the third day, they arrived at Caesarea and disembarked.

"John, the first thing I want to visit is the jail where they incarcerated Paul," Polycarp said. "Joazar please rent us a carriage for the month."

John and Polycarp succeeded in locating the jail. Polycarp talked with the Roman guards. No one knew what he was talking about.

Joazar joined them and they rode, in the carriage, to a large church.

"Welcome to our church," the priest said. "May I help you?"

"Yes, I am Bishop Polycarp and I am attempting to locate scrolls written by Paul," he said. "Do you have any scrolls?"

"Yes, we have them ready for you to copy," he said. "Mr. Philemon sent us a message and told us to expect you."

"I am not surprised," he said. "He does study my itinerary."

"We have several written by Paul and one written to a Roman soldier by Peter's scribe, Mark," he said. "You can make copies of them. We will be pleased to have them displayed as part of your research."

Polycarp began to understand the range of Mr. Philemon's influence. He was prepared for future encounters.

Their first stop was at the Inn in Sychar. Polycarp inquired about any interesting travelers who might have stayed at the Inn while traveling to Jerusalem. Paul, who was the grandson of Abraham, the Inn's founder, joined them for their dinner meal.

"We have had many travelers in this arca," Paul said. "Long before the inn, this was a gathering place because of Jacob's well. You might want to visit it."

"We certainly will," John said. "Do you have a drawing of the area?"

"Yes, I do," he said. "We sell a drawing showing the Roman highways and important sites. I have a few scrolls I might sell you."

"Who wrote the scrolls?" Polycarp asked. "I am interested."

"I think most of them were written by Omar, he was Paul's father," he said. "Paul's father and my grandfather were friends."

"Paul the apostle's father and your grand-father were friends?" he asked. "That is very interesting."

"Grandpa sold many items that Omar provided. Whenever Omar and his family traveled, they stayed here."

John pondered Paul's statement.

"Do you have anything of Paul's?" he asked.

"Jesus, Mary, Joseph, Zacharias, John, and many other friends of Omar's have stayed at our inn," he said.

Polycarp couldn't believe their good fortune. He purchased many scrolls and other items of interest.

The next morning, they visited Jacob's well. Joazar made a drawing of the well site. Polycarp was very impressed by his drawing skills.

Their next stop was Jerusalem. Polycarp planned to stay in Mr. Philemon's house and make short research trips each day. They started locally and after many inquiries, they were told of a retail outlet owned by Paul's sister's grandson.

"We were told you are the grandson of Yona, Paul's sister," John said. "We are interested in any scrolls you might have written by Paul's or Yona. We would be interest in other items that belonged to them."

"I have many things you might be interested in," Solomon said. "Some I will sell you and some I will not sell, but you may look at them."

Polycarp purchased everything Solomon would sell. He purchased scrolls, coins and parchments. They copied many scrolls and purchased more writing supplies. Later they rented a wagon and had the items collected packed, sealed, and delivered to an office of Mr. Philemon's in Joppa.

Their next stop was in Jericho. Polycarp purchased a pile of rubble that was part of the old city wall and had it shipped to Joppa.

Next they visited Bethany. After two days, they located Martha's house. They didn't find anything to purchase so they returned to Jerusalem.

Polycarp was interested in visiting Jesus' tomb and hoped to find the cross to which Jesus was nailed. The tomb was located and Polycarp prayed at the entrance. The cross was another story. Eventually, John was told that Simon of Cyrene had carried the cross, and that it was later given to Joseph of Arimathea. No other information about the cross was available.

It was time for them to journey to Joppa. The servants, at Mr. Philemon's house, prepared a large dinner their last night in Jerusalem.

"You have been wonderful hosts," Polycarp said. "We will tell Mr. Philemon you did a very good job for us."

"Thank you, sir," he said. "We like our job with Mr. Philemon. We only see him a few times per year, but we are always prepared."

Polycarp requested that they travel through Emmaus on their way to Joppa. They spent several hours in Emmaus, but they found nothing of interest.

Their last stop before Joppa was in Lydda. They entered a shop were Polycarp noticed a few items of interest.

"I have pottery that is very old," the shopkeeper said. "That piece is from the time of Emperor Tiberius. I have pottery that is much older than that piece."

"This is the age I am interested in," John said. "Do you have any more pieces of pottery of this time period?"

"I have so many," he said. "You couldn't carry all of it."

"I will take ten pieces," he said. "Wrap them carefully. Joazar will pay you."

"I could have more tomorrow," he said. "I have some coins with Tiberius's face on one side."

"We will take a few of the coins," Polycarp said. "That is all."

The team traveled to Joppa. Before sailing home, Polycarp planned to remain in Joppa for a few days. John had scheduled time to pursue the shops of Joppa. Their ship was, in the port, being loaded. Removing all the cargo and loading new cargo took several days. The team lived aboard the ship as they traveled throughout Joppa. They visited a large church and talked with the priest.

"I am interested in Peter," Polycarp said. "Was he involved with this church?"

"Yes, he was," the priest replied. "This church is built where he raised Tabitha from the dead. The land belonged to her family."

"Do you have any scrolls," he asked. "I would be interested in any items related to Peter or Tabitha."

"We have a few scrolls that were written for Peter," he said. "They are his teachings. You can make of copy of them, if you are interested. Tabitha's family still lives in town. I will take you to them."

"Thank you," he said. "Joazar will make copies of the scrolls."

They walked a few blocks to the house occupied by Tabitha's

descendants. It was a large house, located on a large lot. Tabitha's grand-daughter was home.

"Good afternoon," the priest said. "These are my friends, Bishop Polycarp and his assistant John. They would like to talk to you about Tabitha."

"Come in and have a seat," Mary said.

"Do you have anything that belonged to Tabitha?" Polycarp immediately asked.

"Yes, we have many things she made," she said. "I have about ten tunics and several other pieces of clothing."

No one had ever shown any interest in the items, so Mary sold most of them to Polycarp. She gave the others to the local church.

Polycarp and John returned to their ship.

"When we return to Smyrna, I want to give Mr. Philemon a tunic and a rock from Jericho," Polycarp said. "Put them in my office, and I will schedule a meeting with him as soon as we return."

"Why do you want a rock?" John asked. "Do you think he will want a rock?"

"After I talk with Mr. Philemon, I will tell you," he said.

With his arms full of scrolls, Joazar returned to the ship. As soon as they were aboard, the ship sailed.

On the second evening, they docked at Rhodes. The ship remained in the harbor overnight. Polycarp went ashore and located a restaurant.

"I have heard a colony of writers lived on Rhodes," he said. "Do you know where it is located?"

"It is on the other side of the island," the restaurateur said. "They stay away from people."

"I thought I might visit with them," he said. "I guess we don't have time."

"I think the ship is getting ready to sail," John said. "I enjoyed breakfast."

They returned to the ship.

They sailed toward Smyrna. It was a warm, sunny day. Polycarp sat on the main deck and enjoyed the weather. When they awoke the next morning, the ship docked in Smyrna.

"Captain, we had an enjoyable trip," Polycarp said. "Have all our cargo delivered to me at the university. We will carry the small packs."

"I will have it delivered," he said. "Your carriage and driver from the university are waiting for you."

"Hello, Bishop Polycarp," he said. "My name is Stephen. I have been assigned to care for your house and your needs. Mark made several changes. I will be one of your students."

"Hello, Stephen," he said. "Meet my helpers, John and Joazar. They will help you load the carriage."

Stephen took them to the university. Polycarp informed Stephen that he would return home at sundown. They were glad to be home.

"John, don't forget my two items," Polycarp said. "When you have the other items organized, send me a message. You can have the rocks piled outside our building. I should know about them in a day or two."

After Polycarp talked with his student assistant, he had his assistant deliver a message to Mr. Philemon requesting a meeting. When the student returned, he informed Polycarp that Mr. Philemon would see him midmorning the next day. Polycarp talked with James until sundown and then departed.

Polycarp and Stephen walked to the church. Mark and the priests sat and waited for Polycarp.

"Good evening, Bishop Polycarp," Mark said. "I wanted the priests to meet you. May I introduce you?"

Mark made a very complementary general introduction and then introduced Polycarp to each priest individually. After the introductions, dinner was served. Mark explained to Polycarp how the university was growing and the church was growing as a result. He also acknowledged the importance of the research program. Polycarp was very pleased with Mark's remarks. After dinner, he walked home with Stephen.

The next morning, he arose, ate breakfast with Stephen, and went to his office. He picked up his two presents for Mr. Philemon and then walked to Mr. Philemon's office. The sun shone brightly, and he enjoyed the sounds of the harbor. Polycarp knocked on Mr. Philemon's door.

"It is good to see you. I have great news," Mr. Philemon said.

"I have two presents for you," Polycarp said. "This is a tunic for your wife, and this rock is for you."

"A rock and a rather plain tunic," he said. "You are going to have to explain them to me."

"The tunic was made by Tabitha," he said. "She was a lady, Peter brought back to life. She lived in Joppa and her profession was making clothing."

Philemon inspected the tunic.

"That is a great present for my wife," he said. "What about this dirty rock?"

"The rock was part of the wall at Jericho," he said. "The one Joshua destroyed. I have an idea how to use them."

"Let's hear your idea," he said as a grin appeared on his face.

"You could have a rock cutter, shape about three pound pieces," Polycarp said. "Then we could sell them as door stops and parchment weights. I think it would fund our research. I would provide a parchment with each rock explaining where it was originally used."

"Sell parchment weights and door stops," he said. "I don't know. I will have a rock cutter stop by your office. I only want about ten blocks made. We need to determine if they will sell."

"You said you have news," Polycarp inquired.

"Yes I have finished plans and Roman approval to build our new facility," Mr. Philemon said. "It can only be four stories high, but it is going to be our largest building."

"How large," he asked. "We will need housing for the students."

"It is going to be larger than all our present buildings combined," he said. "I don't plan to build another building for several years."

"That will be a lot of work," he said. "If you send me a plan, I will know how many professors to hire."

"Exactly, It will be lot of work," he said. "I want you to stop traveling. Let someone else gather the research items. I need you at the university."

Polycarp stared at Mr. Philemon.

"I have been planning a trip to Rome," he said. "We can locate many items it Rome."

"Think it over," he said. "When you are responsible for everything, the church and the university, how can you take care of all that and travel. Get back to me next week."

Polycarp doesn't remember the remainder of the meeting.

He went back to his office at the university. James was waiting to see him.

"What about the rocks," he asked. "Do you want me to move them?"

"No, put a parchment on them explaining they are part of the wall of Jericho," he said. "I will know more in a few weeks."

James didn't say anything. He had Joazar make a stack of small parchments explaining the rocks.

The next day, the rock cutter visited Polycarp and took twenty rocks with him. The rock became a topic of discussion around the university. Students and faculty were interested in obtaining one. Soon, Mr. Philemon sent a message to Polycarp indicating the cut rocks sold immediately at a very high price and he would have a wagon pick up all that remained. He also indicated that his wife loved the tunic.

Polycarp exhibited a large smile as he sat at his desk and looked up toward the sky.

The next day, John visited Polycarp's office and inquired about the rocks. Polycarp explained the details of his idea to him. Then he reached under his desk, retrieved a rock and gave it to John.

John looked at him in disbelief and mumbled that he could use a door stop.

Polycarp talked with John about Mr. Philemon's expansion of the university.

"If I agree to stop traveling, would you continue my research?" he asked. "I will still head up the research, but you would do all the planning and traveling. I would work with you before and after each trip. You can take some time to think about this request."

"I don't need any time," he said. "It is fine with me. I think your research is the key to our growth."

"Thank you," he said. "I will talk with Mr. Philemon and then with you again."

Polycarp met with Mr. Philemon and discussed the proposed plans. Mr. Philemon agreed to address a combined meeting of the priesthood and the faculty. He informed them of the changes and Polycarp's new responsibilities. Polycarp sent a message to Stephen, and he arranged for Polycarp and Mark to dine together that evening. Polycarp then worked in his office until sundown and walked home.

After a short rest, Polycarp and Stephen walked to the church.

"I am pleased that you could arrange your schedule to have dinner with me," Polycarp said. "I have a few new items I want to explain to you."

"I like good news," Mark said. "Do you have any more rocks hidden under your desk? I would like to have one of them. That was a great idea."

"Certainly, I'll send you a rock," he said. "Mr. Philemon and I are going to address the priesthood and the faculty and explain our future plans with them. I wanted you to know ahead of time."

"This must be important," Mark said. "I haven't met with Mr. Philemon since."

Mark stopped talking and started listening. Polycarp gave Mark a rough idea of what they planned to say.

Polycarp arranged for the meeting on the next Friday. The group met in the largest lecture room at the university. Mr. Philemon explained how he intended to build a major expansion unto the university. He explained his plans to add medicine to the curriculums offered. Then he explained Polycarp's new role. He extoled that John would be leading the research project and that he would be reporting directly to Polycarp. After the meeting food was served, Mr. Philemon and Polycarp remained to answer questions.

At sundown Polycarp returned to his home. He didn't eat anything, but did relax in his favorite chair. Stephen lit several candles, and they listened to the night sounds of the university.

The next morning, Polycarp ate breakfast with Stephen before he went to the university. When John came to see him, he was working on his research. John was apprehensive concerning his new position. Polycarp spent several hours with him and explained that he would be available to help with any problems. John became comfortable with the thought of Polycarp being available to help. They walked to Polycarp's favorite restaurant at the harbor and ate lunch.

CHAPTER 7

BISHOP POLYCARP TEACHES AT THE UNIVERSITY

After several meetings, John was assigned the task of creating a written log of the items involved with the research project. He was expected to teach one research course the periods he was at the university. All his other duties as a teacher would involve research. When John was ready to travel, Polycarp met with Mr. Philemon and obtained his approval.

Soon, Polycarp met with Mark, who requested the meeting to inform him that he planned to step down as senior priest. He would spend his older age praying and writing. He introduced Polycarp to the new senior priest, Francis. After they exchanged greetings Francis returned to the church.

"It is time for me to be less busy," Mark said. "I am looking forward to writing and reading some of the scrolls you have obtained for the university."

"Are you certain you really want to stepdown from your position?" Polycarp asked. "Your performance is excellent. The priesthood will miss your guidance."

"I have prayed for many hours about this," he said. "I am convinced the end of my tenure has arrived."

Polycarp sternly looked at Mark.

"Tell me about Priest Francis," Polycarp said. "Has he been at the church a long time?"

"He has been with me for twenty years," he said. "He will do a fine job for God, the church, and you. Please attend dinner with us tomorrow evening. I am going to advise the priests of the change."

"I am happy for you," Polycarp said. "When I get older, I hope I take time to reflect."

"I am very fortunate to be in Smyrna," he said. "I can't think of a place I would rather live."

"I hope to be here for a long time," he said. "I will expect you to visit with me."

"Thank you," he said. "I will read for a while. Then I will probably have questions."

"I will see you tomorrow," Polycarp said. "Stephen and I will dine with you."

Mark departed Polycarp's office and walked to the church.

After Polycarp visited with the faculty in their offices, he planned strategy concerning the new building. The ground was cleared and the construction began. Polycarp advised Mr. Philemon of Mark's decision, and he agreed to attend the dinner with Polycarp and Stephen.

The next evening, the three of them, arrived at the dining hall at the same time. They were seated, ate dinner, and then Mark made a short speech. The remainder of the evening was spent talking with Mark and the other priests.

After dinner, the sun disappeared below the horizon and a full moon provided light for Polycarp and Stephen as they walked home.

"Stephen, have you known Priest Francis very long?" Polycarp asked.

"Yes, I have known him for a long time," Stephen said. "Mark rarely made a decision without consulting him."

"It is nice to have a friend like that," he said.

The stars twinkled as crystals in the sky before they reached their house.

The next morning, Polycarp worked in his office when he received an urgent message to come to Mr. Philemon's office. He departed immediately, hurried to his office, and found him slumped in his chair with his head in his hands.

"I have suffered a tragedy," Mr. Philemon said. "One of my ships was destroyed by a storm. It was one of my older ships. I probably should have replaced it. I have known the captain for a long time. He sailed that ship for the last five years. He went down with his ship. I lost ten other sailors. I want you to perform a funeral at the church in their honor."

"I will be honored to do that," Polycarp said. "I will make the arrangements for the day after tomorrow."

"There is another problem," he said while trying not to cry. "We now have ten widows and sixteen children living in rented homes with no income. I want to provide for them. I need your ideas and help."

Polycarp took his hand, and they walked to the church. They prayed for the sailors and their families.

After Mr. Philemon returned to his office, Polycarp talked with Francis about the women. He agreed they could cook and clean at the church. Francis also agreed to speak at the funeral. Not many, of the town's people, attended the service.

After the service, Polycarp talked with Mr. Philemon. He explained that he had some ideas but indicated they would cost money. Mr. Philemon told Polycarp to send him all the bills. Polycarp visited with each of the widows and their families. He was impressed with the capabilities of the women. He began to understand the life of a sailor's family. He met with Francis again and then scheduled a meeting with Mr. Philemon.

"Mr. Philemon, we are going to put the women to work," Polycarp said. "They are going to work for each other and the church. If it works out well, we may have them do chores at the university. I want the two large houses close to the university that you purchased and plan to destroy. You can purchase more houses."

Mr. Philemon looked, in wonderment, at Polycarp.

"Yes, I can always purchase more homes," he said. "What are you planning for the houses?"

"All the widows will live and sleep in one house," he said. "In the other house, they will cook and teach the children."

"The houses are yours," he said. "I will locate other houses to purchase."

"Each woman will have a different chore," he said. "Instead of each teaching their own children about religion, one will teach all the children. That will allow many more chores to be completed."

"That might work," he said. "I will contact the women and have them moved. I knew I could count of you. Keep me informed on how things are progressing."

The women were still in shock and encountered some difficulty understanding their move. They eventually became friends with Francis and Polycarp. Their plan worked out very well. The women became very efficient in their duties. They worked so closely together that they called their comrades "sister." Mary was chosen as the head sister and reported to Francis on a weekly basis. Soon they were doing most of the cooking and cleaning at the church. Their school was quite successful and had enrolled a few children from the community. Francis went to inform Polycarp of their progress.

"Your idea about having the women work at the church was a great idea," Francis said. "The priests like it. They can now spend more time studying and praying."

"This is great," Polycarp said. "I will have to send Mr. Philemon a message."

"A problem has arisen," Francis said.

He looked at Polycarp and said, "Mary would like to attend the university. I know we don't have any women students. Do you think James might teach her?"

Polycarp was very surprised. He was concerned about James' willingness to teach women.

"I will talk with him and visit you before the end of the week," he said.

Polycarp met with James to discuss Mary becoming a student. James was opposed to the idea. He thought it would be very distracting to the other students, and that Mary probably wouldn't be able to maintain the study pace. Polycarp was disappointed and went to see Francis.

"James didn't want to have her in his class," Polycarp said. "I think

I understand his position. Send her to me. I will teach her, and she can work at my office."

A smile appeared on Francis's face. He informed Mary of Polycarp's offer.

"I always have a student helper," he said. "She can be my second student helper. I am certain John and Joazar will also teach her."

"I will have her spend each afternoon with you," Francis said. "She will complete her chores in the morning."

"Send her to my office this afternoon," he said. "I will talk with her."

When Polycarp returned from lunch, he found Mary outside his office. She was dressed in a dark plain robe. It reminded Polycarp of Tabitha's tunics.

"Tell me about your robe," he said.

"We, sisters, didn't have many clothes," she said. "Two of us made the robes. They were simple and inexpensive to make. We now all dress alike and are accustomed to wearing robes. I hope you like it."

"I think they are a good idea," he said. "Everyone will know you by your robes. So, you want to be a student."

"Yes, I am teaching the children religion," she said. "I would benefit from formal education. Then I could do a better job for our children."

"You can spend the afternoon working for me," he said. "I will make it an educational experience for you. I will take you to my class as my assistant. You can start tomorrow. Do you know John or Joazar?"

"No, I don't know them," Mary said. "Who are they?"

"Both of them work for me doing research," he said. "John is an instructor. I am sure he will be a help to you. Joazar is very good at writing Greek. He will teach you how to write Greek."

"Do you think I can learn to write Greek?" she asked. "I haven't had much formal education. I taught myself how to read the Roman language."

"If you taught yourself to read Latin, we will teach you anything you want to learn," Polycarp said.

"That would be great," she said. "I will be here, after noon, every work day."

Mary worked for Francis at the church and for Polycarp at the university. The day school that the sisters managed grew very rapidly. Many women in the community enrolled their children in the school.

Several months passed, before John visited Polycarp's office to talk about a research trip.

"I think I would like my first trip to be somewhat close to home and not very complicated," John says. "I thought I might go to Pergamum. I found no indication that you have been there. I think that would be a good way for Joazar and me to start."

"I don't think you will find much there," Polycarp said. "But starting small has some merit. Put an itinerary together and return to see me."

As Polycarp relaxed, he felt a pain in his back. He stood, stretched, and walked outside to absorb the warm, soothing sunshine. He looked at the new classroom building that was under construction. Mr. Philemon saw Polycarp and approached him.

"I have my construction clothes on today," he said. "After I clean my boots, may I see you in your office?"

"I will be there in a few moments," Polycarp said. "The construction of the building is progressing nicely."

Polycarp returned to his office.

As Mr. Philemon appeared he spoke, "I am very impressed with what the women are doing. I want to ensure they have everything they need. Are you in contact with them?"

"Yes, every week," Polycarp said. "One of the sisters named Mary reports to me every week. She is studying religion and Greek. She wants to be a better teacher for the children."

"If she would teach them useful things, I would find them jobs," Mr. Philemon said.

"Jobs on your ships?" he asked. "Many of the children are girls."

"I always need good men cooks on my ships," he said. "A good cook that is a man is rare. I can also use women who read and can do simple mathematics. It they could read Greek that would be even better."

"I will have a talk with Mary," he said. "Do you think I should start to find additional professors? We may have to attract more students from other towns. Francis will help me."

"I think that is a good idea," he said. "I would hire at least four professors as soon as possible. That will give you time to train them in our methods. When is the next research trip?"

"John's first trip is going to be short and simple," he said. "I am going to approve his taking Joazar and visiting Pergamum."

"That is fine," he said. "If he has troubles, he will be close to home."

Mr. Philemon returned to the construction site. Polycarp considered what he was going to discuss with Mary. When Mary arrived at Polycarp's office that afternoon, he was waiting for her.

"Come in, I want to talk with you," Polycarp said. "Your Greek lesson will wait for you."

Mary had a puzzled look on her face.

"Is everything satisfactory," Mary asked. "I am learning how to write Greek."

"Yes, everything is fine," he said. "I can help you find jobs for your older students. I have been talking with Mr. Philemon."

"Does Mr. Philemon want to hire my students?" she asked. "What does he expect them to do?"

"I want you to teach your oldest male student how to be a good cook; do any of your boys know how to cook?" Polycarp asked.

"We teach them all how to cook," she said. "We also teach them all how to mend their clothes."

She looked at Polycarp.

"I have two students working as assistant cooks in the church kitchen," she said. "They are both good cooks."

"How old are they," he asked. "Is either of them sixteen?"

"Yes, the older one is sixteen," she said. "He is a good young man."

"Do you think he would like to cook on a ship?" he asked. "I am sure Mr. Philemon would make certain he would be safe."

"He might be interested," she said. "We are all very poor. He and his mother have nothing."

"If he works for Mr. Philemon, he will be paid a fair wage," Polycarp said. "I am certain that would help him and his mother."

"If he is interested, I will have him come to see you," Mary said.

"I am going to have Joazar work with your boys to learn basic building skills," he said. "When I find someone that can teach them about sails, I will also have them learn about sails."

Mary thanked Polycarp and went to her Greek lesson. When she found Joazar he was transcribing scrolls into Greek.

The next afternoon, Mary brought a young man to see Polycarp.

"Bishop Polycarp," Mary said. "I would like you to meet Theophilos. He has been cooking most of his life. I will leave him with you. I am going to learn some Greek."

"Sit down, Theophilos," Polycarp said. "Do you like ships?"

"Yes, sir," he said. "My father was a sailor. I want to be a sailor."

"Have you ever sailed on a ship?" he asked.

"No, I have gone aboard a ship with my father," he said. "He showed me where he bunked."

"How would you like to be an assistant cook on a ship," he asked. "I might have a job for you."

"I would love to assist a ship's cook," he said. "You know ship's cooks are sailors."

Polycarp sensed excitement in his manner.

"I will check on the job," he said. "Come and visit with me early next week."

Theophilos excused himself and walked back to the church. Polycarp sent a message stating he had one cook, with experience, ready to help on a large ship. Polycarp had his student assistant deliver the message to Mr. Philemon. When he returned, he had a message for Polycarp. Mr. Philemon was sending Captain Ontimenamus to see him. His ship was in port, and he would be in Polycarp's office in the morning.

That evening while eating dinner at the church with Francis, Polycarp explained his plan. Francis was in complete agreement.

The following day, when the captain arrived, Polycarp was seated in his office.

"May the wind always be at your back," Ontimenamus said. "You have been to see me several times, now I have come to see you. I understand you have a cook for me."

"Yes, I do," he said. "He is only sixteen. He will need your care."

"Mr. Philemon told me the circumstances," he said. "You may have him report to my ship in the morning. I will make a sailor out of him. I knew his father. He was a fine sailor. I will take good care of him. Have him ask for the chief cook."

"They have anchored me to the university," Polycarp said. "I will not be making many trips with you. My research assistant John will probably be traveling with you next year."

"That is too bad for you, sir," he said. "The sea breeze helps a man think."

The captain saluted Polycarp and went back to his ship.

Soon after Polycarp sent for Mary, she arrived at his office. He explained that her first student had just graduated and he had a job.

When the sun pierced the blue sky the next day, Theophilos was at the ship eager to begin his new career.

"I am looking for the chief cook," he said.

"He is below deck, in the galley," a sailor said. "Go through the bulkhead and down two decks. Ask anyone you find on that deck."

The sailor talk reminded Theophilos of his father; he went below deck and found the chief cook.

"I am here to work for you," he said. "I am a good cook."

"Call me, Stew," he said. "This is a very large ship, and I need additional help."

"We serve meals, every four hours, day and night," he said. "Most of the sailors eat during the day. You will work for me during the day. I will show you where to bunk."

"Yes sir," he said. "What do you want me to do?"

"You can start by calling me, Stew," he said. "Then clean the sack of roots."

Polycarp's next meeting with Mary was about teaching the young women how to read Greek and how to understand basic mathematics.

After the study period ended, John prepared to leave on his research trip. Polycarp planned to speak to the priest at dinner that evening concerning opportunities as an instructor.

After he finished his day at the university, he walked home. The weather was brisk and clouds hurried across the sky. Polycarp detected the odor of burning wood. Stephen and Polycarp were soon on their way to dinner.

"Please sit next to me," Francis said. "Before you talk, I will introduce you."

"I guess we need to be somewhat formal until after I speak," Polycarp said. "I understand you employ some of Mary's students in the kitchen."

"Yes, they are doing a fine job for us." he said. "Gentlemen, I would like you to meet our bishop and foremost researcher, Polycarp."

He looked at the priesthood.

"I will keep this brief," he said. "You can see our new building will be completed in a few months. We will be teaching more mathematics, science, medicine, language, and religion. If any of you are recommended by Francis, I will talk with you in detail about a job. It will be a full-time teaching position."

"Do you have any part-time positions." a priest asked. "Some of us priests are very knowledgeable in one area, but are students in another."

"I do have a few part-time positions," Polycarp said. One is in sailing, one is in basic mathematics teaching the sisters, and one is in carpentry."

He paused for a moment and then looked at Francis.

"I will be in my office tomorrow morning, what is for supper?" he asked.

"I believe we are having fish and vegetables," Francis said. "Mr. Philemon sends us fish every Friday."

The next morning after breakfast, Polycarp put on his wrap and walked to the university. He enjoyed the warmth of the sunshine. He was in his office when his student helper indicated the first priest had arrived to see him.

"I would like to see you about a part-time job," the priest said.

"Do you understand, many of your students would be young women?" Polycarp asked. "This is a very important position."

"I would like to teach the sisters basic mathematics," he said. "I think their school is providing the community a great service."

Polycarp breathed a sigh of relief and said a silent prayer.

"Go and visit Mary," he said. "If she would like you to teach the women, you are hired. You can have the administrator send me your papers. Good luck."

"I know a priest who is a good carpenter," he said. "He is afraid to teach. If you ever need anything, send me a message."

The priest thanked Polycarp and departed.

The student helper knocked on Polycarp's office door.

"I have a Dr. Lukus to see you. He says Mr. Philemon sent him."

"Hello, Polycarp," Dr. Lukus said. "I have been teaching medicine and practicing in Rome for about fifteen years."

"I have read about a doctor named Luke," Polycarp said with a smile.

"That isn't me," he said. "I would like to teach medicine and run the medical department for you. I have a letter of reference from Mr. Philemon, and I have a listing of my studies for you."

"You know Mr. Philemon?" he asked. "I will look at your qualifications very carefully."

"I know you will need time to study my material," he said. "If it is satisfactory with you, I will come back tomorrow morning."

"Yes, please leave the material on my table," Polycarp said. "I will see you in the morning."

Polycarp took his reference and transcript to Joazar. Joazar quickly copied them. Then Polycarp took the copy to Francis. Francis was out of town for a week, he had gone to Ephesus. Next, Polycarp went to James. He asked him to review the material and get his comments to him before he went home. Polycarp returned to his office. In about two hours, James came to Polycarp's office.

"It looks like you found one of the best doctors in the world," James said. "If I were you, I would sign his paper work. Thanks for asking me."

"I have prayed God would send us a doctor to teach at the university," Polycarp said. "It is amazing God listens to each of us."

He looked toward the sky, folded his hands, and said, "thank you".

When Dr. Lukus arrived the next morning, Polycarp had everything prepared for him to become a professor. Lukus signed the paper work and stated he would report for work in about a month. Polycarp sent a message to Francis announcing the hiring of a new medical professional to teach at the university. Polycarp hired two more of Francis' priests. One would teach language and the other would teach religion.

John appeared with an itinerary for his trip. He left it with Polycarp for his review and approval. After Polycarp approved it, John and Joazar departed for two weeks in Pergamum, doing research.

Polycarp received scrolls from Mr. Philemon that were written by Marcion of Sinopa. He wanted Polycarp to read them and comment concerning their value.

During the next month, Polycarp carefully studied the scrolls and then visited with Mr. Philemon.

"Marcion has made a few basic mistakes in his religion. I don't agree with his ideas," Polycarp said. "The scroll should only be shared with the most devout orthodox Christians. They will understand his flaws. I would not make them available to the masses."

"What does he believe that you don't believe?" Mr. Philemon asked. "Give me the short version."

Polycarp smiled and said, "He believes the Hebrew God is not the father of Jesus. He is probably going to get into trouble writing about his beliefs."

"I have heard enough," he said. "You can do whatever you desire with the scrolls. If I come across any more scrolls, I will send them to you."

Polycarp remembered the priest, who worked for Mary, mentioned a carpenter, so he sent for him.

"May I build something for you?" he asked.

"Yes, I need a large secure cabinet installed in my office to hold my personal scrolls, and I don't want anyone to be able to open the cabinet. Can you build something for me?" he asked.

The carpenter looked at Polycarp and replied, "I will have Joazar make a drawing."

When he returned, he showed Polycarp a drawing of a cabinet. He then handed him a lock made of timber. It came with a copper key. Polycarp approved the cabinet and the lock. It was installed in his office during the following Saturday.

John and Joazar returned from their research trip and scheduled a meeting with Polycarp. The following day, when they met in Polycarp's office, they delivered several scrolls.

"I think you will really like this one scroll," John said. "It is addressed to the angel of the church in Pergamum. I think in was written by your friend John."

"When I visited him, he was quite old," Polycarp said. "He told me that he would probably never visit many of the churches in that area, so he was going to write to them. On future journeys you might find additional scrolls he wrote."

"I had to make a promise to the church to get the scroll," he said. "I told them I would ask you to put a good word in for them. They are hoping to be assigned a bishop."

"I guess, I will have to approve their request," he said.

"The other scrolls came from the library in Pergamum," he said. "They are very old scrolls. No one had read them in years. I just purchased ten of them for your research."

"It sounds like you had a good trip," he said. "Construction is about completed. The new buildings will soon be ready to open. You will be busy teaching next study period. You can start planning next year's research trip."

"We have one more thing for you," he said. "We met a very wealthy young doctor. He is completing his training at the hot spring baths near the Asclepius."

"Those springs are considered very therapeutic, what does that have to do with me?" Polycarp asked.

"He is planning on coming here after he finishes at the Asclepius," he said. "He wants to study with Dr. Lukus."

"That is great," he said. "We can use another doctor. What did you say his name is?"

"His name is Galen," he said. "It will probably be next year before he arrives."

"You are not the only one who has read an interesting scroll," he said. "The scroll I am studying is a story told by God. He descended into the body of a man named Jesus."

"God descended into an earthly body?" John asked. "Where did you obtain that scroll?"

"It claims Jesus was never crucified," he said. "When I am finished with it, I am going to put it under lock and key. See my new cabinets."

Polycarp pointed to the row of cabinets that have recently been installed in his office.

"I don't understand why anyone would write that," John said. "We have plenty on which to work. We will be seeing you."

Polycarp sent a note to Mr. Philemon detailing the results of the research trip. Mr. Philemon responded by message. He wanted Polycarp to visit him in his office.

The next day, Polycarp enjoyed the warm sunshine as he walked to Mr. Philemon's office. He took a few extra moments and walked to the dock and watched a ship being loaded. Suddenly, he remembered his appointment with Mr. Philemon and hurried to his office.

"It sounds like John had a successful research trip," Mr. Philemon said. "The new buildings are completed. We should plan an opening date. Our new quarters are almost all reserved by new students. I think having nice living quarters is one of our secrets to growth."

"Pick a date that is good for you," Polycarp said. "I will make certain we are prepared."

"I would like to open the buildings in four weeks," he said. "Then I am planning a trip to my home. It is near Colosse. Would you and Joazar like to accompany me? You could do some research."

"I thought you wanted me to be at the university at all times," he said. "You know I like to travel and do research."

"It is not far," he said. "I will receive messages every day."

"I will ask Joazar," Polycarp said. "It is fine with me. He might be busy at the university. I will get back to you."

Polycarp returned to the university and contacted Francis. They planned a joint meeting of the priesthood and the faculty. Polycarp explained Mr. Philemon's plans for opening the new buildings. The faculty went about making last moment plans, and Francis invited Mary to the opening. Joazar told Polycarp that he was quite busy and that this learning period he was teaching Mary more Greek. Polycarp talked with his student assistant. The student recommended a new student named Nascien. Polycarp told his student assistant to make an appointment for Nascien and to send him a message.

The next day, Nascien was at Polycarp's office.

"Come in, Nascien," Polycarp said. "I was told you are a new student and want a job."

"That is correct," Nascien said. "My father has paid to send me here, but he told me I would have to find a job and pay all my university costs. That was fine with me. I am very interested in your research."

"What interests you?" he asked.

"Jesus was my great-grand uncle," he said. "I am a descendant of James."

"That is a good reason," he said. "How old are you? You look very young."

"I am only sixteen," he said. "But I have been working for three years. I am used to hard work. My family is quite poor."

Polycarp stood up and went to his office door and summoned his student assistant.

"I want you to help Nascien fill out the required documents," he said. "He is going to work for me. He will assist you most of the time. He will travel with Mr. Philemon and me in a few weeks. Ensure he has quarters in our new building."

Polycarp noticed a tear in Nascien's eye as he and the other student walked down the hall.

At the opening of the new building, each of the new faculty was introduced, and food was made available to everyone. Interested people, from the town, were invited to tour the buildings after the ceremony and to enjoy the food. Mr. Philemon informed Polycarp they would leave for Colosse in one week.

Polycarp spoke with Nascien the next day.

"Can you drive a carriage?" he asked. "How is your Greek?"

"I can drive a carriage," Nascien said. "I know nothing about Greek."

"We will teach you Greek," he said. "I'll handle the Greek on this trip. Your job will be to take care of the carriage and me. Hopefully, we will return with many more packs than we take."

Polycarp informed Francis that he would be traveling with Mr. Philemon. If problems arose, he and James should handle them. If they wanted a third opinion, they could see Dr. Lukus. He sent a copy of the Didache, he had written, to Francis and asked for his comments.

Polycarp and James joined Mr. Philemon's driver and carriage and headed to Colosse. When they arrived at Mr. Philemon's home, Polycarp and Nascien were shown to their rooms.

The next day, Polycarp visited with Mr. Philemon's family. Nascien was dispatched to Laodicea for two days. He was instructed to purchase everything available that related to their research.

The next day, Polycarp walked along the Lycus River. The sun seemed to dance on the surface of the water. He picked up a stone and skipped it across the surface. He counted every bounce of the stone. He noted a large number of shops which sold traveling supplies, because caravans traveling from Ephesus to Euphrates often stopped. One of the shops was owned and operated by Mr. Philemon's family.

That evening, Polycarp joined the family for dinner.

"I would like you to meet my brothers James and Peter. This is my sister Ruth," Mr. Philemon said. "James will accompany you tomorrow. He has located several items that might be related to your research."

After dinner, they relaxed in the living area. Each reviewed his most memorable experience of the day. Polycarp enjoyed a glass of cool water. After a few hours, he excused himself and went to bed.

The next morning, Polycarp ate breakfast with James. They walked to the shops.

"The first shop we are going to visit has been a family business for many generations," James said. "They wove black wool and provided many outer garments for those that traveled with Paul."

"It looks very warm; do they have any old garments?" Polycarp asked.

"They have made a garment and a pair of sandals like they gave to Paul," he said. "They hope you will purchase them and take them to the university."

"Certainly, that sounds good," he said. "Shopkeeper, I also want to buy old scrolls and old coins. Show me what you have available."

"I have a few coins," he said. "Jesse runs a shop and specializes in old scrolls and coins. You should probably visit him. Do you like this coin?"

"Let me see it. That looks like Nero," he said. "I like that coin. You can wrap the garment, sandals, and the coin."

"I do have one other thing you might like," he said. "It is an old drawing of Michael slaying the Devil."

He handed Polycarp the drawing. Polycarp looked at it carefully and decided to purchase it. He had the items delivered to the Philemon residence.

They walked to Jesse's shop. The walls were covered with old drawings, parchments and scrolls. Polycarp was very impressed.

"Hello Jesse," James said. "I want you to meet my friend Polycarp. He is interested in old scrolls."

"You have come to the proper shop," Jesse said. "You have also come at the right time. My horse is sick, and I need to make some money to purchase a new horse."

Polycarp looked directly at Jesse. He thought, to himself, 'I have heard fish stories, now I have heard a horse story.'

"Show me a few old scrolls you need to sell," Polycarp said. "Do you have any that are signed?"

Jesse disappeared into the backroom of his shop and then reappeared carrying an arm load of scrolls. He unrolled one for Polycarp's inspection.

"This one is signed by Epaphras," Jesse said. "He was from this area."

"What can you tell me about him?" Polycarp asked.

Polycarp knew of Epaphras, but wanted to determine what Jesse knew.

"I think he was a Christian," he said. "He might have been important."

"I am interested," he said. "Just put the others on the table. I will look at them. If you have any old coins, I will look at them."

"I have many old coins," he said. "I have coins that show almost every emperor and some older than that. I have a few that depict Alexander the Great."

Polycarp took James aside and talked with him. James indicated that if Jesses' horse died every time he heard that story, they would be knee deep in horses. Polycarp explained that the signed scroll was important to him, but he was going to pretend a different scroll was really important. If he didn't purchase the signed scroll, he wanted James to purchase it in a few days and send it to him at the university.

"Jesse, I really like the large scroll," he said. "The others are interesting. How much do you want for the large scroll?"

"That is a very large old scroll," he said. "You can see it required much more work than the other scrolls. For thirty denarii, I would sell it to you."

"Thirty denarii is a month's pay for most people!" he said. "The university can't afford that scroll."

"I could make you a better price for the smaller scrolls," Jesse said. "I will sell them to you for five denarii."

"I will take all of the other scrolls," Polycarp said. "I will have James check with you about the large scroll. If you drastically reduce the price, the university might be interested."

"I can't afford to do any more business with you," Jesse said. "I hope you realize, I gave you a special price."

When they reached James' home, they saw Nascien and a carriage loaded with packs. They went inside, sat down, and relaxed. Mr. Philemon asked Polycarp if he had a good day. Polycarp replied that he had a very good day. Then Mr. Philemon asked Nascien about his day.

"It was great," he said. "I purchased about twenty scrolls. I also purchased some old clothes."

"I am glad it was a good day for you," Mr. Philemon said. "I am finished with my business. We will start home early in the morning. Get a good night of rest. We will be on the Roman highway for several days."

They traveled many miles each day and stopped in a few small towns to rest and looked for scrolls.

As the week ended, they arrived back home in Smyrna. Nascien put all their treasures in Polycarp's office. He was busy for several days sorting through the material. Polycarp read a scroll Nascien purchased in Laodicea. He thought it was written by John. It was about hot and cold water. It said both were useful but that lukewarm water was not useful. Polycarp figured John didn't know anything about Laodicea's water supply. He was certain John wrote about the church. Polycarp's student helper appeared in the doorway to his office.

"Bishop," he said. "A wrapped package has arrived. It is address to you and it is from Nascien."

"Bring it in and put it on my desk," he said. "I wonder what it is."

"I will bring it in, but it will not fit on your desk," the student said. "It is larger than me."

Polycarp's curiosity was aroused; he stood and walked to the package. He couldn't imagine what it might be.

"Unwrap it and put it against the wall," he said.

The student assistant struggled with the package for some time. Finally, he was able to untie the rope and remove the protective covering.

"It looks like a door," Polycarp said.

As he stared at the door, giant wrinkle appeared on his forehead.

"Find Nascien," he said. "Bring him to my office."

After one hour, Nascien appeared at Polycarp's office.

"I am sorry it took me so long," he said. "Joazar wanted to finish my Greek lesson."

"I received your door," he said. "Would you like to tell me about it?"

"I found it in Laodicea," he said. "The shopkeeper said it was John's door. I knew you were friends with John. Do you like it?"

Polycarp wasn't sure what to say. He didn't want to hurt Nascien's feelings. He was about to laugh at Nascien when he remembered what Matthew wrote, 'knock and the door will be opened unto you'. (Matt, 7, 7, NIV)

Nascien picked the door up and showed Polycarp both sides of it.

"You can only open it from one side. The other side is smooth. It is a funny door."

Polycarp agreed it was a funny door.

"Nascien, I just wanted to tell you that you did a good job for me," he said. "I haven't taken time to look at the scrolls you purchased."

Polycarp instructed Joazar to replace his office door with the door from Laodicea. He scrutinized the doors and decided the new door would fit, because it was very large and could be resized. After it was installed, Polycarp spoke with his two student helpers. He told them whenever he had a visitor, they should explain that they should knock and it would be open unto them. Francis was excited about Polycarp's new door and brought several priests to see it.

Two days later, Mr. Philemon came to see Polycarp's new door.

"It is a very interesting door," he said. "I am glad you didn't put it on my office. I don't have time to answer the door. I just yell come in."

Polycarp looked at Mr. Philemon but didn't say anything.

A few weeks passed. An eye doctor from Laodicea knocked on Polycarp's door. He opened it.

"I talked with your assistant Nascien when he was in Laodicea," he said. "He told me you have a new school of medicine. Do you have an eye doctor?"

"No, we don't have an eye doctor," he said. "Are you looking for a job?"

"Yes, I am," he said. "A new school interests me."

"Follow me," he said. "I will take you to see Dr. Lukus."

Polycarp requested Dr. Lukus to interview the eye doctor and then to come and see him.

Later that day, Dr. Lukus came to see Polycarp.

"I talked with him," Dr. Lukus said. "He is a good eye doctor."

"Should we be teaching about the eye?" Polycarp asked. "Do you want him as an employee?"

"He must know about people," he said. "I think he could help us."

"I don't know," he said. "Other things seem more important."

"Every old person seems to have eye problems," Lukus said. "He could teach about other things."

"Do you really need him?" he asked. "I don't want to hire him just because he is available."

"We can use him," he said. "I am very busy."

"Tell him to start by assisting you," Polycarp said.

"It will take him a while to relocate," he said. "He has a practice and a family. I will talk with him again and let you know when he is available."

It took the new eye doctor three months to relocate to Smyrna. The school of medicine experienced a growth spurt.

John came to see Polycarp. He had discussed the next research trip with Joazar.

"We think we would like to visit Antioch or Rome," he said. "We should find many scrolls in either location. Do you have any suggestions?"

"I would go to Antioch," he said. "They are more likely to sell scrolls. They are always raising money to send to Jerusalem."

"I will put together an itinerary for your approval," John said. "Some of the scrolls you obtained in Laodicea and Colosse are very interesting. Joazar is copying them for everyone to read."

"I am certain Paul wrote several of them," Polycarp said. "I am also reasonably sure John wrote a few of them."

Polycarp thought about the next fall study period. He planned to use his student assistants in the classroom doing everything except teaching. He also planned to assign Nascien the task of writing a few new lessons. He planned to use his time writing and studying his research material. Polycarp had Joazar make a wooden frame for the drawing of Michael and the Devil.

Polycarp and Stephen went to the church to have dinner with Francis.

"I read the Didache," Francis said. "I would like several copies. Maybe it should be a coarse that all priests are required to take. We need a church manual."

"I will have Nascien see you. He can help you write the course," Polycarp said.

Polycarp reached under his chair and retrieved a package. He handed it to Francis.

"I have a present for you," Polycarp said. "Be careful. It is a little fragile."

"I like presents," he said as he looked at it. "It is a drawing. It looks like Michael."

"Correct," he said. "It is The Archangel Michael killing the Devil. It is quite old. Joazar built the protective edge. If you like it, you can hang it in your office."

"Thank you, Polycarp," Francis said. "The thought of an archangel protecting us is comforting."

Francis visited each priest and showed them the drawing. Then Joazar positioned the drawing so Francis couldn't sit in his office without looking at it.

Before John brought his planned itinerary to Polycarp, summer had begun. He planned to visit the area from Antioch to Tarsus. Polycarp thought it would be a great trip and approved his request. Polycarp wished he was going to visit Antioch and the area where Paul's brother lived. He pushed his chair away from his desk and leaned back and prayed. He thanked God for his many blessings and the university.

CHAPTER 8

CODICES

The university accumulated over a thousand scrolls. The cabinets that contained the scrolls occupied a large amount of space. The research concerning papyrus and other reed materials had progressed, but many writers still preferred skins. The university had learned of a new system of retaining written material called a codex system. Polycarp was impressed with the codex that he received from the university at Tarsus. He obtained permission to interview professors who were interested in developing a new information retrieval system at their university. Francis sent a priest to see him.

"Good day, bishop," he said. "My name is Seth. I have been at the church for several years."

"Come in and have a seat," Polycarp said. "Have you ever seen a codex?"

"Yes, I have," he said. "While I attended the university to become a priest, I worked in a writing colony for a few years. Codices are the way of the future."

"Did you ever make a codex?" he asked. "Can we make codices?"

"Yes, I have helped to made codices," he said. "They aren't difficult to produce."

"What would be required?" Polycarp asked. "I need to create some kind of a budget. It will be part of our research."

"The most important item is a good source of skins or reeds. I prefer skins," he said. "I would use wooden covers. We will cut the skins and use silk to bind them together."

"We should be able to do that," he said. "When can you start?"

"I can start anytime. That is why I am here," Seth said. "Francis is willing to transfer me to the university staff."

"Come and see me at the beginning of next week," he said. "Be prepared to go to work."

Polycarp went to see Mr. Philemon. He explained his plan and how he would hire Seth, a priest, one person to transcribe, and two skilled labors. The remainder of the transcribing would be completed by the existing department. At first Mr. Philemon was skeptical. He thought about his personal collection of scrolls. Polycarp explained to him in great detail the advantages of a codex. He stressed the rapid location of information. After Polycarp demonstrated the convenience of a codex and how quickly he could find information, Mr. Philemon became excited about the idea and approved an increase in the research budget.

On the first day of the following week, Seth was in Polycarp's office.

"What have you learned?" Seth asked. "Do I have a new job?"

"Yes, you do," Polycarp said. "Tell Francis to transfer you to the university."

"When should I start?" he asked. "I located a better source for animal skins."

"Find Joazar and he will help you find a location to create our codices department," he said. "After Joazar hires an additional transcriber, you may hire two skilled labors."

Seth located Joazar and they decided to put the new department next to the existing transcribing department. Joazar worked with Seth to interview and select a new person to transcriber scrolls, and then Seth interviewed skilled labors. He started by interviewing carpenters.

"This is a codex," Seth said. "We want to make wooden covers like this one. We will probably require twenty covers per week."

The interviewee took the codex from Seth and examined it very carefully.

"That doesn't look very difficult," he said. "I can make that. I have a little saw."

"Can you acquire the wood and maintain a small stock of it?" he asked. "We don't want to run out of wood."

"My father sells wood," he said. "We wouldn't need much of a stock. He would keep wood in stock for our use."

Seth looked at the carpenter.

"I will help you fill out the required documents, and you can begin working tomorrow," he said.

"How much are you going to pay me?" he asked. "That is important to me."

"The university has a standard wage for starting skilled craftsmen," he said. "When you fill out the documentation, they will explain university employment to you."

That afternoon, Seth interviewed another skilled laborer.

"This is a codex," he said. "We want to bind the edge of the parchments together like this. Can you do that?"

He took the codex and examined it.

"No," he said. "That is fine work. I know someone who would do that for you."

"Are you certain you couldn't bind a codex?" Seth asked.

"I could do it," he said. "I want a real job."

"It is a good job with the university," he said.

"That is work for a woman," he said. "Not a skilled craftsman. I am not interested."

"You must not really need a job," he said. "This is a good job."

"I need a job," he said. "But I am a man, and I need a man's job."

"You said you knew someone who might be interested, have you known them for a long time?" Seth asked.

"Yes, about twenty years," he said. "I see them almost every day."

"Have him come to see me," he said. "I would like to see him today if possible."

He grinned at Seth.

"He is a she," he said. "My sister would really be good at that. She makes all kinds of clothes and ties all kinds of knots. I will bring her to see you."

"Your sister?" he asked. "Do you think she would work with us?"

"If you pay her a good wage, she might," he said.

He stood and exited the transcribing work area.

After an hour, a lady appeared in the codex area.

"I am here to see Seth, is he available?" she asked.

"I am Seth, what may I do for you?" he asked.

"You want to hire someone to make holes and tie wooden pieces together," she said. "My brother told me to see you."

Seth handed a codex to her.

"This is a codex," Seth said. "Could you cut the skin, make the holes and tie everything together with silk?"

She took the codex from Seth and inspected it.

"Yes, that looks easy to me," she said. "I would do that. I am certain I can do better than this."

"You have a job," he said. "How much would I have to pay you?"

"I don't have a job," she said. "Who told you I had a job?"

"Your brother said you made clothes," he said. "Do you make clothes?"

"Yes, I make clothes," she said. "I make clothes for all seven of us. I guess that is like having a job."

"What is your name?" he asked. "Do you want to work for us?"

"My name is Mary," she said. "Yes, I want a job. Will you pay me?"

"Yes, Mary," he said. "You will be given the starting pay of a skilled worker. You will work the same hours as Joazar and me. You start tomorrow."

The next day, Seth had an office in the codices department. Mary and the other worker were in his office.

"You never did tell me your name," Seth said. "This is Mary. She is going to work with us."

"My name is Noah," he said. "I stopped by the mill and picked up a few pieces of wood. You don't want me to work here where they are using ink. I will be making dust."

"Oh, yes," Seth said. "Have Joazar show you the university shop."

"Make a few covers and I will find a permanent location for you," Seth said.

Noah sawed one cover and Joazar stopped him.

"You can't make dust in this area," he said. "This area must be very clean."

"I told Seth that I would make dust, and he told me to make a cover," Noah said. "Who are you?"

Joazar explained the situation to Noah and then escorted him to the university shop. They found a cabinet for Noah's tools and located a table for him to use.

"That is much better," Noah said. "I will do the sawing and make the holes in the covers in the shop. Then I will take the covers to Mary."

"Before you take them to Mary, clean the dust from the covers," Joazar said.

They returned to Seth and explained Noah's location.

"We have a plan," Seth said. "What I want to accomplish today is to cut one hundred skins and make five codices wooden covers, can we do that?"

"Let's get started," Noah said. "I am going to the shop."

"I will get some skins from Joazar and start cutting," Mary said. "Are we going to make blank codices?"

"Yes, I want to see how large a codex will be compared to a scroll," Seth said. "I am certain a codex that contains the same amount of information as a scroll will be much smaller than the scroll. Tomorrow we will have something transcribed on the skins."

Late that afternoon, Seth checked with Mary. She and James were binding the last codex. There was a small crowd of observers. The university was in the codices business. After the transcribers mastered the technique of writing on both sides of small skins, they produced ten skins and handed them to Mary to be bound. She looked forward to tomorrow.

"The first thing I will do is make the holes in the skins," Mary said. "The holes must align perfectly. If they don't align, they won't fit properly. I want everything to align perfectly."

"I will go and do more transcribing," he said. "It looks like you will be faster than I am."

"This is not a race," Mary said. "A good codex can be like a fine carving. Our codices will be pieces of art."

"I have six wooden covers for you," Noah said. "Tomorrow, I will stop by my father's mill and obtain more wood. Then I will be in the shop making more covers for you."

"Be sure and saw them exactly," she said. "They must fit the skins exactly."

"I will make then the correct size," he said. "You can count of me."

"We will make the best codices," she said. "Seth will be pleased with our product."

She smiled at Noah.

Seth made several measurements and was very pleased with what he found. Codices were going to be much more compact than scrolls. He went to see Polycarp.

"Our new system is wonderful," Seth said. "It will take less than half the space."

"How can that be?" Polycarp asked. "I knew it would be easier to locate the information that you seek."

"You write on both sides of the skin. Many scrolls only are written on one side," he said. "It requires half the parchments or skins. The long tables we use to unroll a scroll so we can work on it are not needed. The cabinets made to store our round scrolls contain a great amount of wasted space. The codices are rectangular and will occupy all the space in a cabinet"

"It is compact, easy to use, and can be custom made," he said. "I am tired of unrolling scrolls trying to find a passage. The life of a scholar is about to become simpler"

"Now, you are getting in the spirit," he said. "Mary was a great find."

"Can we do that?" Polycarp asked. "When can I see a codex?"

"I will have a codex on your desk today," he said. "Take a look at it, and then we can talk."

Seth stopped and talked to Mary. She assured him she would complete several codices before the end of the work day. She stayed busy cutting skins and making holes. Before she went home, she placed two completed codices on Seth's desk. Seth took one to Polycarp.

"That is a nice piece of work," Polycarp said. "Your skilled craftsman did a fine job."

"It sure is," he said. "The craftswoman is named Mary."

"I thought you just made a mistake this afternoon, when you said Mary," he said. "A member of your team is named Mary?" Polycarp asked.

"Yes," he said. "She has experience sewing."

"You hired a woman to make this codex?" he asked. "I saw you interviewing men."

"The cover is made by a fine carpenter," Seth said. "Putting it together is like making clothing. She is quite good. Come by the department tomorrow. I will introduce you to her."

Polycarp rubbed his forehead and a smile appeared on his face.

"I guess it is," he said. "Making holes and putting silk through the holes. I will see you tomorrow."

The day ended and each went home.

When Polycarp visited the codices department, the following day, everyone was working.

"Hello, Mary, my name is Polycarp," he said. "How do you like the job?"

"It is great," she said. "We are doing a good job, but we are still slow."

"Just keep doing a good job," he said. "Efficiency will come with practice."

Just then Noah appeared carrying wooden codices covers.

"Hi, Mary," he said. "I have enough covers for five codices."

"Thank you," Mary said. "Say hello to Polycarp."

"Good morning," he said. "Do you work for Seth?"

"We work together," Polycarp said. "The codices are going to save space."

"It will be a lot easier to use," Mary said. "It will also be a lot easier to carry. I think codices are much better than scrolls."

"We have a lot of scrolls," he said. "Scrolls have been around for a long time."

"I think it is time for change," she said. "We will help you make the change."

Polycarp returned to his office. They produced six codices that day. After two weeks, they were produced ten codices per day. An excited Seth went to see Polycarp.

"Do you want to keep purchasing scrolls?" Seth asked. "I think we should switch entirely to codices. It is much more economical."

"How many codices can Mary cut and bind in a day?" Polycarp asked.

"We can make ten a day," he said. "Three transcribers can't keep up with us."

"Have the codices prepared and stored," he said. "We can add the information at any time."

"We are going to switch to codices," Seth said. "I will keep a few blank scrolls on hand."

After Mary and James were about fifty codices ahead of the transcribers, another transcriber was hired. They proved to be a matched team. They produced ten codices per day. Polycarp had Seth send a codex to the church in Ephesus.

"Be sure and tell them we make ten codices per day," Polycarp said. "Have an artist draw a picture on the wooden cover."

"I will ask Noah if we could use cedar from Lebanon for the covers," Seth said. "A codex with a painted picture on its cedar cover would be impressive."

"Let's not get too fancy," Polycarp said. "Only use cedar for special occasions."

Priest Francis visited with Mary. He planned to eliminate the use of scrolls in the church. He wanted all of his codices covers to have a hand drawn picture. The pictures were to be scenes described in the text. Mary talked with Seth.

"I would like to make a set of matched codices for Francis to use in the church," she said. "If we make a very nice and unique set for him, I believe other churches will hire us to transcribe their scrolls and make codices for their use."

"That sounds like a very good idea," Seth said as he looked at Mary. "I will talk with Polycarp."

Polycarp liked the idea. After he inspected the codices the team made for Francis, he contacted several other churches.

Soon, orders for codices arrived. Several bishops ordered codices with custom cover made just for them. On his birthday, they sent the pope a very special codex. When he first looked at it, he was puzzled why anyone would want a codex. After he used it for a while, he learned to enjoy its convenience. He recommended the use of codices to all the churches and made major changes to his library.

When the Bishop of Ephesus met with, Alexandus, the director of the local library, he showed him a codex and told him it was the way of the future. Alexandus visited with Polycarp in Smyrna. He was impressed with the codices department and the quality of its product. Polycarp showed him a side-by-side comparison of a scroll and a codex. Alexandus understood the library facility and the purpose of a library was about to change. The codices would make information readily available to anyone who could read. Ephesus planned the construction of a new, greater library that would emphasize the use of codices. A new era concerning the availability of information was born.

The following week, Polycarp visited Mary.

"I have a special project for you," he said. "John, who was one of Jesus' disciples, gave me a few scrolls. I treasure them greatly. If we had the scrolls transcribed, you could make a custom set of codices for me."

"If the information is important to you, I could put all John's writings in the matched set of codices, and you could label each cover concerning its content."

"I like that idea," he said. "I will have the scrolls transcribed."

"How many sets should I produce?" she asked.

"I want two set of codices," he said. "I will give one set to Mr. Philemon."

Polycarp had written a set of parchments concerning where and under what circumstances the scrolls had been located. For the more esoteric scrolls, he had written parchments that contained his explanation of the original scroll. His explanation of John's Revelation was very popular. Polycarp planned to have codices of his explanations produced. The covers of the explanation codices would be matched with cover of the codex of the scroll it described. He was certain these codices would become very popular with the students.

When Mary completed the codices, she delivered them to Polycarp. The set was an impressive piece of work. Polycarp made an appointment with Mr. Philemon and delivered a set of codices that contained John's writings. Mr. Philemon was very impressed.

"I want ten more sets," he said. "I am going to give a set to each of the churches I attend."

"It will take us a while to produce ten sets," Polycarp said. "We have many orders from churches to transcribe their scrolls."

Mr. Philemon thought for a moment.

"We can sell the set of John's work," he said. "I am going to investigate the possibility of starting another business. I will get back to you. Don't forget my order."

Polycarp was surprised. He had not thought of producing codices of an author's writings and selling it. He slowly walked back to the university.

Polycarp decided to display his set of codices of John's writings in a very conspicuous location in his office. When scholars visited Polycarp, they saw his codices. He explained the production process and provided tours of the department for those that were interested. Almost all of his visitors placed orders to have their favorite scrolls transcribed. Many purchased a set of John's writings. Mary had an artist added to the staff to decorate custom covers. The artist would create unique lettering for the covers for each of the professor's codices. If a customer wanted a drawing, the artist would produce it for a fee.

CHAPTER 9

POLYCARP AT SMYRNA

When John and Joazar departed on their research journey, they were very excited. Many at the university, considered Polycarp's most important duty to be keeping the Philemon family happy. It was important to the church and to Polycarp that he maintained good relationships with Mr. Philemon, Nichodemus and Jonas. Polycarp was engaged at the university with the new study period. The new buildings opened and many of the classes were oversubscribed, so out of necessity students were assigned to a different class. Francis went to visit Polycarp about a local family's son, Irenaeus, who had just completed his first year at the university and hoped to become a priest.

"Polycarp, your oldest student assistant graduated at the end of the last study period," Francis said. "I want you to meet Irenaeus. He will be a good student to assist Nascien."

Polycarp looked at Francis and sensed how important Irenaeus was to him.

"Thank you for remembering me. I hadn't thought about needing another student assistant," he said. "Irenaeus, where is your home?"

"I am from Smyrna," he said. "My parents have been members of the church for many years. I attended church with them and the last few years, Mary taught me."

"It is my pleasure to meet you," Polycarp said. "I have a lot of work to be completed, therefore you can help Nascien. Do you speak Greek?"

"Yes, I can read and speak Greek quite well," he said. "I can write Greek fairly well."

Polycarp smiled at him and said, "You will be a great help to us. Inform the administrator that you are going to replace the assistant that graduated."

Irenaeus looked at Polycarp and then went to the administration office.

Francis stood and thanked Polycarp, "He is a good student, and I have grand hopes that he will be a great teacher and priest."

Francis excused himself and walked back to the church.

Polycarp continued his studies. He was certain the scroll they found, during their last research trip, was written for John by his scribe. The wording was quite familiar to him. He also read a series of scrolls that claimed to be the teachings of Peter. When Mr. Philemon knocked on Polycarp's office door, he was startled. He opened the door and greeted him.

"I have some news for you," Mr. Philemon said. "This is my son, Nicodemus. He has completed many courses at the university, and he is going to assume control of my businesses."

"What are you going to do?" Polycarp asked. "We count on you in many ways."

"Nothing will change for you," he said. "From now on you will visit with Nicodemus instead of me. Our business will continue to fund the church and the university. He knows all about your research and is keenly interested in it."

Polycarp breathed deeply and then smiled at Mr. Philemon.

"You scared me for a moment," he said. "The research is the heart line of my life."

"It is also very important to the church and he university," Mr. Philemon said. "I think the growth of the university is directly linked to your research."

"It is gratifying to hear you say that," Polycarp said.

"The rock will remain in the office," he said. "As for me, the misses and I are going to do some traveling. I am thinking about purchasing a house in Rome. You will always be welcome."

Polycarp looked at Mr. Philemon and said, "I am happy for you, and I am certain Nicodemus and I will work together just fine."

"I would like to meet your research team," Nicodemus said.

"I will be pleased to arrange a meeting a few days after they return," Polycarp said. "I would also like you to have dinner at the church with Francis, me, and the priests. When you are available, give me a few days' notice."

"Is tomorrow evening agreeable with you?" Nicodemus asked. "I look forward to meeting Francis."

"That is fine with me, and I am certain Francis can be available," he said. "We will see you tomorrow at dinner."

Nicodemus and his father returned to their business, and Polycarp sent a message to Francis. Stephen was also informed that he would attend dinner with Polycarp. Polycarp didn't sleep very well that evening. He prayed several times for God's direction concerning the changes he faced. He knew he would have to adopt his style to satisfy Nicodemus.

The next morning, Polycarp ate an early breakfast and walked to his office. It was a beautiful day, white clouds raced across the light blue sky. The silence was broken as the church bell called the priest to prayer. When Polycarp arrived at his office, Irenaeus was seated at the desk outside his office. He was reading a parchment. Polycarp greeted him.

"You don't have to be here this early," he said. "Someone must have told you, I am an early riser."

"I enjoy saying my prayers very early," Irenaeus said. "I will be here before you most of the time. I checked the class schedule with Nascien, and one of us will be here to help you at all time."

"That is fine," he said. "You might be able to help Nascien with his Greek."

"I will be glad to do that," he said. "We will be a great team."

"Don't allow me to work too late this evening," Polycarp said. "I am dining with Francis and the priesthood this evening. I would be pleased for you to accompany me."

"I generally eat an early meal and then study," Irenaeus said. "If it is agreeable with you, I will study. Thank you for the offer."

Polycarp looked at Irenaeus.

"It is fine with me," he said. "I have to eat many dinners with other people. It is part of my job. Anytime you want a nice dinner, let me know. We can always eat at the church."

Polycarp spent the day at work in his office. That evening, Stephen and he walked to the dining hall. They sat with Francis and waited for Nicodemus. When he arrived, Polycarp greeted him and escorted him to the table.

"This is Francis the senior priest," Polycarp said.

"He probably doesn't know me," Nicodemus said. "I see him every Sabbath."

"I have seen you with your father," Francis said. "Now I know you. It is my pleasure. We look forward to working with you."

Nicodemus sampled his dinner.

"These vegetables are good," he said. "Where is the fish?"

"We have fish on Fridays," Francis said. "Your father sends it to us. On the other days, we rarely have meat."

"Would you like to have fresh fish twice a week?" he asked. "You know my father owns many fishing boats."

"Yes, we would appreciate more fish," he said. "I thought he probably owned a few fishing boats."

"You can have all the fish you want," he said. "Just send a priest to the dock. He will need to look for the boats with a "P" on their sails."

"The boats with "P" on the sails," Francis said. "I am sure we can find them."

"I will tell the captains to look for a priest every Tuesday," he said. "I am not going to change the arrangements father has made for Fridays. If you have special occasions and want fish, just send someone to the boats."

"Thank you," he said. "That is very generous."

"What about Mary's children?" he asked. "Do they eat fish?"

"No, they rarely have any fish," he said. "If we have any extra on Friday, we send it to her. Many of us just eat a half serving. Do you know Mary?"

"Of course, I know about Mary's school," he said. "Father has told me about the good she is does for our community. I will have a mate send enough fish on Tuesdays so everyone at the school will have fish."

"Thank you," Francis said. "After dinner, I want to introduce you to Mary."

It was a joyous dinner. After dinner, Francis, Polycarp, and Nicodemus went to visit Mary. When they found her, she was in the church kitchen helping her students wash dishes.

"Mary, I would like to introduce you to Nicodemus. He is Mr. Philemon's son," Francis said.

"You startled me," she said. "Hello, Nicodemus. It is nice to meet you."

"How often do you and the children eat fish," he asked. "Would you like some fish for the children?"

"Occasionally, Father Francis will give us fish," she said. "When he doesn't have extra, we don't have fish."

"I am going to send enough fish to the church on Tuesdays so everyone can eat fish," he said. "Tell Francis how much you need."

Mary smiled at Nicodemus.

"I am sure the children will enjoy fish," she said. "I will tell them of your generosity."

They talked for a short time and then the men departed.

After Stephen and Polycarp walked home, Polycarp received a message from his sister, Martha, which indicated that his mother had died, and she had buried his mother at the church. Stephen noted a tear in Polycarp's eye.

After he gained his composure, he visited with Nicodemus concerning his mother's death. He hoped to visit Martha and his mother's grave. The university allowed him time away from his position to take care of his family.

Polycarp boarded the next ship to Philippi. When he arrived, he rented a carriage and visited his sister, Martha, who was at home with Rachael. Daniel was at work.

"Good evening, ladies," he said. "I am sorry to have to visit under sad circumstances."

Martha greeted him.

"I am having problems, because I am not a man," she said.

Polycarp looked at his sister.

"What is your problem?" he asked. "May I help you?"

"Yes," she said. "The priest at the church took my money for a grave plot, but he is insisting it be registered in the name of a man, and I want it to remain in our family."

"I think I can help with that," he said. "What else is wrong?"

"I am also having trouble transferring the house to my name," she said. "The town administrator insists the house is yours."

"If I have to inherit it and sell it to you, I will do that," he said. "Tomorrow we will go to the church."

He looked at Rachael and asked, "How are you getting along?"

"I miss your mother," she said while exhibiting a sad face. "Martha and I will be fine."

After breakfast the next morning, they visited the church. Polycarp visited his mother's grave. Seeing his mother's grave was a sad experience and tears filled his eyes. After a few moments, the local priest approached Martha.

"Who is the priest with you," he asked. "He is not one of us."

He pointed at Polycarp.

"This is Polycarp," she said. "He is my brother and the Bishop of Smyrna."

The priest hesitated for a moment.

"It is an honor to meet you," he said. "I have heard of you. You used to be at the university."

"I was raised in this church," he said. "My sister tells me you will not register our mother's grave site in her name."

"It was just a misunderstanding," he said. "We didn't know her brother was a bishop. I will take care of everything."

Martha smiled at Polycarp.

Next, they walked to the town hall. Polycarp inherited the house and then sold it to Martha. He paid the tax and everyone was happy.

When they arrived home, Rachael had prepared dinner. They took their seats at the table. Polycarp prayed for his mother and sister and then blessed the food. They enjoyed a great meal and went to the living area to relax. Polycarp looked at Rachael.

"That was a good dinner," he said. "My dinners in Smyrna taste somewhat institutional. They don't have that home cooked quality. Do you need a job?"

"No, sir," Rachael said. "I am going to stay with Martha. You aren't going to get me on another ship."

Polycarp and Martha laughed. Rachael laughed with them.

The next day, Polycarp said goodbye and sailed to Smyrna. When he arrived, Stephen met him at the dock. They walked to the house.

"Welcome home, bishop," he said. "I trust everything was resolved."

"Yes, my sister is fine," he said. "I can't say the same for the church in Philippi. I might have to write to them."

"We are expecting John and Joazar back from the research trip tomorrow," he said. "We have already received one pack of scrolls."

"Stephen, will you go to the market?" he asked. "I would like fresh fish and fresh vegetables for dinner. Purchase enough so you can dine with me."

"Yes," he replied. "I will be back in a few moments."

Stephen grabbed his basket and hurried to the market. After he filled it with fresh vegetables, he visited the fish market. He found a fish that had just been delivered to the market. He purchased it and took it home. He cleaned it again and prepared dinner. That evening Stephen and Polycarp enjoyed tasty fresh fish for dinner.

Polycarp slept late the next morning. He ate breakfast and then walked to the university. Nascien was at the desk outside his office.

"Nascien, find out when John's ship will arrive," Polycarp said. "I want you to get a carriage, and then we will meet them."

"It arrives this afternoon," Nascien said. "I will get a carriage at noon. While we are waiting for them, we can eat at the dock."

"That will be fine," he said. "We will depart at noon."

Nascien was a good student and mastered the Greek language. He spoke to Polycarp in Greek.

At noon, they went to the dock and ate fresh fish. As John's ship approached the dock, Nascien pointed toward it. Polycarp stood and went to the ship. John greeted them.

"We have many scrolls," he said. "We visited Antioch and Tarsus. Did you ever hear of a town named Mopsuestia?"

Polycarp stroked his beard and said, "No, I don't think so, where is it?"

"It is close to Tarsus," he said. "The town has a very poor church, and they must have had fifty scrolls written by Paul. He often taught there. It was before he went on missions. I purchased all of them but one. I told them to never sell the other scroll to anyone."

"When Joazar has copied everything, send me the originals," Polycarp said. "I look forward to talking with you after you have had time to rest."

After several weeks passed, John and Joazar visited with Polycarp. They brought him a large stack of scrolls. They also brought him a basket.

"I have finally copied all of them," Joazar said. "Here are all the originals. One of these scrolls contains words from Peter. I am not sure who wrote it. He is seeking money for the apostles in Jerusalem."

"I will study all of them," Polycarp said. "What is this basket?"

"It is one of the baskets that Jesus used when he fed the five thousand," John said. "I found it in a shop in Tarsus. I thought you might like it."

"Very interesting," he said. "I guess you can purchase almost anything."

"We were allowed to copy many scrolls at the university in Tarsus," Joazar said. "They have a great number of scrolls written by Paul. I think he wrote them, while he was on mission, and sent them to his brother. His brother gave them to the university."

John looked at Polycarp.

"It was a great trip," he said.

"You can start planning your trip to Rome," Polycarp said. "Next summer will be here in a year. When you get older, time flies. I might have a place where you can live while you are in Rome."

The next study period passed. The university was crowded. Polycarp spent much of his time, reading and studying. He taught two courses. He was informed that a professor was retiring at the end of the term. He visited Francis to talk about a replacement.

"I am going to be looking for a teacher," Polycarp said. "Who can you recommend?'

"If Nascien wasn't so young, I recommend him," Francis said. "In a few years, he will make a good instructor. I would recommend you talk with Stephen."

"Stephen, the priest who keeps the house?" he asked. "Is he graduating?"

"He has already completed his work," he said. "He has been working with me at the church."

"I will talk with him tonight," he said. "You are right, he will do fine."

After dinner, Polycarp talked with Stephen.

"One of our professors is retiring," he said. "I have talked with Francis. He indicated you might be interested in teaching."

"Yes, I would appreciate a change to be a professor," he said. "I will have to ask Francis permission to be transferred from the church to the university."

"Be certain to find a good housekeeper for me," he said. "You can tell him it is a good training ground."

"Francis and I will find you a good housekeeper," he said. "Thank you."

When Irenaeus knocked on his office door the next morning, Polycarp looked up from the scroll he was reading.

"Come in," he said. "How are your studies progressing?"

"Very well," he said. "When Joazar was on the research trip, I did a great amount of work for Professor James. Now that Joazar is back, I will complete more course work. What are you reading?"

"Is Nascien at the desk outside the office?" he asked. "I want to see both of you."

"I was studying," Nascien said. "You wanted both of us?"

"Yes," he said. "I thought you might be interested in this scroll, I am reading. It was written by Jesus's brother, Thomas. He recorded many great quotes of Jesus, but the scroll is not well received. He grew up knowing Jesus, and he has not clearly written that Jesus is God."

"That is too bad," Irenaeus said. "I would, we would like to read the scroll."

"I think I will teach a course next study period using this scroll," Polycarp said. "Both of you can help me write the lessons."

Polycarp's student helpers became excited about helping prepare the lessons. They obtained a copy of the scroll from Joazar and kept it with them.

Polycarp started to write his message to the church in Philippi. On occasion, Irenaeus would assist him with the epistle.

It was a forceful message written to those who were losing their way because they doubted their salvation. Polycarp instructed the priest the church should refrain from teaching anything that wasn't true. He had Joazar make a copy of Matthew, Mark, Luke, and John's writings and a few of Paul's writings, so he could include them with his letter. He warned against abandoning their beliefs and urged them to return to their strong faith based religion. He insisted they stand fast and set an example for God. Love everyone, be kind to women and the poor. When he completed the message, he sent it by messenger to the senior priest in Philippi.

The next time they had dinner with Francis, they discussed his new housekeeper.

"I have a new housekeeper," Francis said. "It is strange, but his name is also Stephen. He will start with you next week. He is studying to be a priest."

"Thank you," Polycarp said. "I am sure he will do a good job. When I visited my mother's grave in Philippi, I was so disappointed with the church that I decided to write a letter of instruction to the head priest."

Francis smiled at Polycarp.

"I received a message from him sometime back," he said. "He wanted to know about your appearance. I told him you exhibited a bushy beard, and I assured him that you had visited your mother's grave. I also confirmed that you were raised in that church. I think he was expecting a message from you."

Polycarp smiled at Francis.

After dinner, he walked home. The moon and the stars seemed especially bright that night.

Another study period passed. Nascien matured in his studies and his faith. Irenaeus helped Polycarp, almost every day, and diligently studied his courses. Polycarp had two excellent student assistants. John sent a proposed itinerary to Polycarp for his review and approval. He requested a month long research trip the next summer to Rome. Polycarp approved his proposal and explained he would be staying at Mr. Philemon's house. Polycarp indicated that he was particularly interested in any scroll written by Paul, Luke, and Peter's scribe, Mark. He said he was also interested in any scrolls available written by Emperor Nerva or any scrolls written about the destruction due to the eruption of the volcano.

Nascien looked at Polycarp.

"When will John be traveling to do research for you?" he asked. "I am very interested in the scrolls that have been acquired."

"We have an unwritten agreement," Polycarp said. "They will teach spring and fall study periods and travel during the summer. Our plan seems to be working just fine."

"Where will they be going this summer?" he asked. "Are they planning to go to Egypt?"

"Not this year," he said. "They are planning to go to Rome. Rome is a great place. Someday, I might go to Rome."

"I am sure many interesting objects exist in Rome," he said. "I don't know if they will be able to purchase many."

When Polycarp visited with Nicodemus, he was well and very glad to see him. He indicated his father lived in Rome and had purchased a few old items for Polycarp's research. Polycarp asked Nicodemus to send his father a message telling him that John and Joazar would like to stay with them this summer while they visited Rome. The message was aboard the next ship to Rome.

After two weeks, Polycarp received a message and a pack of coins from Mr. Philemon. He carefully looked at the coins. When he found a coin with Nerva's likeness on it, he smiled and looked toward the sky. Mr. Philemon said they enjoyed living in Rome and looked forward to John and Joazar's visit.

"John, I have communicated with Mr. Philemon," Polycarp said. "He said he expects you and Joazar to live with him and his wife while you are in Rome. He has already purchased a few things for you to consider."

"I will tell Joazar," John said. "I am sure he will be a big help to us. It wouldn't be long before the study period is over."

"Be very courteous with Mr. Philemon," he said. "He is a great benefactor of the university."

"I know," he said. "We will work carefully with him."

John went back to writing and Polycarp returned to his office.

Polycarp studied a series of scrolls written to the Corinthians. He was particularly interested in what Paul said about his discussion with God. He asked Irenaeus to come into his office. Polycarp showed him the scroll and told him to obtain a copy from Joazar. Then Irenaeus was instructed to write a lesson concerning what he thought God told Paul when he was with him on the Road to Damascus.

"I want you to read the entire set of scrolls," he said. "I don't want you to ask anyone else what they think about what Paul is saying. I want to know what you think."

"It may take me a few days," Irenaeus said. "After I have written the lesson, I will come and visit you. I am certain it was a profound discussion."

Two weeks passed, before Irenaeus approached Polycarp. He stated he was ready to discuss his assignment.

"I think God told Paul something that allowed him to gain great wisdom about Him," Irenaeus said. "Paul didn't include the exact words spoken to him."

"Can you and I learn these words?" Polycarp said. "Is that what Paul was trying to teach people without saying the exact words?"

"Yes, I suppose it was," he said. "We will have to study all of Paul's writing to be certain."

"That is part of what my research is all about," Polycarp said. "I recommend you have Joazar make you copies of the scrolls we know Paul wrote. They will be yours. You can keep them in my office."

"God's message, delivered by Jesus to Paul, is a great research topic," Irenaeus said. "When we understand God's message, we should all become as spirited as Paul."

Polycarp continued to read all the scrolls they could acquire, and

Irenaeus' reading became more focused on Paul's scrolls and his university studies.

That evening, when Polycarp returned home from the university, Stephen was waiting for him.

"You received a message today," he said while handing Polycarp the message. "I will finish preparing dinner."

"Thank you," he said. "I am not expecting a message. I wonder who wrote to me."

Polycarp took the message from Stephen and read it.

> Polycarp
> Bishop of Smyrna
>
> May God bless you and your university.
> Your sister Dianna is very sick and is dying.
> Our three sons are married and have their
> own families.
> Dianna, our youngest and only daughter, is
> very well trained.
> After her mother dies, she plans to come to the
> university.
> Please look for her and help her.
> Her future is in God's hands.
>
> Abraham
> Dianna's Husband

Polycarp hadn't kept in touch with his oldest sister. The message was a surprise. He also had no way of knowing exactly what had happened. He decided his best plan of action was to contact Mary.

The next day, Mary went to visit Polycarp at his office. Polycarp smiled at her.

"Mary, my sister's daughter, Dianna, will be coming to the university," he said. "I have never seen her, but I received a message that she is well trained. Do you have room for her?"

"Yes, we have room," she said. "Originally, Mr. Philemon gave us ten houses. I have three and Francis has seven houses."

"Francis has seven?" he asked. "What does he do with seven houses?"

"Some house student priests," she said. "The others are rented and the money helps the school."

"I am trying to understand," he said. "What do you do with the houses?"

"One is occupied by a few of the women who had infants, when the ship was destroyed," she said. "They are still with me. One is occupied by two older women, who are still with us, but can't care for themselves. The last house is home to me and the women that decided to remain with me. We run the school, cook, and clean for the priest at the church."

"I never thought about what happened after you started supplying cooks to Mr. Philemon," he said. "Can my niece live with you and help with the priests?"

"Yes, she can," she said. "I need help. When will she arrive?"

"I don't know," he said. "I think she will be here soon."

Before Dianna arrived, a few weeks passed. She proved to be very well trained and went to work directly for Mary. Mary scheduled Dianna a meeting with Polycarp.

When Dianna went to see Polycarp, he was in his office reading. She knocked on the door. Polycarp opened it.

"It is not necessary for you to schedule a meeting with me. You are always welcome. Come in and be seated," he said.

"Thank you, uncle," Dianna said. "I like my job and Mary is great. I want to learn how to help the doctors. I used to care for an older couple."

"I can help you get started with classes," he said. "We don't have any women helping the doctors. This is a university, we teach, we don't treat patients."

"I thought you had doctors and a hospital," she said. "Does it always rain like this?

"No," he said. "This is unusual."

It rained for the next four days. The older houses in the lower part of town flooded. Nicodemus came to see Polycarp and explained his office was flooded. Polycarp rescheduled classrooms and provided Nichodemus space to use as an office. Many homes flooded, and the people came to Mary for help. She assisted them in every way possible. She provided living quarters, food, and clean water. Dr. Luke instructed Mary concerning how to prepare the drinking water. Many people in the town became sick, and the doctors at the medical school helped the local doctors provide aid to the victims.

After about ten days, the water retreated. Polycarp was in his office when Nicodemus appeared. His face exhibited a grand smile.

"I have returned to my office," he said. "I wanted to personally thank you and all those who helped you. The school provided much needed assistance to the community."

Polycarp smiled and nodded his head in the affirmative.

"We are pleased that we were able to help," he said. "That is a primary goal of this university. Helping our community is number one."

A month passed, the university and the town returned to preflood routines. Nicodemus came to see Polycarp.

"When I moved my office over here, I sent a message to father," he said. I explained how the university and the day school helped the community."

"How is your father?" he asked. "Can he still care for himself?"

"Yes, he is fine," he said. "Mother is more confined."

"I am sorry to hear that," he said. "Send my regards to your mother."

"Father told me to come and visit you," he said. "He wants to know what the university needs to prepare for the next flood. He also wants to know if you are ready to grow."

Polycarp realized a great opportunity had just been presented to him. He wanted to take the fullest advantage of it. He looked at Nicodemus.

"I will meet with my staff," he said. "I will also meet with Francis. We will develop a detailed answer for your father."

Polycarp met with James, John, Mary, Dr. Lukus, and Francis. They decided the school was ready to grow. To be prepared for the next flood, they needed another large kitchen and a building to house patients and displaced people. Polycarp informed Nichodemus of their desires.

Another month passed. Nichodemus invited Polycarp to see his new office located on the second story of the building. It was located where his father once had an office.

"How do you like my office?" he asked.

"It is very nice," Polycarp said. "I have been here before."

"I have heard from father," Nicodemus said. "We are going to build a new separate school of medicine next to the last large building. It will include many classrooms, a large kitchen and dining room. It will also have beds for fifty patients."

Polycarp hesitated for a moment.

"That is very generous of your father," he said. "I am sure Dr. Lukus will make good use of it."

"He wants you to manage it," he said. He also wants to double the size of Mary's school."

"That will take a lot of planning," he said. "Mary is a one man operation."

He smiled at Nicodemus.

"I mean a one person operation," he said.

"He will build whatever is needed for the school," he said. "Father told me to follow his example and things would be up to me going forward."

Polycarp was pleased that they had not rushed to answer Nicodemus.

"If we work together, I am certain we can do it," Polycarp said. "I need a little time."

"When you decide about Mary's school, schedule a meeting with me," Nicodemus said. "We are going to start building the new medical school. I purchased more land several years ago."

Polycarp, Mary, and her assistant, Dianna, scheduled several meetings to discuss what they needed to double the size of Mary's school. They decided they needed living quarters for twenty-five women. The women would be trained to help the doctors and help with the day school. They would use one of the available classrooms vacated by the school of medicine.

When he met with Nicodemus, Polycarp explained Francis' need for living quarters for the program to train priests. This was to be a new program associated with the university's college of religion. Nichodemus obtained his father's approval, and it was a busy year of construction at the university.

Nicodemus spoke to Polycarp about his son attending the university and joining the research team.

"If you could find a place on the research team for Jonas, it would make his grandfather very happy," Nicodemus said. "We decided it is time for him to leave home and study with you."

Polycarp stared at the floor for a short while. He realized he couldn't refuse.

"I will talk with John," he said. "He plans the research trips. I am sure he could use another team member."

Polycarp and John met several times. John wanted to reduce his traveling and become a full-time instructor. Polycarp agreed if John would help the research team prepare to travel, when Nascien was trained to manage the research trips, Jonas would be a research helper. John said the timing was good and everything would be just fine. Polycarp exuded a gasp of relief.

Before Polycarp discussed the training of the women, who would assist the doctors, he slowly walked to Dr. Lukus' office. They greeted each other.

"The new medical school is under construction, and we are also going to teach women how to help doctors," Polycarp said. "I want you to assign someone to teach them."

Dr. Lukus frowned.

After a few moments, he said, "That is not going to be easy," he said. "I don't think the doctors will like having to teach women. I'll get back to you."

Polycarp's fears were realized and his joy disappeared.

"Why would they care if their students are women?" he asked. "That doesn't make sense to me."

"Many doctors think they are very important and only have to teach doctors in training," he said. "Let me work on it."

Polycarp was disturbed by Dr. Lukus comment.

"If you need any help," he said. "Come and visit me."

After a few weeks, Dr. Lukus spoke with Polycarp. He had spoken to the eye doctor, and he wouldn't teach anything except about the eyes. Dr. Galenus didn't want to teach women, and said he would leave the university if he had to teach anything other than anatomy and logic. Dr. Lukus agreed the doctors would teach a priest what he needed to know, and when he was trained, the priest would teach the women. This plan allowed the doctors more time to train doctors. The teacher of the women would be one of the priests that was about to graduate from the medical school and knew Mary.

When John presented Polycarp with the itinerary of the summer research trip to Rome, he was seated in his office reading. He put down his scroll and glanced at the parchment for a few moments.

"I think this is a good trip for a new research team," John said. "Mr. Philemon is there, and we have good routes of communication with Rome."

"Rome is a great destination," Polycarp said. "I am sure Mr. Philemon is looking forward to having the team stay with him. Ensure they bring us back many scrolls about the recovery effort instituted after the volcano erupted near Pompeii and after the fires in Rome."

"I will personally check on those items for you," Nascien said. "We will miss John. He has been a great help with our preparation."

Polycarp went to see John.

"Are you ready to become a full-time instructor?" he asked. "I am certain you have the research team ready to travel."

"I am ready to teach, and they are ready to travel," he said.

"The students will appreciate your stories," Polycarp said. "I am pleased you decided to become a full-time professor."

Polycarp asked his student assistant to have Mary and her assistant come to his office.

When Polycarp returned from lunch, they were seated outside his office.

"Hello, Mary," he said. "It is good to see both of you."

"I see the new buildings are under construction, will you explain the intended function of each building to us?" Mary asked.

"That is part of why I asked you to come and see me," he said. "We will have new buildings, and we will have new duties."

"I am sure we will," Mary said. "Tell me about ours."

"One of the new buildings is living quarters for women," he said. "One is living quarters for priests, who are students, not assigned to the church. The other building is a new College of Medicine."

"I didn't know about the new living quarters for priests," Mary said. "Are you going to teach them?"

Polycarp smiled at Mary.

"Yes, we will have a series of courses just to train priests," he said. "They will also take some of the courses we currently offer."

"Tell us our new duties," she said. "I am glad I brought Dianna along."

"In addition to your current duties," he said. "You will operate the kitchen and dining room in the new College of Medicine."

Mary looked at Dianna.

"Ok, I expected that, what else?" she asked.

"You will clean all the new buildings," he said. "We will allow students who can't eat with the priests to eat in the dining room."

"It is good we are getting twenty-five new women," Mary said. "I will have jobs for all of them. What about training for women who want to help the doctor?"

Polycarp hesitated for a moment. He wanted to analyze Mary's reaction.

"A priest will be trained to teach them," he said. "When the new building opens the beginning of next year, we will offer a series of courses."

Mary didn't say anything. She and Dianna departed.

At the end of the summer, the buildings were mostly built. The twenty-five women were identified and started training. The new class for priests was oversubscribed, and a list of future students was created. The research team was due back at the university the following week. Polycarp received three packs of scrolls from the team. The scrolls were sorted and organized by John. Dr. Lukus advised Polycarp he had filled his faculty needs, and that many more students planned to attend when the new school opened. When Nascien and Jonas returned they gave all their materials to John to be cataloged. John brought Polycarp a detailed list of the material obtained.

"It looks like it was a very successful trip," John said. "They obtained or copied scrolls containing Paul's lessons, several parchments Paul sent to the Roman government, and scrolls concerning Paul's imprisonment at Caesarea and eventual transfer to Rome."

"I am interested in reading them. When you have them copied, send me the originals," Polycarp said.

"They also obtained scrolls written by several other interesting people," he said. "We filled one pack with twelve scrolls written by Luke."

Polycarp looked at John.

"I knew Luke was with Peter in Rome," he said. "They were both killed about the same time."

"I think some of the scrolls contain lessons Luke heard Peter deliver," John said. "Joazar is transcribing two scrolls that were written about relief for the victims of Vesuvius. We also have a scroll Nerva wrote to John when John was on Patmos."

"I consider both Nerva and John good friends," Polycarp said. "Deliver the scrolls written by Nerva directly to me."

Mary requested a meeting with Polycarp. They met in his office.

"I have a problem," Mary said. "We agreed on twenty-five additional women in our program, and I have thirty women I would like to admit."

Polycarp ran his fingers through his beard.

"That is a problem," he said. "We built living quarters for twenty-five women. That is what you requested. I can't ask for more. We have planned on twenty-five in the classrooms."

"The living quarters have twenty-five rooms," she said. "I could easily fit two women into many of the rooms."

Polycarp appreciated that Mary provided a solution.

"How you use the living quarters is your decision," he said. "I will have the priest who is going to teach the women check with you about class size."

"They should be able to teach thirty," she said.

"If you can make it work without changing the budget, it is acceptable with me," he said.

Mary thought for a few moments.

"You might be able to convince the priest to teach thirty women," she said. "Maybe one of our more advanced students could grade homework for him."

"We could do that," Polycarp said. "Instruct your student to visit with me."

She looked at Polycarp.

"Please ensure that you inform the professor how much time we are going to save him," Mary said. "If you convince him, he will do less work with thirty students, our chances are good."

As Polycarp considered Mary's comment, she continued to speak, "I have jobs for all thirty. That should help your budget."

"Thirty will help our program." Polycarp said.

Polycarp visited with Nicodemus concerning the opening ceremony for the new buildings. He explained he would like Francis to speak first. Then he would speak, and after he was finished Nichodemus would speak. Nichodemus informed him he wouldn't speak. He said his wife, Julia, would speak and they would attend the ceremony together. Nicodemus indicated they would provide the normal banquet after the buildings were opened. Polycarp agreed and offered his help to Julia. He then returned to his office.

The next ten days passed rapidly. When Francis began his speech, they stood before the new clinic.

"I would like to thank Mr. Philemon, his son Nicodemus, and his wife Julia for the new living quarters for the priests," Francis said. "This will allow us to have a new enlarged academic program to train priests."

Polycarp spoke next and thanked the family for the new School of Medicine and the enlargement of the university's programs to train women. Then, Julia began her very polished speech.

"It is our great honor to provide our town with these new facilities," she said. "We intend to carry forward the traditions started by Mr. Philemon."

She then explained in detail how the new medical clinic would function.

"Any citizen who has lived in Smyrna longer than one year can obtain medical help at the university clinic," she said. "The medical service will be provided by doctors who are students and the care and meals will be provided by women who are students. If you can't pay the modest fee charged by the university, Nicodemus and I will pay for it. Our family will be using the clinic."

Nicodemus stood beside her. As they entered the new building, they preceded Francis and Polycarp. The banquet began. Before the afternoon was over, the people in town who hadn't attended the opening of the buildings were visiting the clinic. Nicodemus, Julia, and Polycarp were sought out by the community. They wanted to express their appreciation.

The first patient for the clinic was a young person.

"My son has something in his eye and he can't see," she said. "Can you help him?"

"Yes, we can," Dr. Lukus said. "I will have our eye doctor look at your son."

Dr. Glidus successfully helped the boy. His sight returned to normal. The news of the doctor's success was quickly carried throughout town. The clinic was graciously used by the citizens of Smyrna.

The next year went by very rapidly. Many learned their new jobs. The clinic was full and the women and men students were working well together. Nichodemus paid for about ten percent of the patients. Many of the other patients were paying their bills and making donations to the university. The new programs flourished.

After Polycarp finished his day at the university, he walked home. Dianna visited with him and Stephen for dinner.

"Hello, Dianna," Polycarp said. "Stephen has prepared us a nice meal."

"I have wanted to visit with you," she said. "I have been very busy."

"I know Mary's school has really grown," he said. "I can imagine you are very busy."

"Mary has officially made me her assistant," she said. "She has given me responsibility for the new building."

"Are you managing the new kitchen?" Polycarp asked. "I hope a lot of our students will use that dining room."

"Yes, the new kitchen is very popular," she said. "We are busy all day."

"I hope you enjoy, Stephen's cooking," he said. "We are having fish this evening."

"If I didn't have to cook it, I will like it," she said. "This is a beautiful piece of fish. I think Mary utilizes most of the fish Nicodemus' boats catch."

"That is a good arrangement for everyone," he said. "He donates his fish, and we eat fresh fish. Let's go into the living area and relax."

"I can't stay a long time," she said. "I get up very early in the morning. We serve a large number of students breakfast, and I am training many new workers. One of the new students, Florinus, is sometimes difficult."

Polycarp became concerned.

"You may always send students that are difficult to me," he said. "I would be pleased to assist you and Mary."

"I think I will have Florinus speak with you," she said. "One of your religion courses might do him some good."

Polycarp listened intently.

"He has some strange ideas," she said.

Polycarp smiled at Dianna. He felt good about being able to help her.

"I am glad you came to see me," he said. "You are always welcome. Come back."

They talked for a short while, and then Dianna walked to her living quarters. Polycarp and Stephen discussed the new aqueduct being built in Smyrna.

The next morning they arose early and after breakfast, Polycarp walked to his office. When a messenger arrived from Nicodemus' office, he was reading. The message explained that one of the ships had suffered a serious fire. Another ship was dispatched to tow the disabled ship to port. Polycarp was informed seven men with burns would be brought to the medical school.

The next day, the burned men arrived at the school.

"Polycarp, I want these men to receive the best care," Nicodemus said. "We are going to repair their ship, and you are going to repair the men."

"Your men will receive the best care," he said. "As they recover I will have them returned to you."

"Do you have room for all of them?" he asked. "The clinic looks full."

"Mary has made arrangements," he said. "She will provide for all of them."

After one week, three of the sailors returned to Nicodemus. The other four remained at the clinic. Their injuries were more severe and took more time to heal. Finally, the last sailor was returned to Nicodemus. His ship was repaired and he visited it. Nicodemus and all seven of the sailors returned to the clinic to thank the doctors and the women.

"We are very grateful for your hospitality," the head mate said. "We are now well and will return to our families and to the sea. We thank you."

"It was a pleasure to care for you," Mary said. "Have a safe journey."

Word of the good care the sailors received was transmitted throughout the Roman Empire. Mary advised Polycarp that each of Nicodemus' sailors should be taught how to care for injured or sick mates.

"We should add another course," she said. "Each sailor would be required to provide care in our clinic for ten days."

Polycarp wanted to hear more about what Mary had in mind. She explained that sailors often experienced cuts or broken bones. Immediate fundamental medical procedures would provide a much better recovery. She went on to talk about sea sickness and proper food preparation. She insisted that each ship be issued a box of medical supplies and have a sailor trained to use them.

"I will check with Nicodemus," he said. "Is there anything else?"

"Yes, when they complete the course," she said. "The university should give them a box of medical supplies."

"I think Nicodemus will like that," he said. "I will get back to you in a few days."

Polycarp scheduled a meeting with Nichodemus.

Two days later, Polycarp was in Nicodemus' office explaining Mary's idea.

"I think that is a great idea," Nicodemus said. When your students graduate, you give them degrees. I should give my sailors something."

"You could give them a pay raise and a medical symbol for their uniforms," Polycarp said.

"They are sailors," he said. "No medical symbols for them. I don't remember the details of your program for our sailors."

"This would be the fifth course required," Polycarp said. "Making and using sails, making and using anchors, and how to care of their mates."

"Yes, I will give them a pay increase," Nicodemus said. "I will also personally give each one that completes all the courses an anchor symbol to wear of his uniform. Give my thanks to Mary."

"You could give the anchor to them at graduation," he said. "I am sure your direct involvement in the program will increase the number of sailors who attend."

"I am not going to graduation," he said. "I will give you jumpers with anchors attached that you can give to them."

"I will be pleased to present the jumpers to them," Polycarp said. "Your involvement is important."

"I will meet with each of them," he said. "I will talk with them one-on-one. Will that help?"

"I suppose it would help," he said. "If you change your mind let me know."

"I don't plan to address or stand before any large crowds," he said. "I expect you to teach my son how to do that."

Polycarp began to understand Nicodemus concern. He looked at him and smiled.

"I will make sure your son is a good public speaker," he said. "I think I can teach him to like lecturing."

Polycarp scheduled a meeting with Jonas. He planned to give Jonas opportunities to practice his public speaking.

"Jonas, I want you to give a verbal presentation to the faculty about your research trip," he said. "We will meet in a large lecture hall. If you need help, you may visit me."

"You want me to explain what we obtained, when will the meeting convene?" he asked.

"Bring a few copies of scrolls to pass around for them to glance at," he said. "We will meet next Friday."

The following week, Jonas spoke to the faculty. He explained that the scroll that was passed around was written for Peter by Luke. Each faculty member unrolled the scroll and examined it. The faculty enjoyed seeing the scroll and gained a better understanding of Polycarp's research. It was a successful meeting. Polycarp didn't have to be concerned about teaching Jonas how to prepare and deliver a public speech. He ensured that Jonas had several additional opportunities to speak before a class. It was about time for the study period to end, and Polycarp spent many hours planning the next study period.

After Irenaeus read and studied most of the scrolls obtained during research trips, he scheduled a meeting with Polycarp. He was eager to make a good impression on him.

"I am certain many of the scrolls that have been obtained have been written by Paul," Irenaeus said. "If Paul didn't write them, someone traveling with him wrote them. Luke also wrote proper Greek."

"When I read the scrolls, I thought the same thing," Polycarp said. "I traced the route of Paul's mission trips by where we obtained the scrolls."

"I think he visited some places twice," Irenaeus said. "Some places like Corinth he wrote to after he had visited with them. I think he was answering a message sent to him."

Polycarp looked at Irenaeus.

"When they were with Paul, both Apollos and Luke wrote lessons and corresponded with church members," Polycarp said. "We have located a few of their scrolls."

"I am going to continue studying," Irenaeus said. "We can learn a lot about Paul from our scrolls."

"If you find any links to Matthew, Mark, Luke or John, let me know," he said.

"Paul spent time with Luke on several occasions and at different locations," Irenaeus said. "Luke ministered to Paul's physical ailments, and he endured his style of missionary work."

He looked at Polycarp and scratched his head.

"Paul wrote about what Jesus said to him," Polycarp said. "He doesn't directly quote him. He does a fine job of explaining Jesus' message. His major concern is that we understand grace."

Polycarp stood and started out of his office.

"I don't think he ever wrote exactly what Jesus told him," he said. "It is one of the great Christian secrets."

Irenaeus smiled at him.

CHAPTER 10

A TRIP TO ROME

Many years after the university church, in Smyrna, became a very influential Christian church; the church in Ephesus still struggled with their second place status. Polycarp was old, but in good health, and he was considered a bishop of long standing. He was very well respected among his fellow bishops. His student priests led churches throughout the Roman Empire. When Anicetus was The Bishop of Rome, the churches fiercely competed with each other for members. Different messages about Jesus were being taught. Anicetus sent a message to the Bishop of Smyrna, Polycarp, asking him to come to Rome and discuss the differences between their churches. When Nascien delivered the message, Polycarp was in his office.

"Good day, sir," he said. "I have a message for you. When you have an opportunity, I would like to talk with you."

"Give the message to me," Polycarp said. "I must read it. I wasn't expecting a message."

The Bishop of Smyrna
Polycarp

May God always bless the church at Smyrna.
I have heard many good reports about the
church and the university.
I would appreciate your advice about the
different messages concerning Jesus being taught

in Rome.
I would also like to discuss several other issues such as the date on which Easter should be celebrated.

The Bishop of Rome
Anicetus

After Polycarp read the message, he decided to visit with Francis.

That evening Stephen and he walked to the church and dined with the priests. Polycarp greeted Francis.

"Pope Anicetus has sent a message to me, do you know him?" he asked.

"I know about him," Francis said. "He was in Antioch before he went to Rome. I am certain things are much different for him in Rome."

"He wants me to travel to Rome to discuss how we teach religion," he said. "I was thinking of telling him to come to Smyrna and take a course with us."

"If he goes too far from Rome, I believe he would be replaced," he said. "He is spending all his time defending orthodox Christianity."

"I didn't realize his situation was that difficult," Polycarp said. "He is probably just trying to teach the correct message about Jesus."

"I understand, in Rome, if you don't like the message a church is teaching, you go to the next church," Francis said. "They would benefit from a unified understanding and expression of Jesus. A constant message, maybe from different viewpoints, like the message you allow our priests to study."

"I really believe the interviews and research have been a great help," Polycarp said. "I could probably help him."

"You might want to ask Nicodemus," he said. "I think his father attends Anicetus' church."

Polycarp hadn't considered that Mr. Philemon knew him.

"Thank you for your advice," he said. "I will schedule a meeting with Nicodemus."

After two weeks, Nicodemus returned home and answered Polycarp's message. He had visited his father and scheduled a meeting for that afternoon. Immediately after lunch, Polycarp walked to Nicodemus' office. The sounds of the busy harbor filled the air. The sun shone and a cool sea breeze washed his face. He tugged on his beard with vigor. He felt great. When he arrived at Nicodemus' office building, he climbed the stairs and knocked on the door.

"Come in, I didn't see you sooner because I was in Rome visiting father,"

Nicodemus said.

"Visiting your father is generally mutually beneficial," Polycarp said. "I have a question about Rome, do you know Bishop Anicetus?"

"Yes, we know him," he said. "Religion in Rome can be confusing. Father told him to contact you. Father attends his church almost every week."

"Your father told him to send me a message?" he asked. "The Pope didn't tell me he knew you or your father."

"He seems like a good man," Nicodemus said. "We like him, and we think you might be able to help him."

"It is a long way to Rome, do you think I should visit with him?" he asked.

"I think father would like you to visit him," he said. "He always liked your interpretation of Jesus' message."

"When do you think I should visit with him?" Polycarp asked. "How long should I remain in Rome?"

He looked at Nicodemus.

Nicodemus smiled at Polycarp and answered, "You can stay with father. He loves to have visitors. His large house has plenty of rooms, and he employs a large staff of helpers. You could remain as long as you desire."

"I would enjoy visiting with your father," he said. "He always had a few questions for me."

"I want you to sail on the flagship of our fleet," he said. "The ship will sail, for Rome, in about three weeks. I will send you the exact date."

"I am certain my staff and students will complete my work while I am in Rome," Polycarp said. "They could always send me a message."

"Father has special quarters on this ship," he said. "He will make them available to you. I think he is having a special flag made for your trip. The flag will inform everyone that the Bishop of Smyrna is aboard."

Polycarp envisioned a ship's flag with a Christian symbol on it.

"I will have my own flag!" Polycarp said. "Do you have a flag?"

"No, they fly father's flag for me," he said. "I want to talk to you about your assistant."

Polycarp focused his attention on Nicodemus.

"Nascien has been my assistant for many years," he said. "Your son works with him doing the research."

"Jonas says he is a great man, and he told me he is a descendant of Jesus' brother," he said. "Father and I would like you to give him special training so he can manage the university. Someday, you will want only to read and teach a course."

Polycarp was surprised.

"What about Irenaeus?" he asked. "He is a very good man and has been with me a long time."

"We think having a descendant of Jesus manage the university will be a good influence on the entire university and church," he said. "You can transfer Irenaeus and eventually appoint him a bishop."

Polycarp became agitated with Nicodemus' suggestion.

"That doesn't seem kosher to me," he said. "Irenaeus has a much better understanding of how a successful university functions.

"Father asked me to discuss this with you," Nicodemus said. "I think it is important to him."

"This is a big step for me," he said. "I will pray about it, and I will talk with Irenaeus about his plans. I haven't promised him anything."

Polycarp could see a frown on Nichodemus' face. This was the first time Polycarp bulked at his suggestions.

"This is important to us," he said. "Do a lot of praying. I am counting on you."

Polycarp thought 'I will need a lot of guidance. Two good men and one position, I must spend a great amount of time at the prayer rail.'

With his head bowed, he slowly proceeded to the church.

After he prayed, Polycarp returned to his office. He thought about how generous Mr. Philemon and Nicodemus had been to the university. He didn't want to lose their support and trust. That evening, he slept only a few hours. He awoke early and started walking to the university. It was still dark, but as he walked along the living quarters of the priests, he saw candles flickering through the windows. He remembered nights, long ago, when he studied all night. By the time he reached his office, the sun peeked over the horizon and brightened his day. He scheduled a meeting with Irenaeus.

When Irenaeus arrived, he knocked on Polycarp's office door. Polycarp opened the door.

"We haven't talked for a while," Polycarp said. "The door has been opened unto you."

Polycarp smiled at Irenaeus and then sensed seriousness in Irenaeus' manner.

"I want to see you," Irenaeus said. "I have been busy studying and lecturing."

"What are your long range plans?" he asked. "How do you like teaching?"

Irenaeus looked at Polycarp and answered, "I think I would rather be assigned to a church. I have wanted to tell you, but I didn't want to disappoint you."

Polycarp knew his prayers had been answered. He looked at Irenaeus and sensed he was worried. He placed his hand on Irenaeus' shoulder.

"I am surprised, but I am not disappointed," he said. "Ensuring that Jesus' message is taught correctly is our most important objective."

"I promise I will always teach, as you have taught me," he said. "We are in complete agreement. I like the research. It adds a lot to our university."

Polycarp patted Irenaeus' shoulder.

'I will talk with Francis, and we will have you assigned to a large church," he said. "You can do research wherever you are sent. I will miss you."

"I will send you messages," Irenaeus said. "If you would have Nascien keep me up-to-date, I would appreciate it."

"I will communicate with you, on a regular basis," he said. "You must keep me up to date."

They prayed together and then Irenaeus returned to his office. Polycarp was relieved. He had worried about talking with Irenaeus, and

Irenaeus worried about talking with him. Now they both could relax and move forward with their lives. Prayer had brought peace into their lives. Polycarp met with Francis and asked him to assign Irenaeus to a church, where he would have the opportunity for rapid advancement. He hated to lose his friend, but wished him the best at his new church position. Before he departed, Polycarp scheduled a meeting with Nascien.

When Polycarp arrived at his office the next morning, the sun shone brightly. A cup of steaming hot tea sat on his desk. He told Nascien to come in.

"We need to do some planning," Polycarp said. "Have a seat. Have you mastered the Greek language?"

"I am doing well," he said. "Joazar doesn't have time to work with me directly. I have completed all the university language courses."

"You completed all the courses?" he asked. "That must have been a great amount of work."

"I can read and write Greek better than most of your professors," he said. "I have completed all the required course work. I do a considerable amount of lecturing."

"Have you transitioned from a student to a faculty member?" he asked. "I must have signed your paper work when I was signing a stack for graduation."

"I am still a student," Nascien said. "I am also a full-time faculty member. I teach and do research."

"We have a lot of opportunity, are you planning to make education your career?" he asked.

Nascien smiled at him.

"Yes I am," he said. "I hope to work for you for a long time."

"I plan to be in Rome for about a month," he said. "While I am away, I would like you to work with Francis and Nicodemus to manage the university. I will schedule a meeting for next week. I will provide you with a copy of my daily schedule."

A huge smile appeared on Nascien's face.

"That is great," he said. "I am certain Mary will also be a big help. She knows everything that goes on around here."

"I want you to remember James," he said. "He is retired, but he is available through the church at almost any time."

"I will have one of the priests-in-training assist me while you are gone," he said. "I am sure Jonas will want to go to Rome with you."

"You are probably correct," he said. "Fill out the paper work, and we will make the priest-in-training a student assistant."

During the next few weeks, Polycarp and Nascien visited with Francis and every member of the faculty. When they visited with Nicodemus, he was delighted that Nascien was being promoted to an assistant management position. He was also delighted that Jonas was going to Rome. Polycarp advised Nicodemus that Irenaeus had been assigned to a church. Nicodemus didn't respond. He informed Polycarp the flagship would be leaving in seven days. The next week was a busy week at the university. Polycarp spent extra time training Nascien. He listened to Polycarp's every word and worked very diligently. When he wasn't certain what to do, he would ask questions. He proved to be a quick learner. Polycarp's fears were assuaged, and he slept much better.

When Polycarp walked home, the sun slipped below the horizon. He took time to enjoy the evening and the beautiful pink sky. Stephen had dinner prepared for him. He also had him packed for his journey to Rome.

The next morning, after breakfast, they walked to the dock. The flagship was easy to locate. It was much larger than the other ships. Polycarp's flag was hoisted. Stephen remarked he was proud to work for someone who rated a ship's flag. Polycarp agreed it was a nice gesture by Mr. Philemon. The captain waited on the main deck for Polycarp to arrive.

"Good morning, bishop," he said. "It is an honor to fly your flag. Please note that every mate on this ship has an anchor on his jumper. I believe you know a few of my mates."

Polycarp looked at a sailor's uniform and then the ship's large mast.

"It certainly appears to be a fine ship," Polycarp said. "The wood is beautiful."

"The entire hull is made of cedar from the Lebanon forest," he said.

"The ship was constructed for Mr. Philemon at the shipyard in Tyre. Your quarters are also made of hand worked cedar."

Polycarp smiled at the captain.

"I could get used to living in this environment," he said. "I just couldn't afford it."

"You will have a mate in your quarters at all times," he said. "They are there to assist you. If you need me, just send the mate to look for me. I will be checking with you on a regular basis."

"How many stops are we going to make?" he asked. "Are we carrying a lot of cargo?"

"We will make one stop in Crete," he said. "We should be fully loaded and have all the paper work completed in about one hour. Then we will sail. Your assistant Jonas will be in the quarters next to yours. The head mate will show you to your quarters."

"Thank you, captain," he said. "I guess you know Jonas is Mr. Philemon's grandson."

"Yes, we know," he said. "He was provided first class passage as a member of the family."

Polycarp followed the first mate. His living quarters was a very large suite that comprised several rooms. There was a bedroom, a living room, an office, a private bathroom, and a kitchen with cook. Polycarp was especially impressed with the wood. Everything was carved and signed by the artist. Wooden religious symbols hung on the walls.

During the first day at sea, Polycarp had his mate give him a tour of the ship. The ship was loaded with raw materials, copper and silver for Crete and grain for Rome. During his tour, every sailor thanked Polycarp for their training at the school. Polycarp sensed how proud each sailor was of his accomplishments. Even their work shirts displayed an anchor. This ship was large and didn't hug the coast. It handled waves larger than Polycarp had ever seen with little problem and maintained a good speed. They finally arrived in Crete. The mate informed Polycarp that they would be in Crete all day and overnight, and that he had been assigned to be his tour guide.

Polycarp and his mate disembarked and found a carriage. They spent part of the day touring the buildings that the Romans had built, and then traveled to an ancient site that had been occupied for fifteen centuries. Polycarp enjoyed visiting ancient ruins. That evening, they enjoyed the local cuisine and music. The mate and Polycarp enjoyed their walk back to the ship. The sunset was beautiful. Polycarp sat on the deck for two hours and watched the flickering candles of a busy city. A group of sailors played simple musical instruments and sang about the sea. Finally, he became sleepy and went to his quarters.

The next morning, Polycarp was wakened by the sound of men loading the ship. He dressed and went outside. He stood by the rail and watched the men as they carried a large bag of grain on each shoulder. Polycarp's back ached just watching them work. The sailors supervised the loading operation. The men that carried the grain were dock workers. Soon the ship was loaded and they started to Rome.

"Bishop, I hope you like to eat lamb?" his cook asked. "Mary taught me how to prepare it. When I visited the market last evening, I found a nice fresh lamb for you."

"I like lamb," Polycarp said. "Lamb will be a nice change."

"I will also prepare vegetables and bread for you," he said. "It will be ready for dinner tonight. The captain would like to join you for dinner."

Polycarp smiled at his cook.

"That is fine with me," he said. "Do I have to dress in formal attire?"

"Not formal," he said. "I am sure the captain will wear a fresh uniform to dine with you. He will not expect you to ware formal dress for him. Your robes are always very impressive."

It was a beautiful day at sea. The ship seemed to cut its way through the glimmering water. It looked like some of the fish flew out of the water to escape from the ship. The sails fluttered and the waves splashed as the ship sailed its way to Rome.

Mr. Philemon's carriage and driver waited at the dock for Polycarp. It was a long ride to Mr. Philemon's house. His house was a large stone building with many rooms. Mr. Philemon greeted Polycarp, and the servants showed them to their rooms. After unpacking, Polycarp decided to take a walk. The buildings and the streets were very impressive, but Polycarp wasn't thrilled. He found the temples and the sporting arenas to be oppressive. When he returned to Mr. Philemon's for dinner, Anicetus was waiting for him. They agreed that they would meet in the morning at Anicetus' church office.

Early the next morning, Polycarp and Jonas walked to the church.

"We have water, hot tea, and bread," Anicetus said.

"When good water is available, I drink a lot of it," Polycarp said.

"My first question for you, Polycarp, is about the divinity of Jesus," Anicetus said.

"This is not a question for me," he said. "John was with Jesus throughout his ministry, and he lived a long time after Jesus was crucified. I talked with John about his strong belief that Jesus was divine."

"Not all his brothers considered him divine," Anicetus said.

"They knew him too well," he said. "They couldn't see the forest for the trees."

Polycarp stared at Anicetus.

"I believe Jesus is God," he said. "He is eternal and divine."

Polycarp paused and sensed Anicetus' manner.

"When I visited him the first time, John was in the process of writing down his recollections of being with Jesus," he said. "If it were not for his church in Ephesus, many would not believe Jesus was divine."

During the next few days, Anicetus and Polycarp discussed many of the points of differences among the churches of Rome. Anicetus was faithful to his Bible on Jewish points and was trying to be orthodox in his Christian teaching.

The last day of meetings was on a Friday.

"I have one more question," Anicetus said. "I have sided with Justin Martyr. He is a local Christian teacher. Let's discuss resurrection Sunday."

"I think the Lord's last supper was a Passover Meal," Polycarp said. "Passover Meals are always on the fourteenth of Nican (April). I don't understand the confusion. The Bible clearly states Passover is the fourteenth of Nican."

"We don't believe resurrection Sunday has a fixed date," Anicetus said. "We believe Jesus was killed on Friday and resurrected on Sunday."

"That is interesting," he said. "I prefer Biblical."

"Friend, I guess we will have to agree to disagree on this point," Anicetus said. "I will continue to use the first Sunday, after the first full moon, after the spring equinox as resurrection Sunday."

"I don't agree with you," Polycarp said. "As long as we agree on the meaning of the last supper, the date is not important."

"We have covered all the questions I wanted to discuss with you," he said. "Please join me in celebrating Jesus' last supper."

The three of them communed. Polycarp later stated to Jonas that immediately after communion he felt the grace of God. Polycarp and Jonas returned to Mr. Philemon's house. Jonas stayed busy transcribing his notes.

The next day, Polycarp updated Mr. Philemon about the great progress of the church and university in Smyrna. After dinner, they went to the living area of the house to relax.

"Did you and Anicetus come to agreement?" Mr. Philemon asked. "Am I going to see a lot of change?"

"We agreed every time," Polycarp said. "Sometimes our agreement was to not agree. I think you will notice some change. I hope you see more confidence in his teaching methods."

"Did you agree on a fixed date for resurrection Sunday?" he asked. "The fourteenth of Nican was so easy to remember."

"No we didn't." he said. "Someone will have to tell you each year when Easter is going to be celebrated."

"We have one church in town that doesn't celebrate Passover," he said. "They only emphasize Jesus' resurrection. We shouldn't forget our past."

"It is a week until the ship will arrive," Mr. Philemon said. "I have arranged for a carriage and driver to take you to see the destruction caused by the volcano. I am too old to travel that far. The driver will stop for you and Jonas after breakfast in the morning."

"Thank you," he said. "Working for you has been an honor. I think we both have a few more years."

Polycarp and Jonas arose early and ate a large breakfast. After sunrise, the carriage arrived at the house. The sky was blue and large white clouds raced across it. They put their packs into the carriage and headed to Vesuvius. Polycarp knew that Mount Vesuvius had been an active volcano for many years. He read an account of the mountain spouting flames. The scroll was written about a hundred fifty years ago. Records from the time of the eruption, about seventy years ago, indicate it was also preceded by earthquakes. The local people had become accustomed to Vesuvius shaking and shooting fire, so many didn't react before its most recent violent eruption. After traveling for two long days, they were in the area influenced by the volcano. They rented lodging at The Inn at Atelia. They would take day trips from that location.

"I have my writing material," Jonas said. "I will put them in the carriage."

Polycarp motioned to Jonas.

"I want to visit a few shops," he said. "They may have a few old scrolls or parchments."

Atelia was a small town. They located a shop on the main street.

"Come in and I will help you find what you need," the shopkeeper said.

"I am looking for old scrolls," Polycarp said. "I would like anything written by those who fled the eruption."

"I have a few scrolls you might like," he said. "I have one written by a native of Naples who fled by boat. It is not very well written, but it gives you a very good idea of what happened."

While perusing the scroll, Polycarp said. "You are correct; will you extend a reduced price to our university?"

The shopkeeper ignored Polycarp's request. He was accustomed to requests for a lower price, but Polycarp's request was different. He smiled at him.

"While you were reading the scroll, I thought of another scroll," he said. "I have a pack full of scrolls written about the volcano eruption. I have one that a fellow wrote about his uncle who died. He was trying to save people. I will sell you the whole pack for a day's wage."

"That sounds reasonable," he said. "I will have Jonas put them in our carriage."

"I put a parchment in the pack," he said. "It is a record of how one family spent the relief money they were given by the Roman government."

"Thank you, I don't know much about the relief program," Polycarp said. "Did Titus require a record to be kept?"

"I think it was a request," he said. "Unfortunately, he died before he could return."

"Right, I remember," he said. "Many people thought his older brother poisoned his food."

"That was the rumor," the storekeeper said. "No one knows for certain. It is not unusual for us to lose our emperors under unknown circumstances."

"I must be going now. Thank you for all your help," Polycarp said. They returned to the inn.

During the next two days, Polycarp and Jonas visited small towns close to the mountain. They stopped at many shops and purchased many scrolls. When they went south of the mountain, there was very little to see. The towns were covered by seventy-five feet of ash. A few important building had been cleared and valuables removed by the government.

They returned to Atelia to rest before starting their journey back to Rome.

"Driver, we want to leave tomorrow morning as soon as the sun rises," Polycarp said. "Have the carriage loaded and ready for us. The inn keeper will prepare you an early breakfast."

"Thank you," he said. "I will have everything ready. I see you found a few items to take back with us."

"It has been an interesting trip," he said. "I like scrolls written by people who actually were involved with what they wrote about. It is amazing how stories of the same event differ."

The next morning, Polycarp arose with the sun. When he checked on the carriage, he realized he was the only one not sleeping. He made a loud noise and the inn keeper appeared.

"I guess I didn't wake up," he said. "I will have the servants cook breakfast for everyone. I need to awaken your driver. I forgot about him."

"Cook our breakfasts first," Polycarp said. "We have a long journey today."

"I will go and help grandfather's driver," Jonas said. "He is probably upset. Soon, we will return for breakfast."

"I always have a plan," he said. "Some days I follow it, on other days things just don't go as I planned them. This is a type two day."

Polycarp looked at Jonas, who smiled.

After an hour, they had eaten their breakfast and were headed north. When it started to rain, the day had about ended. Before they found lodging at an inn, all three were wet. Polycarp went to his room to put on dry clothes. Jonas helped the driver with the carriage. He checked the scrolls to make sure they were all dry. Then he went to his room and put on dry clothes. Polycarp and Jonas enjoyed a large dinner meal. After dinner, they went to the public room of the Inn and relaxed.

The next morning after breakfast, they started to Rome. It wasn't raining and the road was smooth. When they arrived home, they had many stories to tell Mr. Philemon. Jonas and the driver unloaded the carriage. They prepared the materials that had been collected for shipment to the university. Polycarp went directly into the house.

"Polycarp, did you find anything of interest to take to the university?" Mr. Philemon asked. "A few scrolls, I hope."

"Yes, we actually purchased quite a few," Polycarp said. "The one shop owner wanted to get rid of a whole pack full of old scrolls. When we get home, it will take Jonas a while to sort through them."

Jonas came into the house.

"Almost everything is ready to be shipped to the university," he said. "I am ready to go home."

"Jonas, did you learn anything?" Mr. Philemon asked. "I hope this trip has been a good experience for you."

"Yes, I learned every day," he said. "One day, I learned all about a type two day."

Mr. Philemon looked at Polycarp and then at Jason.

"It was about time you learned about a type two day," Polycarp said. "I have experienced them on occasion."

They looked at each other and laughed for a while.

The following day, Jonas and Polycarp finished packing their scrolls for shipment. A mate came to the house and helped them. The mate then took the scrolls to the ship. When they all arrived at the ship the next morning, Polycarp's flag was flying.

"I hope you like your flag," Mr. Philemon said. "I had it made special for you. You are probably the only bishop with a ship's flag."

"The flag was a thoughtful touch," Polycarp said. "Your ship is beautiful. It is the best ship on the sea."

When they boarded the ship, the mate was waiting for them. Everything was in its place and Polycarp was on the main deck when he noticed many Roman soldiers approaching. He watched as they marched aboard the ship. The mate informed him they had been ordered to Crete.

Polycarp thought, 'There are many places they could be shipped that are worse the Crete.'

Polycarp noticed a gentle figure heading his way.

"Good day bishop," he said. "My name is Rogus. I am going to the church in Smyrna to see the senior priest named Francis. Do you know Francis?"

Polycarp hesitated for a moment. He looked at Rogus.

"Yes, I know Francis," he said. "What are you going to see him about?"

"I am planning to finish my studies at the university," he said. "His message says he has a job for me. I will be working for Mary, do you know her?"

Polycarp smiled at him.

"Yes, I know Mary," he said. "She teaches students while they work under her direction, what skills have you learned? Mary's students cook and clean for the priests at the church and they work for the university."

"I can cook," he said. "I hope to earn enough money to pay for my lodging, food, and education as a cook."

"I am sure Mary can use a cook," he said. "Will you have dinner with me this evening?"

"Yes, I will look for you in the mess-hall," he said. "I think dinner is at four bells."

"Come to my cabin," he said. "I am in Mr. Philemon's cabin. Just ask any sailor, and they will help you find me. You can explain the bell system to me and my assistant, Jonas, and I will explain the university to you."

At six o'clock that evening there was a knock on the door of Polycarp's cabin. The mate announced Rogus.

"Come in," Polycarp said. "This is my assistant Jonas. I owe you a few explanations. First, I am in this cabin because I have known Mr. Philemon, who has owned this fleet of ships, for a long time. Second, I am The Bishop of Smyrna. Call me Polycarp. We will be eating in our cabin. We have a cook assigned to us."

As Polycarp watched, a worried look appeared on Rogus' face.

"The Bishop of Smyrna, you have a cook?" he asked. "If I have been to bold, I am very sorry."

"No, sit down," he said. "I will have Jonas tell you all about the university. I will be back in a few minutes. I promised the captain that I would bless the food in the mess-hall this evening."

He then went to the mess-hall, blessed the food, and prayed for a calm sea and a good breeze. The captain acknowledged him and he went topside. Many of the Roman troop were not familiar with the Christian religion and discussed it among themselves. Polycarp returned to his cabin. The cook was prepared to serve dinner. Polycarp, Jonas, and Rogus enjoyed their dinner. After dinner, they sat in their living area and discussed the school.

"The cooks on this ship completed our school that helps train sailors," Polycarp said. "Mary teaches them all a little about cooking. The one's that want to become cooks, work in our kitchens at the university."

"I like cooking, but I am planning on becoming a priest," Rogus said. "I want to be in the program that trains priests."

"We start a new group of priest-in-training every year," Polycarp said. "If you have been talking with Francis, I am certain he has planned your studies."

Polycarp motioned at the cook.

"Yes, bishop," the cook replied. "You are correct. I spent a year and a half at the university. That helped qualify me for this job on our flag ship. Rogus, see the anchor on my jumper. When we complete the courses, we get these jumpers. I am certain when you complete the priest-in-training classes, there will be a job waiting for you."

"I am excited," he said. "I can hardly wait to become associated with the university and obtain additional information."

"When you are at the university, you can visit with me," Polycarp said. "I have a special door on my office. If you knock, it will be opened unto you. If I am not in my office, Jonas will make an appointment for you. Please visit with me."

When the ship docked, the Roman soldiers marched off the ship. It took much longer to load the lumber, going to Nichodemus. Each piece had been carefully hand formed and wrapped for protected. When the sun appeared, they sailed toward Smyrna. Polycarp received a message from the captain. He had referred one of the families traveling, to The Bishop of Smyrna. When the family approached him, Polycarp stood at the ship's rail on the main deck. He watched the waves the ship created in the ocean.

"Good day, bishop," he said. "This is my son, Spockus. He has graduated from our local college and is going to Smyrna to study medicine. The captain explained that you might tell him about the school."

"Join me," Polycarp said. "Watching the ocean brings peace to me. We have a fine school of medicine."

"How familiar are you with the college of medicine?" he asked. "Are you a professor?"

Polycarp hesitated for a moment.

"I manage the program. Dr. Lukus and his staff teach the courses," he said. "I am certain your son has made a good decision. He will have to study very diligently and practice his skills in our clinic. Our medical school provides care to our community. It is a great learning opportunity."

"I am looking forward to meeting Dr. Lukus," he said. "I am going to start my studies very soon. The next study program is about to start."

"I believe Dr. Lukus starts about thirty student doctors a year," he said. "You will be with us several years. When you complete your studies, you can work for Dr. Lukus and the community, or you can obtain a job anywhere you want to live."

"I am planning on returning to Crete," he said. "This is my home. I want to help this community."

"Good luck to you," Polycarp said. "Dr. Lukus will teach you everything you will need to know. Helping your home community is a good thing."

The sunset that evening was particularly beautiful. The sun appeared as a large orange ball as it slipped below the western sea. After a few days, they arrived at the port in Smyrna. Stephen arrived with a carriage. A mate helped Jonas and Stephen carefully place all the material and their packs into the carriage. Polycarp found the captain and thanked him for a pleasant journey. Polycarp went to the house, and Jonas took the material to the university.

After a good night of rest, Polycarp walked to the university.

Jonas greeted him, "As soon as I copy the scrolls I will have the originals delivered to your office."

Polycarp thanked him and entered his office. After a few moments, Nascien knocked on his office door. They discussed Polycarp's trip and Nascien's experiences at the university."

The university had progressed as expected. Whenever Nascien needed any help, Francis provided it. Polycarp and Nascien walked around the university. John talked with them about the research trip. Then Polycarp returned to his office and scheduled a meeting with Nicodemus.

Two days later, he walked to Nicodemus' office and discussed the trip. Polycarp gave him a message from his father and expressed his gratitude for his treatment aboard the flag ship. On his way back to the university, Polycarp walked through the harbor and visualized his cabin on the flag ship.

After a week passed, Jonas brought the original scrolls to Polycarp's office.

"John said to tell you that you have a scroll written by an eye witness to the eruption of the volcano," Jonas said. "He said it was written by Pliny the Younger about his uncle. His uncle was trying to help people escape, but they didn't make it. They were all killed."

"I have heard of Pliny the Elder," Polycarp said. "He was a historian. I think we have some scrolls written by him."

"Many of the scrolls were written by someone who felt or saw the destruction," he said. "It must have been a terrible thing. Large stones flew through the air. Just going outside and trying to escape was dangerous."

"We are lucky," he said. "We might have a flood occasionally, but we don't have a volcano."

Jonas looked at Polycarp and said, "John indicated he plans to visit with you this afternoon concerning the scrolls."

Later that afternoon, John went to Polycarp's office. He seemed excited.

"I took a quick look at some of the scrolls that the university purchased," John said. "The one scroll is just like another scroll we have except a few sentences have been added."

"Tell me more," Polycarp said. "Who wrote the scrolls?"

"It looks like a scroll that Mark wrote," he said. I am certain he was writing for Peter."

"Did the added sentences change the meaning of the message?" he asked.

"No, they added more detail," John said. "I want to show you the scroll."

Polycarp read the ending of the scroll. He was familiar with what John had noticed.

"I prefer the unembellished version of the scroll," he said. "The scroll should be labeled, so we can find it and determine who wrote the ending."

A month passed, before Francis entered Polycarp's office. He was accompanied by several high ranking Roman soldiers. He explained to Polycarp they wanted to inspect the church and the university. The soldiers spent the entire day looking at the university and making notes. They were polite, but never explained their intentions.

The next day, Francis went to visit Polycarp.

"The Roman soldiers gave me a creepy feeling," he said. "They didn't say what they wanted, but I am sure we will be finding out."

"It is surprising," Polycarp said. "The Romans are pagans. I wouldn't expect them to have much interest in a Christian church and university. I think I will tell Nicodemus they visited us."

The following morning, Stephen and Polycarp had breakfast on the dock. Polycarp then went to visit with Nicodemus. He was not in his office. Polycarp returned to Nicodemus' office the next day.

"I was here to see you yesterday, but you weren't available," he said. "A few days ago, a group of Roman soldiers visited with Francis and me."

"I guess they visited everyone," Nicodemus said. "What did they want?"

"They never said what they wanted," Polycarp said. "They spent the entire day making notes and then they left. We thought you should know."

"I didn't know they had visited you," Nicodemus said. "They visited me yesterday. They must be making notes to tell their superiors about Smyrna. I hope this is not bad news. I will send father a message."

"They are probably going to impose another tax," Polycarp said. "They must need another building somewhere."

"I hope it is just a tax," Nicodemus said. "How is the clinic?"

"It is doing well," he said. "It is almost always full of patients. It is a great asset to our medical school. The doctors are gaining real experience. We have students coming from far away to be trained."

Polycarp returned to the university. He stayed busy reading and writing. After two weeks, Nicodemus invited him to lunch. They met at the harbor and enjoyed a meal and the sunshine. Nicodemus said he had received a message from his father.

"He had no idea what the Roman soldiers wanted," Nicodemus said. "He said he was concerned. He suggested we build a new separate library to house all the scrolls."

"A new larger separate library would be a nice addition for the university," Polycarp said. "We could make it look like all the research scrolls and codices were in the library."

"That was father's idea," he said. "We would have different rooms for different scrolls. Maybe, we would arrange them, by author or by subject. All the originals would be kept out of sight next to your office."

"I like that idea," he said. "We could even include some of the more common originals in the library."

"He sent me a plan for the new library," Nicodemus said. "It matches the other buildings and includes a few areas to study and a few lecture halls. When the university grows, we could use those rooms for library space."

He took the drawings and carefully studied at them.

"This looks very good," Polycarp said. "When do you plan to start construction of the new library?"

"We will start clearing land next week," Nicodemus said. "We now own all the land around the church and the university. Father said to tell you to have a type one day."

"It is an inside situation," he said. "We had a little fun with Jonas."

They finished their meal and then walked to the university. Nichodemus showed Polycarp where the new library would be built. He explained they would start building a large number of secure cabinets for the new library. At the end of the day Polycarp went home.

Later he and Stephen dined with Francis and informed him about the new library. He was very pleased.

"I prayed for a new larger library," Francis said. "Now that we use primarily codices, I hope we relocate some of our scrolls and material into the new library. That would give us more space, for prayer, in the church."

"I will work with you," Polycarp said. "We will do whatever you need. I think the student priests would do a lot of their studying in the library. I want to make it a quiet, well lighted space to read and study."

After a month, Francis could see the outline of the new building. He visited with Polycarp, and they discussed how to move the scrolls from the church to the library.

They decided it would be best to have the priest hand carry them.

After his day at the university, Polycarp and Stephen went to the church.

"Polycarp, I have an idea," Francis said. "I want one of my priests to be the administrator for the new library," he said. "He will be responsible for teaching all student priests how to write Greek. He will also be responsible for teaching them how to maintain scrolls and will keep a cabinet full of blank codices available for your students."

"That is a good idea," Polycarp said. "The team that is responsible for transcribing has been making a few blank scrolls. We use mostly codices."

"The library will have to be able to handle a large number of codices," Francis said. "If we build the proper cabinets, it should be significantly easier for the students to use codices than scrolls."

"It will allow them to complete more transcribing," he said. "Determine how many codices are needed each week, and I will have the students transferred to work with your priests."

"I am going to locate the room used to make blank codices in the back of the first floor of the new building," he said. "That way he won't have to transfer the raw materials upstairs."

"I am planning on using a third of the third floor for a medical library," Polycarp said. "The student doctors will be able to read and study in that area."

"I am excited about the library," he said. "It will provide us with many new opportunities."

Before the next study period started, the walls for the new building were completed. Polycarp planned to convert the existing library space into classrooms. More students enrolled every study period. The studies of medicine and religion increased the most rapidly. When Nascien appeared with a student, Polycarp was seated in his office.

"Good afternoon," Rogus said. "We met sailing from Crete to Smyrna. I am now studying to be a priest and work for Mary. She is wonderful. She gave me a job in the kitchen and dining room at the medical building. I wanted to see you and to thank you."

"I am glad you are happy," Polycarp said. "I thought she might use your cooking skills."

"She told me, in many churches, the priests do their own cooking," he said. "I must go to class now. Come over and eat with us."

Polycarp returned to reading and making plans for the new library. He began to see Roman soldiers on a regular basis. The situation was unusual because it was a time of peace for the Roman Empire. He became very concerned and sent a message to Irenaeus.

Irenaeus

May God bless you and your fellow priests.
I hope your church is growing rapidly.
Recently, I have noticed many Roman soldiers.
I am fearful they are considering destroying the
material I have collected for my research.
You were the only student who read every
scroll, more than one time, and enjoyed their
content.
I am going to ship my original scrolls to you,
for safe keeping.
I will keep the copies, both scrolls and codices.
I will have Nascien contact you and accompany
the scrolls.
If things change here, I will want them returned.
While you have them, make copies of them
and use them to train new priests.
I will have them shipped to the port where the
Rhone River meets the sea.
Arrangements are being made to have them
delivered to you.

Polycarp
The Bishop of Smyrna

Polycarp received a message from Irenaeus.

Polycarp
The Bishop of Smyrna
May God bless you and Francis.
I will be very pleased to receive your scrolls.
We will secure them for you and we will
make a copy of each scroll for our use.
Our church and our community is growing
very rapidly.

I am looking forward to seeing Nascien.

I hope your situation improves.

Irenaeus

Cyzicus, an area north of Smyrna, was struck by a major earthquake. The new very large temple that the Romans had recently built to Hadrian was destroyed. Collections were made by the Romans to provide relief for the people and to rebuild the temple. Francis and Polycarp were in favor of helping the relief and had no choice but to contribute toward the rebuilding of the temple. The Roman soldiers departed Smyrna and remained busy helping the people of Cyzicus. Polycarp and Francis met for dinner at the church.

"Now that I don't see Roman soldiers every day, I am feeling better," Polycarp said. "Have your priests return from Cyzicus?"

"Yes, they have returned," Francis said. "We are back to a more normal schedule.

We are glad you decided to dine with us."

"After dinner, I want you to pray with me," Polycarp said. "I need your help to bolster my faith. Old age is getting to me. It seems all I want to do is read and write. I no longer do much lecturing."

"That is fine," he said. "We have your leadership. You are a great asset to the church and the university. If you need help, Nascien will help you."

"You are correct," he said. "He is a great help to me and the university."

After dinner, they went to the alter rail and prayed.

CHAPTER 11

TRIPS TO GAUL

The research trips resulted in many hundred scrolls and other items being collected. The university became recognized for a large collection of Christian artifacts. Polycarp feared that the pagan Roman Empire was plotting to confiscate the research material. After two codices copies of each scroll was made, Nascien prepared to take the original scrolls to Irenaeus, in Lagdunum, Gaul, so they would be stored at the church. Polycarp was certain the scrolls would be safe with Irenaeus. Carefully packing the scrolls for shipment required a month. Finally, the first shipment, of the scrolls was secured. They were loaded on one of Nicodemus' ships.

"Nascien, Irenaeus will be expecting you," Polycarp said. "He will take good care of our scrolls."

"They are packed, and I am ready to sail," Nascien said. "The scrolls and I will be transferred to a smaller ship. This ship goes to Rome."

Polycarp looked at Nascien and wished him a safe journey.

When the ship reached Rome, Nascien and the scrolls were transferred to one of Mr. Philemon's smaller ships. Nascien walked along the long line of ships docked in Rome. Finally, he found his ship. He walked up the gangplank and boarded. He saw a sailor and asked, "Will you explain to me where my cabin is located."

"On the starboard side at the bow," he said. "We only have one cabin and transport a few passengers."

He walked forward looking for a cabin. The captain of the ship saw him.

"Can I help you?" he asked. "We are sailing to the Rhone River."

"Good, I'm on the correct ship," he said.

They greeted each other.

"I don't want to be away a long time, how many days are required for the voyage?" Nascien asked.

"It depends on loading and unloading of cargo," he said. "The dock workers only work ten hours a day. It will take about seven days. We have several stops to make."

"Where are we stopping?" he asked. "I didn't know we would be stopping."

"We will sail to Corsica today," he said. "Tomorrow they will off load some material. After noon, we will sail to Posea."

Nascien suddenly realized his voyage would be long and tedious.

"Why do we make so many stops?" he asked. "It makes the trip much longer."

"This ship is a cargo ship," he said. "We make money hauling cargo."

"You are transporting me," he said. "I am not cargo."

"We take a few passengers," he said. "Many of our passengers are friends of Mr. Philemon's family. Most small ships don't carry passengers."

Because the ship was primarily a commercial cargo ship, Nascien shared quarters with seven other passengers. They eat in the mess-hall with the sailors. The seas were high and the ship groaned loudly as it sailed to Corsica. Nascien and the other passengers stood on the main deck. They grasped the railing and tried not to be sick.

"I see land," Nascien said. "We have finally made it."

"That is Corsica," the mate said. "We will dock in Aleria. I would recommend you stay aboard. We have a small amount of cargo to deliver. We will spend the night here and sail about noon."

"Why do you recommend we stay aboard the ship?" Nascien asked.

"If you disembark the ship, we can't provide security for you," the mate said. "You will be safe aboard the ship. We have sailors on guard duty at all times. Meals will be served in the mess-hall."

Nascien didn't appreciate the situation, so he went to his cabin and prayed.

The next day, the ship sailed to Posea. More cargo was unloaded and a small amount was loaded. The remainder of the week saw the same routine, dock, stay on board overnight, unload, load and sail during the day. Nascien was glad when the ship finally arrived at the confluence of the Rhone River and the Great Sea.

Irenaeus met Nascien and welcomed him to Gaul.

"We made so many stops, walking might have been faster," Nascien said. "I have scrolls for you."

"I did walk," Irenaeus said. "It was very slow, but very rewarding."

Nascien wasn't aware of the fact that Irenaeus had walked from Smyrna to Gaul. He stared at Irenaeus.

"The journey to Corsica was quite rough," he said. "During the day, I stood in the sea breeze. The remainder of the trip was smooth sailing, but long and tiring. I hope you haven't waited too long."

"I arrived yesterday," he said. "They told me you would be here yesterday or today. The smaller ships don't keep an exact schedule. The material is going to be loaded aboard a river boat. I have checked our cabin and it is fine."

"We are going to take another boat, how far do we have to go?" Nascien somberly asked.

"It will take three days, and we will make many stops," he said while trying not to smile.

"I am not used to this type of traveling," Nascien said. "I am used to sailing long distances."

"We will encounter many barges on the river," Irenaeus said. "We won't be traveling very fast. The river current is quite fast going south, but we are going north. They will use horses to pull the barge."

The river barge stopped at every port along the way. Avignon was the first stop, then Viviers, Tournon, Vienne, and finally, Lagdunum (Lyon). The journey took three days, but the river was smooth and they visited each town.

"I think you will like our church," Irenaeus said. "It has grown rapidly. When I arrived, the church employed two priests. Now, the church has five priests. The senior priest is quite old."

"I will help you unload the scrolls," Nascien said. "I hope they all survived the trip."

"We will take the carriage to the church," he said. "The other priests will bring the material."

Nascien and Irenaeus rode to the church. Then Nascien went to his room, cleaned himself, and went to sleep He was awakened at dinner time.

"The priests unloaded all the packs and placed the material in the church for us," Irenaeus said. "After we eat, we can inspect it."

"It is nice to have real food," Nascien said. "I don't know how the sailors make it eating in the mess-hall every day."

"One of the packs is damp," Irenaeus informed Nascien. "We should probably open it first."

"I was afraid of that," he said. "I hope the scrolls are not ruined."

"Do you think Polycarp is in any danger?" Irenaeus asked.

"Not at this time, but he is getting older and resists change," he said.

Nascien stood up and headed straight for the packs. When he arrived, the priests unpacked the damp scrolls.

"We don't know how they became wet," the priest said. "We will have to carefully dry several of the scrolls. I will get a rack."

"This is not good," Nascien said. "Polycarp never considered the scrolls might be damaged in shipment."

"If we carefully unroll the scrolls and stretch them on this rack, they will dry," a priest said. "They might become a little more brittle."

"I will help you," Nascien said. "I will work on this one."

"I have done this before," the priest said. "It is not as bad as it looks."

It was determined that only four of the scrolls were damp. All of the damp scrolls had been written by Luke. After they were stretched to dry, Nascien returned and finished his dinner. He was glad the scrolls weren't totally destroyed.

The next morning, Irenaeus took Nascien on a tour of the church. After lunch, they walked around Lagdunum. The following morning, after breakfast, Nascien boarded a river boat for his return trip. His trip was similar to his trip to Lagdunum, slow and uncomfortable.

When he reached Smyrna, Polycarp met him at the dock. They greeted one another.

"It was a difficult trip," Nascien said. "All we did was sail for a while and then stop for a day. I am glad the first trip is complete."

"Did you deliver the packs to Irenaeus?" he asked. "I am certain he was pleased."

"I delivered everything, but four scrolls became damp," he said. "We put them on a rack to dry."

"I am glad we made several copies of everything, which of the scrolls were damaged?" he asked.

"The scrolls were written by Luke," he said. "When he wrote them, I think he was traveling with Paul. I left a parchment indicating that I had read them before they became damp. I wrote what I remembered."

"That should help who ever reads them next," Polycarp said. "Thank you. I don't know why, but after you departed, I developed a feeling something was going to happen."

Polycarp met with Nicodemus.

"When Nascien traveled to Gaul, he encountered a few problems," he said.

"What kind of problems did he encounter?" Nicodemus asked. "Maybe, I can help."

Polycarp explained the many stops and the four wet scrolls. Nichodemus said he would look into the situation and ensure things were better on the next journey to Gaul.

Nascien planned to make two additional trips to Gaul. Polycarp didn't want to chance losing too many original scrolls at once. Nascien wasn't looking forward to his second journey. When the time arrived, Polycarp accompanied him to the ship. They saw the captain and waved to him.

The captain greeted them.

"Has Nicodemus talked with you, captain?" Polycarp asked. "Last trip we encountered a few problems."

"Yes, he talked to me," the captain said. "He is sending two escorts with your assistant. They will load and unload your packs. They will remain with your assistant until he returns to Smyrna."

Nascien thanked the captain and inquired about the names of his escorts.

"Just call them mate one and mate two," he said. "They will call you sir."

Two of the largest sailors Polycarp had ever seen joined them. The captain explained that the mates were picked by Nicodemus. The packs and the three travelers shared a cabin. Mate two spent most of his time next to the packs that contained the scrolls. Nascien walked to the ship's rail and enjoyed the sunshine, gentle rocking motion, and sea breeze.

When the ship docked in Rome, the mates escorted the scrolls and Nascien to the next ship. After they were transferred to a smaller ship, they were the only passengers. Mate one explained to the captain of the smaller ship, they traveled under Nicodemus' flag. They received the best of everything.

When they reached the Rhone River, Irenaeus met them.

"I have purchased us passage on a barge," Irenaeus said. "Who is that with you?"

"This is mate one," Nascien said. "We won't be taking a barge. Mate two and I will remain with the packs. I will rent us a carriage. You are welcome to travel with us."

"Thank you," Irenaeus said. "Did they come from Smyrna with you?"

"Yes," Nascien said. "They work for Nichodemus."

"I understand," he said. "I will be glad to ride with you. Traveling overland might be easier and quicker. Going north the barges fight the river current the entire trip."

"We will take good care of you and the packs," mate one said. "If you need to stop, just tell me."

Very early the third day, they reached Lagdunum.

"Where should we stow the packs?" mate one asked. "We will carry them."

"Please place them in the church," Irenaeus said. "Just follow the priest."

The mates carefully took the packs into the church. They then went to dinner with Irenaeus and Nascien.

"Mate one," Irenaeus said. "Would you like a tour of Lagdunum tomorrow?"

"No thank you, sir," he said. "When I don't feel the sea breeze, I get nervous. We will start home. You can say a prayer for us."

The return trip was completed without incident, and Nascien was less apprehensive about trip three. He prepared scrolls for the trip. After two weeks, he notified Polycarp he was ready to travel.

Two days later they went to the dock. Mate one and mate two met them.

"How many scrolls will we be transporting?" mate one asked. "We will take them to the cabin."

"Three packs," Nascien said. "I hope we have good weather and a calm sea."

The trip was uneventful and they returned safely. When Nascien talked with Polycarp, he was very complementary about the mates and the ships.

The next day, Polycarp visited with Nichodemus. He thanked him for his assistance.

"I knew the mates would do a good job," Nichodemus said. "They have been with me for several years. They are my problem solvers."

Nascien and Polycarp returned to their jobs of managing the university. The walls for the new library were completed and the roof structure was built. Polycarp visited with a cabinet shop to begin construction of the cabinets for the codices and the scrolls. The cabinets were installed before the rooms were completed, and then the rooms were built to fit the cabinets. When the first set of cabinets was completed, Polycarp met the installers and carefully observed the installation.

"The cabinets you built are different for each room," Polycarp noted. "They house the scrolls we have accumulated and the codices we produce."

"These cabinets are all the same," the carpenter said. "They are labeled "blank codices". They were built for this room on the ground floor."

"Yes, that is correct," he said. "I forgot about the preparation room. It might be better if I just watch."

"You may watch us today," he said as he smiled. "We watch Francis every Sabbath."

By the time the cabinets were installed in the third room, the first room was completed. Nascien informed Polycarp that the priest could start moving scrolls the following week. Polycarp talked with the student priests and joined them in transporting the scrolls. After his first trip, Polycarp found a chair and watched the precession. The new facility was a great improvement over existing reading and studying areas. The scrolls kept under lock and key in his office were all copies. Very few people knew about the change.

CHAPTER 12

POLYCARP'S DEATH

Nascien entered Polycarp's office.

"How do you feel?" he asked. "Would you like to go outside and take a walk?"

"It is a beautiful day for a walk," Polycarp said. "I would like to walk over to Mary's school and visit with Mary and my sister."

Polycarp kept his cane propped against his desk. They started across the campus to visit Mary.

"Don't go too fast," he said. "I think I can make it."

"We are almost there," he said. "I see Mary."

"Hello, Mary," Polycarp called. "Is Dianna here?"

"I will get her," Mary said. "Dianna, Polycarp is here to see you."

"How are you?" Mary asked. "You look weak."

"I am getting old," Polycarp said. "I needed a walk, and Nascien said he would walk with me. I decided to visit you."

"We are glad you came to see us," Mary said. "You are always welcome."

They visited for a short time, and then Dianna went back to work.

Nascien and Polycarp started the return walk to his office.

"I remember when I thought that was a short walk," Polycarp said. "Now it is all I can do without stopping to rest."

"Here come some Roman soldiers," Nascien said. "I think more soldiers have moved into our area."

"It is troublesome that you can't go anywhere without seeing soldiers," Polycarp said. "This is a peaceful town, we don't need them."

"They seem to be investigating the university," he said. "I wish they would go away and allow us to worship and teach in peace."

"Whatever they want, I am sure it won't be good for us," he said. "I hope it is just tax."

Soon they arrived at Polycarp's office, went inside, and sat down. Polycarp groaned and looked at Nascien.

"That was a good walk," he said. "Thank you for helping me."

"It was good to talk with Mary," Nascien said. "She is always busy."

"Do you dream?" Polycarp asked. "I had a dream the other night."

"I have short funny dreams, what did you dream?" Nascien asked.

"I dreamed that I am going to die. I am going to be killed. My death will be very similar to Jesus' death," he said.

"Someone is going to turn you over to the Romans, and the Romans are going to execute you?" Nascien asked.

"I can't remember all the details," he said. "The Romans are going to kill me. The dream scared me so bad, I awoke."

"The Romans have no reason to kill you," he said. "They are here to insure the peace."

"The building shook, did you feel it?" Polycarp asked.

"I felt it," he said. "It was a small earthquake. This area experiences earthquakes."

"We don't need any earthquakes," he said. "I wobble enough."

He looked at Nascien and smiled.

When the day ended, Polycarp was exhausted and slowly walked home. When he arrived, Stephen had a nice dinner prepared for him. After dinner, Polycarp went into the living area and sat in his favorite chair. Soon, Stephen woke him and helped him into bed.

The next morning, after breakfast Polycarp walked to his office. Nascien was waiting for him.

"Do you remember yesterday when we felt that earthquake?" Nascien asked. "It shook the building a little."

"Yes, I remember," Polycarp said. "What happened?"

"About fifty miles north of town, the earthquake destroyed a Roman fortification," he said. "Many soldiers have been killed and many have been injured."

"We should pray for them," Polycarp said.

"Dr. Lukus and Mary are getting the clinic prepared for those that have been injured," Nascien said. "Francis and several priests are going to the fortification to help them."

"You can help Mary," Polycarp said. "If I need you I will send for you."

"The injured should arrive tomorrow," Nascien said. "We will need to get as much rest as possible this evening."

"I don't think I will be much help," Polycarp said. "I'll just stay out of your way."

"You can pray for us and for the injured," he said. "We need prayers."

"That I can do," he said. "That is a good job for me."

That evening Mary's staff and Dr. Lukus' staff finished preparing the clinic for the injured men. Polycarp was able to get a good night of rest.

The next morning, the injured men arrived in a steady, endless stream of wagons. "These men need help," a soldier said. "A few of us are not injured and will help you."

"This one has a broken leg," the doctor said. "Mary, wash it and have a splint put on it."

"Soldier, if you would erect several tents for your soldiers that are not severally injured, it would help," Nascien said. "That would allow more room in the clinic for those that need constant medical care."

"I will do that," he said. "I will erect two large tents."

"Be careful with him," the doctor said. "Put him in a bed in the clinic."

"I hope we have enough room," Nascien said. "Hurry with those tents."

After six wagons loaded with injured men arrived, a Roman soldier announced the last of the injured had been transported. Mary and Dr. Lukus' people worked all night. By morning, everyone had received medical attention. Part of the staff was told to go home, sleep, and return in eight hours. The others would rest later.

Several days passed, before Francis and his priests returned from the area of the earthquake. It was a Sabbath, and Polycarp led the service in the church. Francis went to visit Polycarp.

"We did a lot of praying," he said. "We also helped to bury many soldiers."

"I am pleased you have returned," Polycarp said. "We need your help at the clinic and at the church. I have been doing the praying."

"We had one problem," he said. "Many of the soldiers that worked with us wanted to become Christians."

"That doesn't sound like a problem," Polycarp said. "What is the problem?"

"The head soldier told me not to baptize anyone," Francis said. "He was afraid."

"What else did he say?" he asked. "Did he come here with you?"

"No, he stayed at the fortification," he said. "He said his men thought our God was stronger than their God. He protected us from earthquake."

"He could cause us some bigger problems," Polycarp said.

Polycarp went to the church and prayed for hours. When it became dark, he slowly walked home.

After three days, an excited Francis came to see Polycarp.

"One of the soldiers came to see me today," Francis said. "He informed me that several of them, led by the head soldier, are coming to look for you."

"Why do they want me?" Polycarp asked. "I don't know them."

"You are the Bishop of Smyrna," he said. "I think you should leave town and hide with some of our members."

"Why should I hide?" he asked. "They probably just want to know about our God."

"I have been informed they plan to arrest you," he said. "You need to pack."

"I'm not afraid," he said. "I haven't done anything wrong."

"They are pagans," he said. "They want your recognition."

Francis eventually convinced Polycarp to visit with a member of the church for a few days.

A driver took Polycarp into the country.

"Hello, I am your bishop," he said. "I would like to stay with you. I will visit with the people in this area concerning the earthquake."

"Come in, Polycarp," Euseus said. "We know you. We are members of the church in Smyrna. You are welcome to stay with us. We have a room upstairs."

Polycarp entered Euseus' home.

"If Roman soldiers come looking for me, tell them I am in the upper room," he said.

"Why would they be looking for you?" he asked. "I thought they were here to protect us."

"Their pagan God didn't protect them from the earthquake," he said. "So they are unset with our God and me."

"I thought Francis and his priest went to the fortification and helped the injured," he said. "They should be thankful for the help."

"While they helped those that were injured, many of them wanted to join the Christian Church," he said. "Claudius, the leader, is not happy. He thinks we are confusing his soldiers."

"I could tell him that I haven't seen you," Euseus said. "Then they would move on and look elsewhere."

"I don't want you to jeopardize your family," he said. "Just tell them I am here trying to help."

The next day, the Roman soldiers arrived in Smyrna.

"My name is Claudius," he said. I'm responsible for this legion of the Roman Army."

"We are sorry for your loses due to the earthquake," a priest said.

"Where are my injured soldiers?" he asked. "I want to visit them."

"The clinic is the building at the end of the street," he said. "Proceed straight down the street."

As the soldiers rode their horses toward the clinic, they saw military tents.

"Why aren't my soldiers in the clinic?" Claudius asked. "They are as good as a Christian."

"The clinic is full of your soldiers," Mary said. "The two tents are full of your soldiers that are healing and need less care."

"I want to talk with them," he said. "I want to determine when they can be sent back to Rome for proper treatment."

"I am certain they will be pleased to see you," she said. "You can talk to Dr. Lukus about when they will be able to travel."

Claudius walked into the first tent. He watched a doctor check his soldiers.

"When will he be able to be shipped to Rome," Claudius asked. "Can he walk?"

"I will get Dr. Lukus for you," he said. "He is over there giving medical care to another soldier."

Claudius walked toward Dr. Lukus.

"Tell him Claudius wants to talk to him," he said. "I don't have all day."

The young doctor returned with Dr. Lukus.

"I want to thank you for helping my soldiers," he said.

"We are pleased we are able to help them," Lukus said. "A few have died since they arrived."

"I plan to ship them home to Rome," he said. "When will they be ready?"

"By Monday, I think all but a few will be able to travel," he said. "You can check with Nicodemus about a ship."

"I want to see him, where can I find him?" he asked

"His office is in the large building at the dock," he said. "He has ships going to Rome."

"He will do what I tell him," he said. "I'll find him."

Claudius and two of his soldiers went to visit Nichodemus. Seven soldiers stayed with the injured and the remainder rode around the town.

"I am looking for Nicodemus," Claudius said. "I need a ship."

"I will get him for you," he said.

The soldiers were escorted to Nicodemus' office.

"I need a ship," Claudius said. "Can you help me?"

"Yes, I can," Nicodemus said. "I have an agreement with the Roman government. I have ships sailing to Rome every week."

"My legion was struck by an earthquake and needs to return to Rome," he said.

"I will have a ship for you on Monday," he said. "We will make room for everyone but will only carry a small amount of grain."

"I will bring them to you on Monday morning," he said.

The three soldiers returned to the clinic.

"Mary, I talked to Dr. Lukus and to Nicodemus," Claudius said. "Most of my soldiers will be returning to Rome on Monday. Have them ready."

"Yes, sir," Mary said. "We will have them ready for you."

"I want to see the bishop," he said. "Where can I find him?"

"I don't know," she said. "I haven't seen him for a day or two. You can check at the church."

Claudius and his two soldiers walked to the church.

"I am looking for the bishop," Claudius said. "Where is he?"

"He is not here," a priest said. "He went to visit with a sick family in the country."

"Which way did he go?" he asked. "I want to see him."

"He went north," he said. "I don't know exactly where he went. He is probably checking to see if they were injured by the earthquake."

The three of them met with the other soldiers at the edge of town. Claudius decided to form several parties to search for Polycarp. They split into groups of ten soldiers each. Those that didn't hunt Polycarp remained in town. Claudius and his group headed north. After a few miles, they came to a small farm house.

"I want to stop here," Claudius said. "I don't think he is trying to avoid us."

Claudius dismounted and walked to the house. The farmer's wife answered the door.

"Can I help you," she asks. "My husband is in the field."

"We are Romans," Claudius said. "We are looking for Polycarp."

"Who, did you say?" she asked. "I don't think I know him."

"He is a bishop," he said. "He runs the church."

"He is not here," she said. "I know of him, but I have never met him. We are not Christians."

"We are going to search you house," he said. "It is important that we find him."

"Allow me to get my husband," she said. "I will be back in a few minutes."

"I don't have time to wait for your husband," he said. "Move out of our way."

The soldiers searched the house and found nothing. They got a drink of water and rode to the next farm.

After a few hours, they arrived at Euseus' farm. Claudius knocked on the door.

"I am looking for Polycarp," Claudius said. "Is he here?"

"Yes, he is staying with us," Euseus said. "He has been comforting those that were frightened by the earthquake."

"Where is he?" he asked. "I want to talk to him."

"He is in the upper room," he said. "I will get him for you."

After a few moments, Polycarp appeared.

"Euseus said you want to speak with me?"

"Yes, come with us," he said. "Can you ride a horse?"

"No, I am too old to ride a horse," he said. "I have a carriage."

"Get your carriage," he said. "I will escort you back to Smyrna."

Euseus went to the barn and prepared Polycarp's carriage for him.

"Polycarp, it was nice to see you," Euseus said. "We feel much better."

"I will be going to Smyrna," Polycarp said. "God be with you."

"You better hope he is with you," Claudius said. "You are going to need help."

Polycarp looked at Claudius.

"Where are you taking me?" he asked. "I did nothing to you."

"You are my prisoner," he said. "I am taking you to the arena."

Polycarp exhibited no fear.

"I want the public to see you. We will see how good an example you can set for them."

"I am a Christian," he said. "We should all be examples for God."

"The lions will like you," he said as he grinned at Polycarp. "Do you like animals?"

They returned to town. The soldiers kept Polycarp a prisoner in one of the tents next to the clinic. The soldiers murmured.

"I wonder what they are going to do to him?" the injured soldier asked. "If it weren't for him, we wouldn't be getting such great care."

"The way they are watching him, I think he is in trouble," Dr. Lukus said. "I hope everything will be resolved."

"The head soldier isn't a Christian," a soldier said. "He might have him killed."

The next morning, the soldiers took Polycarp to the arena. The arena was full of people expecting to see wild animals and races.

Claudius introduced Polycarp to the crowd.

"I want you to meet the Bishop of Smyrna," Claudius said. "He is here to recognize our God, Jupiter. I am willing to give him a chance to repent."

Polycarp looked at Claudius.

"Repent of what?" he asked. "I have done no wrong."

"When your people helped my troops, they didn't recognize Jupiter," he said. "All I ask is that you admit Jupiter is God."

"I can't do that," he said. "I am a Christian. I don't worship Jupiter."

"You are making a mistake, bishop," Claudius said. "I really don't want to kill you."

The mostly pagan crowd began to jeer.

"If you do not acknowledge Jupiter," Claudius said. "I will turn the wild animals loose on you."

"I will not say Jupiter is God," Polycarp said. "Bring them on."

Claudius decided not to turn the wild animals loose. He wanted to keep them for later. He spoke to the crowd.

"What do you think his punishment should be?" Claudius asked. "He won't recognize Jupiter."

"Burn him alive," the crowd answered. "Burn him alive."

Claudius looked at his troops.

"Maybe we should burn him," he said. "Gather twigs and sticks and we will burn him."

The crowd built a large stack of wood.

Claudius glared at Polycarp and said, "I have decided to burn you."

He then instructed his men, "Soldiers, bind him and place him on top of the wood."

"You don't need to bind me," Polycarp said. "Just have someone help me."

They placed Polycarp on top of the wood.

"Light the fire," he said. "This will end our problem."

The fire was lighted and it burned with great heat. Polycarp lay on top of the pile of burning wood.

"The fire isn't getting to him," Claudius said. "It is dancing around him."

"His God is protecting him," someone in the crowd yelled. "You can't even burn him."

"Kill that trouble maker," Claudius yelled. "No one can talk to me like that."

The soldiers weren't sure who yelled the remarks, so they killed several people. The wood was almost all burned and Polycarp was still lying in the middle of it.

"My God has been with me for eighty six years," Polycarp said. "Now I will be with him."

As Polycarp's soul entered a state of eternal peace, the fire was extinguished.

A priest approached Claudius.

"I would like his body, so we can give him a proper burial," he said. "He is dead."

"You can't have his body," Claudius said. "I am not finished with it."

"You don't need the body of a dead man," the priest said. "I will take care of it."

Claudius had the soldiers remove the body from the arena. They took it away and built another fire and burned the body. After the body was burned, the soldiers returned to the arena.

The priests went to Polycarp's body.

"Gather his remains," Francis said. "Take them to the church."

"I will gather them," Nascien volunteered. "He was my friend."

"For the next three days, I want at least one priest praying, on his knees, at the altar in the churches," Francis said. "Then we will celebrate Polycarp's life."

"I will miss him," Nicodemus said. "He was like an angel on earth. He was a saint."

On the third day, most of the people in Smyrna came to celebrate Polycarp's life. It was unofficially the first saint's day. Nicodemus talked with Francis.

"I want to build a memorial at the church in Polycarp's honor," Nicodemus said. "Find a place for it and advise me."

"When it is finished, I will put his bones in it," Francis said.

The following day, a ship sailed to Rome. It carried many soldiers who owed their lives to Polycarp and his staff of workers. The watch had changed. It was Irenaeus' time to carry forward Jesus' message.

ABOUT THE AUTHOR

The author served in the U.S. Navy and then went to college. After graduating with an engineering degree, he enjoyed careers (50 yrs.) as an engineer, businessman, and professor. He is now retired but writes novels.

While reading the New Testament for over sixty years and teaching Sunday School Bible classes for twenty years, John Mench Ph.D. has been conflicted by the lack of personality within the testament. He endeavors to add perspective to the message of the testament by creating lives for those who wrote and developed Jesus' message.

Printed in the United States
By Bookmasters